Dick Richards
Private Eye

Chris Wong Sick Hong

Dragon Moon Press

Dick Richards
Private Eye

Chris Wong Sick Hong

Dick Richards, Private Eye

ISBN 978-1-897492-44-4
Printed in the United States

www.dragonmoonpress.com

Acknowledgements

To Dragon Moon Press for taking a chance on a first-time author.

Gabrielle for her editorial acumen and inexplicable approval of some jokes I was certain would be redacted.

Maggie and Kevin for their help regarding the non-writing side of writing.

Jeff, whom I still haven't met for lunch. I haven't forgotten, but, well, schedules.

Andrea and Patti for their feedback, as well as Justin and MisCon. That's where the rabbit hole opened up wide enough for me to squeeze through.

Dedication

To my wife, Joyce, who endured all the jokes that didn't make it in here. I don't know anyone else who would have been as patient. I love you.

Chapter 1

They call me a dick because I am one: Dick Richards, Private Eye. Though there's more than a little truth to it, at least I'm less of a jerk than this guy:

"The issue," Count Fantabuloso says, leaning closer across the table between us, "is armament not *of* my issue." He's mastered that tone of voice that makes you feel stupid for asking a reasonable question, or in this case simply making conversation. I've been working with him long enough that I should probably expect it, but it still stings.

If you didn't know the man, you'd laugh. Outlandish hat complete with wide brim and ridiculous feather, baby-blue alligator suit, indoor sunglasses rimmed with diamonds—his dress sense would put any pimp to shame, and he likes it that way. It makes people underestimate him. They don't see the man in the opera cloak as a threat until it's too late. This, along with his intelligence and ruthlessness, was how he became Tipton's sole magical weapons dealer. If a dwarf in Tipton wants to brain a goblin, he gets his runic shotgun from the Count. If an elf needs components for a magical poison, she gets them from the Count. And if a troll thug looking to go up in the world even thinks about increasing its arsenal, it first gets permission to have that thought from the Count.

That's why he's concerned. One of his lieutenants, the Baron Marcus, recently found a handgun in a Dumpster. Count Fantabuloso keeps meticulous records so he knows it isn't his. He doesn't know where it comes from either, which is where I come in.

He nods and the Baron Marcus, who's been hovering nearby, places the gun on the table in front of me. Beyond him several esquires, grunts in the Count's organization, maintain a cordon of privacy.

You might wonder why I work for a guy like this at all, but while he's very much a warlord, he qualifies as an enlightened one. Since he'd supply both sides in any war, with careful accounting and the persuasive application of force he can shut troublemakers down cold. In his own words: "Peace is a fool's dream; tranquility learned." The Count honestly thinks people will eventually become tame enough to think twice about violence. I doubt it will work in the long run, but I can't argue with his results so far. If weapons start freely streaming into Tipton, the delicate balance of power the Count has carefully cultivated will topple like a fat man with one leg. Millennia-old racial tensions, hanging in the air like gunpowder, will explode the first time someone fires a warning shot. All in all, he's a lot better than the other assholes I could be working for.

I glance at the gun, then take down specifics in my field notebook. When. Where. How. The Count doesn't have much info, but it sounds like someone dumped it to avoid getting caught. I don't know why the Baron Marcus was snooping around in Dumpsters, but I don't ask. Everyone has their reasons and few are beautiful under close scrutiny.

"Please find this fool," the Count concludes, "so I can beat him like an MMA poseur wannabe." He brandishes his omnipresent Differance Stick, a heavy-duty cane topped with a brass knob. A small plaque on the side reads, "Martin Luther King, Jr. High School. Making a Differance Since 1831." The feather in his hat—long, bright green, and hopefully fake—wobbles in agreement. I'd hate to meet the bird it came from.

After checking the safety, I tuck the handgun under my right armpit, into the spare holster Raven insisted I wear today. It feels reassuringly heavy in my hand, but there'll be time to inspect it in more detail later. My favorite sidearm, a business gift from the Count, is stashed under my left.

Our business concluded, I excuse myself and make my way past the cordon of esquires. Tharaveir, the owner of this fine establishment, is making a rare appearance behind the counter, checking the till and scowling daggers at the Count. While the Pub, as it's called, gains a certain cachet from being the Count's favorite watering hole, whenever the Count actually shows up most patrons are too scared to stick around. With his gaunt, almost hollow cheeks and aquiline features, not to mention his five-foot-eight stature, it's not hard to make Tharaveir as elven, but there's more than the normal amount of casual menace leering from his blue eyes. He's managed to get kicked out of both Alfheim and Svartalfheim—the elven and dark elven homelands, respectively—and if he ever decides the Count is more trouble than he's worth, the shit will shower down like an avalanche and the fan won't have a chance. Tharaveir will never win, but he'll never give up either.

I exit without incident and humanity explodes around me. Evergreen Court is only four stories tall, but the incessant squawking of specialty shops, restaurants, and ATMs, all clamoring for attention like hyperactive four-year-olds, is barely contained by the sound-absorbing foam embedded in the safety railings. A middle-aged man, in the slack-jawed, head-slightly-tilted posture that comes standard with vidscreen sunglasses, glides past on the moving walkway like a digital zombie. He's far from the only one.

I shoulder myself into the tide of flesh, letting the walkway take me where I want to go. A "public service announcement" from a tattoo parlor informs me that the first five people to get a phoenix stenciled on their liver will win an all-expenses paid trip through the daytime talk show circuit, as if there aren't enough attention whores already.

My next stop is an express elevator nearly filled to capacity. It smells faintly of deodorant. The corporate logos in the sound-absorbing carpet are worn flat and a kid lost in an e-book nearly elbows me in the stomach. It can be hard to tell whether those kind of moves are on purpose, but unspoken etiquette allows retaliatory knees to the junk. I don't. Unspoken etiquette and legality are not the same. A panel near me displays the elevator's maximum capacity and I stifle a sharp laugh. Every year, maximum occupancy goes down while maximum load goes up.

I take the Jennings Court exit and, a short walkway later, arrive at the entrance to my office. Or, more accurately, the entrance to my office complex, even though I'm the only tenant. Situated in a corporate red light district, it's a modest beige door set into a beige wall. Self-help corporations, financial advisors, maid services, and the occasional franchised ethnic deli flaunt themselves around me, corporate whores all. Judging from the crowd gathered in the central open space, the guy in the hippo costume is about to make his annual bungee jump. It's one of the more successful marketing promotions, and one year there was no one inside. When it hit the floor, the stuffed hippo costume exploded into coupons and vouchers to a shocked silence, and then applause. That was the year I stopped watching. I think about joining the tourists, but the odds of him getting caught in the cord are too low to make it worth my while.

I touch my door and the reactive film laminate shows a numeric keypad at eye level. I punch in the security code and the door slides aside. The narrow hallway beyond leads to six doors, three on each side, before dead-ending at a seventh. They're all the deep, rounded red of convincingly fake wood, all sport decorative brass hinges, and each bears an inexpensive plaque with my name. The decoy doors also lead to offices, but those are trapped. Of everyone who's tried to kill me, only one group has guessed the right door—the second on the left—on the first try, and they were as surprised as we were. The paranoia might seem like overkill, but word of mouth counts for a lot, and that word says anyone who wants to hire me presses "0" to leave a message at the outer door and waits for me to get back to them. Anyone else is probably trying to kill me. I could just move my office, true, but even though the Count pays extremely well, and even with the help of a black hat who owed me a favor, buying this much space was a hefty investment. I'm not letting it go unless absolutely necessary.

The inner door, as always, is locked. I trace a pattern on it with my finger and it swings outward.

I'm not sure why, other than her sense of humor, Raven's office is decked out the way it is. Lightweight aluminum filing cabinets, stained a mottled brown, line the walls, but all they do is look impressive. There's nothing inside and I don't even know if they actually open. A ceiling fan with three blades turns slowly, churning air-conditioned air. Cheap blinds hang over two wide LED panels, filtering a dirty yellow light into the room. Raven's desk, authentic wood from a certified, carbon-negative tree farm down in Ecuador, looms against the rear wall, its left end flush with the empty doorway to my office. For some reason, she thinks there's still enough nature left to be worth saving.

I slide my field notebook, a thin brick with limited memory and an electrosensitive screen, into its holster in the armrest of my desk/chair. Stiffened fiber optic cables, woven into a surprisingly comfortable chair, sprout processing elements molded into arm- and headrests. A thin screen always hangs at just the right angle. The entire thing glints, beads of light moving through the cable like an ethereal ant farm, as the notebook copies itself to permanent storage. As usual, I almost forget that the stylus doesn't stay with the notebook; it has its own slot where it can recharge.

I place the Count's mystery gun on my table. It has a black surface, gridded with white lines, and I whip out my phone to take a few pictures of the gun from different angles. An app calculates its dimensions, distills a silhouette, and appends everything to the message I send Raven.

"You ever seen anything like this?" I say. The grip's wooden, but the barrel is metal. There are no obvious markings, magical or otherwise, but no obvious seams either. The wood joins the metal perfectly, as if the two were grown together, and any magic capable of that usually leaves a physical trace, a sigil or at least a mark.

Raven's head appears on the wall in front of me. Her hair is black with dark purple highlights, wound into a prim bun, and she's wearing thick-rimmed emo glasses to match. My phone interfaces with my desk, and it's projecting her response. Sophisticated algorithms, or so I've been told, filter out the background for her privacy.

"Nope," she says. "What does it shoot?"

Biting back the urge to say *people*, I go with, "Haven't checked yet. I wanted your general impression first."

"Aww...how sweet," is the reply. Her head morphs into a giant yellow smiley face.

I shake my head. Emoticons are back in fashion as retro kitsch, and of course Raven joined the bandwagon as soon as possible.

The face morphs back into her head, and her hair is now orange. It changes colors along with her mood, even in person, but her eyes always stay green.

I pick up the gun and pop the clip. Nine shaped-quartz rounds in a wicker magazine appear. There's room for ten. I check the chamber. Empty. I snap pictures of the clip, then an individual bullet, and send them to Raven too. This gun is definitely odd.

Crystal rounds are typically the province of dwarves, but these show none of their trademark precision. The blunt ends still carry traces of the rock matrix they were hewn from and the facets, while they taper to a point, are ridged and glassy, like they've been chipped off or even melted. Plus, dwarves wouldn't bother with wood. Living, or even once-living, things have an aura that interferes with their craftsmanship.

The metal barrel makes elves unlikely—their magic fails

around iron and steel—but I can't be sure it's actually steel without testing. Silver can be hardened remarkably and elves love silver. (It's shiny.) Still, there are none of the leafy decorations elves festoon absolutely everything with, like flower children deprived of Ritalin. The handgrip, while sporting a fetching two-tone effect, might as well be sanded smooth. That doesn't leave many other factions with the technology to produce something like this.

"Dark elves?" Raven suggests. "They've picked up a lot of dwarven habits down there."

"Maybe," I say, but I hope not. Things turn vicious for absolutely no reason at all when dark elves are involved. Their glamour plugs gleefully into humanity's bestial instincts. Thankfully, immigration agreements keep their numbers in check. If they're making a move to change that, bloodshed will be unavoidable.

"Anyway," Raven says, "I've got enough to start searching the databases. Oh, and btw," she actually pronounces each letter, "David's going to stop by later." Her head morphs again into that yellow smiley face, which winks at me before dissolving.

Gee, thanks for letting me know, Raven. She really needs to stop giving David the code to the doors. I'll be there to meet him anyway, but first I need to test-fire this thing and see what it can do.

❀

Count Fantabuloso likes to spot check at least one weapon in each incoming shipment for quality, and one of the ranges built for this purpose hides behind the counter of Jimbo's Porn-n-Pawn, down in the Sawyer district. The ones for field-testing rocket launchers and other heavy ordnance are a bit intimidating, to be honest—sleek, chrome deathtraps with unidentifiable dents and stains—but those are in sound-proofed warehouses surrounded by nightclubs. Most testing takes place after ten P.M. so no one notices a thing.

The Sawyer district itself is grungy and low-traffic. You almost always have elbow room and, in the quieter hours, you can almost stretch out your arms without hitting someone. The businesses here eschew advertising. When the signs themselves read "Five Dollar Store" or "Pawn Shop," not much more needs to be said. The primary occupation in this area of Tipton is loitering, and the denizens are very good at what they do. Hundreds of impassive faces on five floors, perched on every available surface, swivel blankly like buzzards to watch me walk by. It's a small fraction of the thousands here, but uncanny nonetheless.

The exterior windows of Jimbo's Porn-n-Pawn, as well as those of Jimbo's Foodie Mart next door, each bear a green sticker proclaiming official security protection, but grilled bars are still mounted just behind them for insurance. While the windows are security glass unbreakable by anything short of multiple .50-caliber rounds, the Count sees no reason to openly display his wealth. People have enough reasons to hate him already.

I open the door and the digital doorbell rings, an annoying techno remix of Beethoven's Eighth. The current Jimbo—the Count swaps them out every three to four months—glances at me. There are no lines of sight or fire between the door and the black counter, but I see his head swivel in the hyperbolic mirror discreetly mounted near the ceiling. I head down an aisle filled with ancient video games and computer cables on the left and remaindered romance novels on the right. A short left later I come face to face with a very bored esquire.

Like every other esquire on duty, he wears the official street uniform. The full-length arms of a black, undermesh shirt project from an overstuffed coat whose sleeves have been ripped off. The coat lies open to display a black T-shirt with the Count's logo, a fist over crossed lightning bolts in white outline. Black jeans and combat boots complete the ensemble, and the esquire looms among the bric-a-brac like an angry bull sent to the corner for bad behavior.

"What you want?" he says.

This one has made himself quite a nest behind the counter. A collapsible metal chair leans at an angle against a dusty, rolled-up rug. The front legs are propped atop a cooler and a thick stack of old magazines, respectively. A small dumbwaiter with a missing wheel is at just the right place and height for an armrest. He can kick back, relax with his elbow propped up, gangsta-style, and watch the antique CRT TV mounted in a pile of clothes, all while still technically keeping an eye on the door. He notices me glancing at his nest, looks me over, then glares as if daring me to say something. I don't. He's either good enough to pull it off or will be gone before too long.

"I have a test coming up," I say.

He's supposed to reply with "We don't sell textbooks" and wait for my "Really. I must have been misinformed," but he just reaches under the counter between us, pushes a hidden button, and a door set in the wall to my right glides silently aside. Compared to the shop's shabby wallpaper, the metal walls in the corridor beyond gleam. I step between a power tools bin and a display case filled with musical instruments, through a softly hissing curtain of air, and the door slides shut behind me.

The Baron Rutgert, a skinny man around fifty-ish who looks extremely out of place whenever he goes to staff meetings, is in his office. Balding and bespectacled, he looks and acts like a college professor. I have no idea how he came to work for the Count, but he's all right if you don't mind the random jumps and pauses in his conversations. You'll be talking and then an idea will strike him. Minutes will pass and he won't even realize he's stopped talking.

He's in charge of R&D and his office has every kind of electronics known to man, all of them linked together in nearly every way known to man. He doesn't have a desk because he doesn't need one. Projectors in his glasses display anything he calls for as he rolls around on his chair. On four wide counters, thinfilm displays alternate with processing stations, and in the center of it all is an optical switching station that lights up like a cubist Christmas tree when things really get going. He explained it all to me once—blast pressure, emission and absorption spectra, temperature fluctuations, projectile deformation—but I'm most comfortable with the analog devices in the corner. Even dwarves haven't figured out how to fully integrate magic and electronics and for some things you just can't beat a crystal pendulum. Or seven of them, diamonds all the colors of the rainbow, hanging by leather thongs from a bank of wooden pegs. Below them a compass with a mithril needle, a small crystal ball, and some coins to test I Ching deviations are stacked on a Ouija board. The Ouija board is new.

I nod at the baron.

He looks blankly in my direction. I can't tell if he's looking at me or something projected directly onto his retinas, so I remind him why I'm here.

He blinks, his eyes refocus, and he nods. "Ah yes. The Type 5-S morphology with hand-loaded magazine. I've been wanting to see the emission spectrum. The metallorganic interface, do you think it's homogenous down to the cellular level? If I could reproduce that..." He rolls his chair over a row and it seems like he's waiting for me to reply.

"Instead of standing around here wondering, why don't we find out?" I venture.

The Baron Rutgert breaks into a smile. "Excellent idea. Let's get started." He rolls himself over to the analog corner, takes the blue diamond pendulum and the crystal ball, and puts his chair on autopilot.

"Why the Ouija board?" I ask on our way to the test range.

The baron grins. "I tell the new Jimbos that if anything goes really bad, they can use it to write home one last time."

❃

The targets are pretty standard. A thin sheet of paper sprinkled with holy water leads off, followed by low-thread-count cloth-of-mithril. It already has a few holes and the baron folded it double before hanging it up. Third in line is a two-inch sheet of steel alloyed with 0.5% adamantine. And, just in case, mounted to the far wall is a panel stolen—I have no idea how and have never gotten anyone involved drunk enough to find out—from a decommissioned tank that's supposed to stop anything less potent than depleted uranium shells.

The preparations complete, Rutgert taps the frame of his glasses and the targets slide down the range, spacing themselves at optimum intervals. A side area, outside the main lines of fire, holds a complicated pedestal that looks like a mechanical spider sexually assaulting a metal traffic cone. The baron carefully places the crystal ball atop the contraption. The spidery arms click as he fixes them into place, and with another tap to his glasses they hum to life, invisible lasers crisscrossing through the quartz.

The thing always creeps me out, moving subtly like breathing. The arms further adjust themselves. When they stop, satisfied, the baron manually pushes the contraption along its track, leaving it even with a point halfway between the sheet of paper and cloth-of-mithril.

Next, he hangs the pendulum from a metal bar attached to the ceiling a few feet from where I'll be standing. The bar is three and a half feet across, filled with notches at half inch intervals. It lowers smoothly and Rutgert hangs the pendulum near the left side. He taps his glasses again and the bar rises, more slowly this time, until the diamond's clear of all reasonable bullet trajectories. It swings slowly in the air, tracing tiny arcs. Rutgert leaves without a word, his chair's motor making no noise, off to further calibrate the sensors.

As always, I feel strangely exposed. Most ranges are divided into semi-private stations and have measures, usually waist-high partitions, to keep idiots from wandering into harm's way. Here though, the range itself is barely ninety feet from end to end, and there's absolutely nothing between me and the targets. Spherical camera nodes studding the walls, floor, and ceiling observe everything. A red X on the floor, electrical tape helpfully marking the optimal firing point, always seems like the real target.

I don the shooting goggles the baron has left behind and adjust the fit of the integrated earguards.

They're always tight around my temples, and they let out a stretched, electronic groan as the contacts detect a human head and boot the thing up. It always reminds me of the whistle suddenly depressurized air makes when it streams out a punctured window. A yellow tint bleeds across the world and an icon in the upper left corner of my vision indicates that a recording session has been started.

"Almost done here." Rutgert's voice booms in my ears, the speakers adding a nasal inflection. "Are you ready yet?"

"Just about," I say. I lift the lapel of my jacket and draw the mystery gun. It feels solid in my hand, dependable. Not the made-for-you feeling common to magical items with an agenda, but tried and true. I toggle the safety back and forth a few times, enjoying the way it clicks. The smoothed wood feels fresh against my skin and I find myself looking forward to using it. I start to reholster it until Rutgert's ready, but a sensation of alarm sounds inside my head.

I smile. Nice try. It's subtle, but that flash of fear isn't mine. This gun *wants* to be fired. Well, it can wait.

"The pendulum's nearly settled into Brownian rhythm," Rutgert says. "Just a few more seconds and the last sensors will be—damn it. Diagnostics are showing a boot error in the shrapnel accelerometer pads. I just rewired the damn things last week...Okay. I just had to smack the table. It's probably the connection. They're showing good now. The pendulum's in Brownian 6b, pretty standard for blue."

The gun tries to use my irritation at needless technobabble

to convince me to fire it early. I'm smarter than that.

"Whenever you're ready, Dick," the baron concludes.

I nod though there's really no reason to, and the goggles superimpose a red target on the sheet of paper. I aim and a reticule appears on the goggle display, an estimate of the bullet's most likely point of impact. I take a deep breath and the reticule steadies. I squeeze the trigger slowly.

The world doesn't stop, and there isn't a huge fireball when the round punches through the targets. Instead, my vision dims slightly, probably the goggles protecting my eyes from excessive muzzle flash, and then there's a hole in the sheet of paper. Even the gunshot report's muffled. That's it. A little disappointed, I holster the weapon again, ignoring the sense of alarm, and take the goggles off.

❀

It will be a while before the results come back, so I leave the handgun with Rutgert and head back to my office, wondering what David's gotten into this time. The thing you have to understand about him is that he doesn't have much going for him. He's more annoying than anything else, but I figure as long as he's with me he's not huffing bubble wrap or extorting D-List celebrities. And even though I change the door codes every month, I'm positive Raven keeps him updated. He certainly shows up often enough.

He's into ceremonial magic, which isn't a bad thing by itself, but somewhere along the line he decided that the hallmark of a powerful magician is wearing a goofy hat *all the time.* I've seen at least five, each a vaguely Egyptian hybrid cowl/beret dyed in primary colors. He is only sixteen at most, and how he manages to survive high school while wearing these things is beyond me.

He's gangly, awkward, and stops by about once each week to give me dubiously useful tips. Once it was a raiding party of hobgoblins who turned out to be high on parsley, so focused on headbutting each other that the only way they could do real damage was if anyone got close enough to be knocked out by their stench. Most of them were passed out for good by the time David and I got there, lying in contorted poses like little hardcore lotus eaters. David and I just tossed them all in the Dumpster by the Italian restaurant, closed the lid with a solid clang, and let nature take its course.

If I got rid of my office I could easily avoid him, but I'm not that much of a dick. Plus, I have too much money tied up in the place and as the world gets larger and more interconnected, people's individual worlds get smaller. I'm not so self-absorbed that I think the purpose of the Internet is to show me everything I want to know, while spam filters keep the real world handily at bay. A physical location helps ground me. It's also nice to have a place to escape from advertising. I resent psychological manipulation of all kinds and that's all that is. And strangely, once my enemies learn I have an office, they focus any retribution there, rather than searching out my apartment or hunting me down in the streets. Having a physical office and keeping regular hours is unusual enough that they assume I must have something extremely valuable hidden away.

It's not a bad assumption because I do: the most expensive traps I can afford.

Raven's back at the office when I arrive. Every day at four P.M. she waters the plastic plants with a hipster's dedication to irony. She's in professional mode as usual, sporting an attractive suit whose jacket follows her waist and flares out slightly at the hips. More retro. She says that the baggy, peasant style of clothing is back in style but that if she wants to look like a sack of potatoes she'll just wear a sack of potatoes. It's just as stylish and she'll have lunch too.

At her insistence, I once bought what she called a "dashing, single-breasted coat with matching elbow patches and trousers, conceived in earth tones and completed with power tie." I honestly couldn't tell if she was being sarcastic.

My other suits are pretty much the same style, all some shade of dark brown. It helps with stains and I actually like the look. Modern business attire has literally been inspired by speed skating. "Your business moves at the speed of thought," one ad proclaims. "Shouldn't you?" Personally, I think a sane person has better things to do than take an early monorail to the next city to ensure that electronic paperwork's been filed properly, but it won't be long before the FDA approves the first subcutaneous caffeine injection system. The black market version, hacked to use amphetamines, is already a best-seller among aspiring VPs with severe emotional issues.

"How'd it go?" Raven asks. She pauses to check her work and, satisfied, sets her spritzer on her desk.

"A little disappointing," I say. As always, I find her presence to be invigorating and a little uncomfortable.

"No demons appeared? No holes in the fabric of reality itself?"

"You know that only happened once," I reply. "You were there." I solved that particular problem by using the carcass of the demon to plug the hole it crawled out of. It's amazing how many things go down when exposed to fully automatic fire.

"You're not still sensitive about that, are you?" Raven teases.

I ignore that. "Baron Rutgert's still analyzing. He should be done in a few days."

Thankfully, she takes the hint. While it was technically my fault the demon was able to break through, I fixed it before it had a chance to get out of hand.

"How long do you think it'll take the Count to get impatient this time?" she says.

"A few days."

Raven grins wickedly. "I'll let you know when he leaves another angry, barely understandable voicemail."

I feel like I've been punched in the gut. "You don't answer those calls?"

"Isn't that what caller ID is for?" she says as she returns to spritzing the plastic plants. "Besides, you never interrupt a soliloquy and voicemail's the best way to preserve them for posterity."

"You don't answer the Count," I repeat, slowly.

"I'm just about ready to release a compilation, actually. The Count's Classic Rants, Volume 1."

Belatedly, I realize she's yanking my chain and I relax, decide to play along. "Really? How does it start out?"

Raven perches on her desk, legs crossed, and places her left hand on her chest. She tilts her head back, hair turning the Count's shade of black, and flings her right arm out into a melodramatic pose. "While inquiry into iniquity," she recites, "is inevitable in time's due course, the thrust of your course is marked by quickness. I will no coarseness yet, but hurry your—" Raven mimics the Count excellently, but she's speaking too deeply for her voice, "—ass up," she finishes while coughing. "Sorry, I'm out of practice."

I give her a golf clap for effort. "When's David showing up?"

"About an hour, I think. I have a research appointment at Miskatonic. You planning on sticking around?"

"Yeah. Paperwork. You know how it is."

❀

Along with a tendency to exaggerate absolutely everything, one of David's many quirks is that he always announces his presence by knocking on the doorframe to my office. I've only drawn down on him once, and hadn't even been close to shooting, but ever since then he's made sure to be as conspicuous as possible. It's a thin, weak knock, and next comes, "May I be granted leave to enter your domicile?" in a reedy voice. I doubt he knows "domicile" means "living quarters."

"Come in, David," I say. I get up from my desk/chair and it goes to standby, beeping once as the shaped fiber optic cables dim. The light show has nothing to do with how it works, but I like the effect anyway.

In addition to his omnipresent hat, David's wearing dark blue jeans and a T-shirt from some obscure band I've never heard of. Apparently, their name's Whimsical Death and their logo, front and center, is a skull in profile wearing a winged helmet. A laurel wreath above two crossed candy canes form the background. The broken straps of his backpack are knotted together, so close to his neck it looks like they're trying to strangle him.

He glances around, then darts inside. His favorite place in the room is next to my tool bin; one of the strongest protective sigils is etched into the wall behind it, underneath the paint. David always stands there if he has a choice.

"What did you find this time?" I say.

He puffs himself up, easing the backpack straps away from his throat, and proclaims, "I have uncovered a Brotherhood jewel, hidden deep in the Under and most fair."

That actually surprises me. The Brotherhood, or Brotherhood of the Unspoken Secrets, is always a wildcard. No one knows much about them. A magical fraternity sworn to silence, most people know them as street mimes, but they're rumored to predate history, and some whisper they predate human civilization itself. Even a drunk dwarven war party would quiet down and cross the street upon spotting a Brotherhood patrol.

I'm tempted to squelch this in its tracks. There's no reason for David to be poking into this kind of thing. He'll just get hurt. On the other hand, my job involves poking around into exactly this kind of thing, and you never know when extra information will come in useful. Either way, he's probably just exaggerating and it won't hurt to humor him.

I press him for more details, but he's preening with pride and wants to surprise me. Fair enough.

"Tell you what," I say. "I have another place to investigate first. Why don't you come along and then I'll look at this jewel." I can at least keep him out of trouble for a few hours.

His eyes light up. "With certainty. The night aids stealth."

❃

I have no idea why David talks the way he does. I assume he knows regular English, so maybe it comes with the hats. Raven thinks he's trying to impress me but she jokes around way too much for me to take that seriously. Besides, if he wants to be an esoteric detective, why doesn't he just say so?

According to my notes, the Baron Marcus found the gun at the old Thriftwood Shopping Court, in the Dumpster just behind Antique Motor Sandwiches. I know the place. All three stories are decked out in chrome, and pictures of hot rods line the walls. There'd been a bit of a PR disaster a few years ago when they started cutting up classic cars for booths, but since the general public has the attention span of a hyperactive three-year-old everything has already been forgotten.

David and I are unable to avoid the greeter, an attractive young woman in mechanic's overalls. David stares just a bit too long.

"Thanks for coming to Antique Motor Sandwiches. Your grease monkey will show you to your table shortly. Your name, please?"

Instead of answering, I cast a simple spell which makes David and I much less noticeable. Power breezes lightly through me and the greeter blinks before deciding she must be seeing things. The spell doesn't make us invisible, just so low on everyone's list of priorities that we might as well be. Tapping David on the shoulder, I indicate he should follow me.

Weaving our way through the beginning of the dinner rush, we head for the kitchen. The sounds of conversation cover us in the fluffy blanket of everyone else's self-absorption. Everyone has layers of thoughts and concerns that usually dominate their mind. Ask them, and they'll call it their personality, but among other things it prevents them from seeing anything they're not expecting to see. The spell encourages them to stay that way, then whispers in the back of their minds that we're so far from their day-to-day concerns that we're not worth paying attention to.

Halfway through the kitchen, David speaks. "What are we looking for?"

I shush him immediately. Just because we're less noticeable doesn't mean no one will notice us. True, no one would ever expect a teen to dress like David, let alone go out in public looking like that, but it's not worth taking chances. We make it to the back exit without incident and step into another world.

Opposed to Thriftwood's faded consumerism, the professional polish of the utility corridor is jarring. It's one thing for what's basically a glorified maintenance hallway to be well-kept, and another for the metal beams supporting the fifteen-foot ceiling to be noticeably gleaming. I'd heard that the dwarves were making forays into the invisible professions, mostly through front companies, but I wasn't expecting this. When I think about it, though, it's a perfect match. They have an aptitude for technology, don't mind getting dirty whether it's coal dust from mining or the efflux from a backed up sewer, and they're almost neurotically hard-working.

The main road is a wide two-lane, paved with a shiny gray metal-ceramic blend. Each lane is marked by a series of reflectors, with long stripes of fluorescent lighting in the ceiling casting soft shadows. Garbage stoops and truck loading/unloading bays dot the corridor like apartments and, remarkably, there's no trace of gang graffiti. Knowing dwarves, they probably spent a week or so coating every surface with spray-paint resistant coating.

I wonder briefly what the Count's men were doing back here, then judge the question irrelevant. Everyone has their reasons, and few are beautiful under close scrutiny. There's sporadic activity in the corridor, but we're in no danger of being noticed.

"We're going in the Dumpster," I tell David.

It's seated in a special groove, and like all city Dumpsters since time immemorial is a magnificent shade of green with a black plastic top. A readout on the side estimates it at 20% of capacity, and I'm not looking forward to jumping inside. Restaurant garbage is nasty garbage. Thank God for dry cleaners.

David lifts the top and a smell that's best described as reluctant vomit assaults our noses like a mugger bored with parole.

"Let's make this quick," I say. "I hope you've got a change of clothes in that bag."

He smiles uncertainly, then nods. I make a stirrup with my hands to hoist him up and in, then grab the lip myself and clamber over.

I land on something that squelches and slips under my feet. It takes me a moment to right myself, and as I do David says, "I believe I've uncovered the object of inquiry."

"Satan's biscuits!" the object in question says. "Either the trash came twice or I have company."

The head of a gnome, poking through the upper layer of trash, is staring at David, who's trying to carefully edge away. I nearly burst out laughing.

Gnomes are elemental spirits that, quite honestly, look and act as if the detritus from some forgotten corner of creation cobbled itself together with nothing but determination and resentment. Less than one foot tall, this one emerges completely from the trash and fixes us both with a truculent stare. With limbs carved from battery casings and woven together with small wires, it's obviously an electronics gnome.

"Well?" the gnome insists. "I asked you a question." It folds its arms over its chest and the small plastic fan embedded in its head whirs impatiently.

I again stifle the urge to laugh at David's bemusement. Gnomes are as random as lava lamps and laughter has been known to set them off. They don't negotiate, can't be reasoned with, and rarely make sense. They also never lie, so on the rare occasions when you can get something out of them, it's as good as gold.

"Ask it about a gun," I whisper to David. "We're looking for one that was dumped here a few days ago."

The gnome turns to face me, the fan in its head picking up speed, then turns back to David. "Yes," it says. "Ask me about your toilet paper options."

The look on David's face screams, *What do I do now?* but I stay quiet. The only way to learn to deal with gnomes is to deal with gnomes, as frustrating as that always is.

"Have you resided here a fortnight past?" David asks it.

The gnome stamps its foot. Something crinkles underneath. "Well excuse me, red-eye. I must have forgotten my breathing papers." It spins around, arms raised in astonishment and disgust.

David just stares at it, completely nonplussed.

Me, I'm thinking. Gnomes are always looking for parts to build more gnomes, but this one shouldn't be here. I'd expect it to be nosing around the back of an electronics store. Still, gnomes have an instinct for these things and when they're looking for something in particular, they're as obstinate as politicians being asked to vote against major campaign contributors. For all I know, this gnome caught a whiff of something he likes, and will now stay here for the next few decades looking for it.

It's too much to hope for that the gnome was dumped here by the same person who dumped the gun. Judging from the readout and the level of the trash, the garbage trucks have been by since then. On the other hand, the gnome's first comment might mean it's been here for a while.

"If it's in here, it's looking for something," I tell David. "If we help it out, it might tell us what it knows."

"Like what?"

"A rhinoceros fart, obviously," the gnome chimes in.

"Something electronic," I say.

While David pokes around the garbage, avoiding the especially damp spots, I quietly cast a charm which attunes my eyes to magical auras. David glows slightly, as does the gnome, but nothing else. I scan the walls, the lid, and the top layer of garbage. Nothing but ordinary Dumpster.

"Why not just conjure the necessary parts?" David asks.

"It doesn't work like that." I start poking around too. The

gnome starts gnawing its way through a trash bag, obviously enjoying itself. "Besides, how would you do it?"

"Like this," he says proudly. He mutters some words filled with Ls and Rs. There's a slight breeze and the smell of loam flirts briefly with my nose, making the stench of garbage that much stronger when it fades.

Great. Of all things, where did the kid learn elf magic?

David grins and holds up an Antique Motor Sandwich Card. The gnome, attracted by the flash of magic, stops chewing plastic and stomps over. David hands it the card. The gnome licks the magnetic strip on the back, then nods in approval.

"150 points left. Eat classy, you sons-of-bitches."

"Was that elf magic?" I ask David. I hope I'm wrong, but his smirk tells me all I need to know. I hate to jet now, after giving the gnome what it wants but before we have a chance to get something in return, but first things first. I need to make sure David will be all right. He looks a little confused when I order him out, but he complies. As we leave, the gnome yells, "God damn pasty-faced hippies!" and starts banging ineffectually on the sides of the Dumpster.

Chapter 2

We stop back at my apartment. It's in Waverly Court, a decent residential area with more than a touch of class, if I do say so myself. Clear boundaries between the kitchen, living room, and bathroom will do that. Much of Tipton is so space-starved that efficiencies are the name of the game. I sit David down on the couch across from the big-screen TV. My collection of tiki people watch us impassively.

They're from those old cartoons, really old, where hostile island natives are nothing but pointy, oblong heads attached to arms and legs. They run around like crazy, poking people with spears and boiling hapless explorers alive. Pounding drums and maniacal laughs figure heavily into the soundtracks.

"You know that was elf magic, right?" I say, sharply.

Like most teenagers, David does a good job of rolling his eyes with just his voice, even with his head down. "Yes."

I instinctively want to smack him, but instead say, "And you know that, right about now, you're going to shit until it feels like your colon turned itself inside out?"

His eyes widen as the pain hits and he bolts for the bathroom without asking for directions. He finds it on the second try.

When he finally stumbles out I ask him if he flushed the toilet. He hasn't, so I send him back in.

In the meantime, I rummage through the kitchen cupboards and choose a can, Beefy-Os, basically at random and pop it into the microwave. It should still be good.

I finally hear the sound of flushing, twice, and David emerges.

I tell him to take a shower and get changed, toss his backpack to him. It almost knocks him over. Luckily for both of us, he does have a spare change of clothes, including an extra hat, and after his shower the Beefy-Os are ready and steaming. He takes the bowl gratefully and eats like he hasn't seen food in days.

"Good," I say. "Eat it all. It will keep your intestines human. If you're still hungry, there's more above the sink." He nods and I continue, "So, what color was it?"

He looks at me blankly.

"The dump you just took," I repeat. "What color was it?"

When he just stares, I say, "Come on. Don't tell me you didn't look."

"Blue," he mumbles.

"Good. As long as it's not red or orange you'll be fine." Leaving him with the Beefy-Os, I head for my bedroom. After I strip down, my Dumpster-diving suit lands in the emergency dry cleaning trash bag, as does my shirt. I skirt the edge of my bed on my way to the closet and, opening the doors, I'm ambushed. A dark mass, about three feet tall, lunges from the top shelf, speeding for my face. A spell comes to mind unbidden and a concussive blast sends my assailant flying back into the row of jackets. For a moment it hangs there with wide eyes, an impossibly pleased toothy grin, and a plastic spear.

"God damn it, Beaufort," I swear. I stashed him in there last week for reasons now lost to me.

He takes the whole closet with him on the way down, everything clattering to the floor in a heap.

My pulse pounds in my ears, I taste metal on my breath, and a sinuous whisper wends through my mind. Why stop here? All the edges in my bedroom are razor sharp yet bleed into each other dizzyingly, colors assault me, and electricity like raw nerves on my left shoulder blade lets me know without looking when David enters. I'm tempted to blast him just because, but with a nauseating, unheard click I regain control and all the extra life drains out of the world. David's watching me with a worried look.

"I'm fine," I say, more than a little annoyed. "I stashed one of the tiki people in here last week and it came unbalanced. That's what you heard."

"Oh." He's holding his empty bowl and steadfastly aims his gaze over my shoulder.

"If you're still hungry, feel free to help yourself."

"Your generosity is well received." Without looking me in the eye, he pivots back toward the kitchen.

I look down and realize I'm still in my boxers but not, thankfully, hanging out. That would have been awkward.

This blind rage always surfaces when I use mid-level magic, especially when I'm surprised, so I try my damnedest not to. It's like a floodgate opens in my mind, unleashing a realm of silence and psychedelic fury.

Massaging my temples, I pick some clothes off the closet floor. I'll pick the rest up when I don't run the risk of making them smell like garbage too. That taken care of, I head for the shower. David's watching TV when I finish, and after I eat we head for this jewel of his.

❀

It's deep in the Under, that much I know already. We start at Orptic Court in Cirrus and wind our way down into the empty, hulking remains of a meat packing plant. Large hooks still hang from the ceiling and the remnants of white paint flake off metal walls. Most of the climate control ducts are still intact, and David follows them to where the main system used to be. He retrieves a crowbar that he'd stashed carefully out of sight and jimmies up a hatch in the floor. Traces of a yellow and black pattern still line its edges. With a grunt of exertion, he manages it open and it swings abruptly on rusty hinges, screeching. I'd help but since it's his discovery, he might take it like I was trying to intrude.

The maintenance shaft below has obviously been reworked. Where it originally banked left to allow access under the plant, it now continues straight down in a chimney of crumbling drywall, masonry, and support superstructure. Not for the first time, I wonder how David manages to survive in the Under long enough to find anything interesting. Or, more accurately, how he manages to survive finding something interesting. He claims to only skulk occasionally, but he knows too much odd, timely information not to be sneaking around regularly. I ask him about it as we climb down and he tells me, with more than a hint of pride, that it's his Cloak and Shield.

It makes enough sense, on the surface. While the Cloak prevents people from noticing you, the Shield creates a buffer zone that keeps the ignorant at bay. I guess it's good he remembered both. There are urban legends of people who practice the Cloak and neglect the Shield getting run over on the walkways. And even with his choice of headgear, David isn't the kind of person you'd be likely to take second notice of in the first place. Nobody expects an awkward, skinny kid to be lurking in dark corners, so David had a pretty good thing going. Unfortunately for this line of reasoning, elves are immune to most glamour-type spells humans can cast and it's impossible to learn elven magic without an elven teacher. David isn't coming completely clean, but I let it go. There isn't any point in pushing him. Yet.

After a cramped, winding descent, the chimney tilts into a cluttered corridor, which opens out into a huge space. It's at least four stories tall, similarly long and wide. The walls have been shorn of protrusions, as has the floor. There's no detritus or cover anywhere, making me glad that our tunnel breaches the area at the top, near the seam between the wall and ceiling. The Brotherhood either hasn't found it yet or decided it wasn't worth acting on. Or, the thought flits through my mind, they've left it there on purpose. Provide an easy way into your house and that's exactly where an incompetent thief will strike. The hairs on the back of my neck rise, but I have to admit David's actually found something this time.

A huge greenhouse nestles in the concrete floor like an engagement ring diamond. Cubical and tilted, its steel and glass walls reveal a green explosion—vibrant, gyroscopic life. Streaks of red and blue shimmer through the foliage like fairy dust, and it seems to spin gently. I shake my head to clear the vertigo and refocus.

A group of mimes patrols the floor like a clutter of eerie beetles.

It's all I can do to keep from laughing out loud. Even in the smoky, paranoia-drenched bar that serves as Conspiracy Theory Heaven, anyone who even mentions the thought that the Brotherhood of the Unspoken Secrets is ultimately a militant gardening club would be bounced out, then shot in the back by mysterious assailants for good measure.

The mimes below are definitely patrolling a perimeter, right arms cocked as though cradling rifles. Rumor has it their imaginary weapons pack the same punch as the real deal. Two mimes, closer to the greenhouse, play cards on an invisible table, seated quite comfortably on invisible chairs. Other than that, it's hard enough to tell what mimes are doing in the first place and I'm certainly no expert.

"Verily, the Brothers have flocked to this jewel like pilgrims to a shrine," David whispers.

"When did this start?" I whisper back.

"A fortnight and half thereof hence."

Three weeks? "How long have you been sneaking down here?" I say, a little accusingly.

"True beauty of any kind is rare enough that a man may be excused for drinking his fill." He glares at me, then turns back to the greenhouse. Not good.

I've seen that faraway look before, the one that says, *Whatever's down there, it's got to be better than my life is now.*

Those who don't grow out of it end up doing something really stupid, like selling their soul to a demon for limitless cosmic power. For his sake, I hope David grows out of it. Soon.

Focusing again on the greenhouse, I decide against casting a farseeing spell. Why waste the time and energy when good, old-fashioned binoculars will work just as well? Plus, one brush with magical berserker rage is enough for the evening. Unfortunately, I don't have either of my pairs on me, but I didn't expect David to stumble on anything this big. I'm a little worried that he has, and make a mental note to talk to him about it later.

Our voyeurism is cut short by metallic clinking, amplified to near gunshot volume by the bare walls and absolute silence. It's hard to see what's happening at first, but when thick white smoke starts to fill the room, I know what's going to happen next. Two more tear gas grenades roll in, and there's a frenetic, yet deathly silent, burst of activity as the mimes brace against their assailants. Gunshots follow.

Normally I'd stick around as long as possible, but the hairs on the back of my neck rise in the way they do when really powerful magic is being used, and I don't want David getting in over his head. He objects, weakly, but we leave.

❀

"You say there's been a recent increase in activity?"

Back at my office, David looks irritated at my questions but pleased by the attention. I've been jotting down notes in my field notebook, and I hope he doesn't think this means he can tag along with me more often.

"Verily, only four guards habitually patrol the jewel. This even there were at least ten."

"Have you seen them changing shifts?"

"All the Brothers I've espied have been fully clothed."

This catches me off guard and I have no idea how to respond. I'm halfway sure David's joking, but he deadpanned that line like a pro. Then he starts to smirk, which gives it away.

"You spend too much time with Raven," I say, shaking my head.

After a bit more questioning, an interesting picture emerges. The greenhouse appears to be a safehouse. Injured mimes, some carried on invisible stretchers, are brought there, and the guards outside have more than doubled since David started spying on them. David also thinks their patterns have changed, but unless he's observed them at the same times each day, there's really no way to tell. Though he's the one who stumbled onto it, I don't trust his gut instincts just yet. I probably won't as long as he keeps wearing those hats.

David wonders out loud who the assailants were, everything from mecha-pixies to battle gnomes and beyond. It's obvious the kid watches too much anime.

"Don't you have school tomorrow?" I reply.

He glares at me, but of all the groups I know with the means and will to strike at the Brotherhood, none of them are good people for a teenager to be around. This isn't some cartoon where brightly-colored, big-mouthed heroes join forces to save the world. When people get hurt, they die, and when they die they stay dead. He's better off not getting involved.

A little after David leaves, my phone rings. It's Raven. I recline in my desk/chair, press the button on my phone, and her face appears on the far wall, still sans background.

"So?" she says. "What did David find?"

"A Brotherhood greenhouse of all things."

"Doesn't that clash with their color scheme?"

I start to brief Raven on the evening's events, but she cuts me off halfway through.

"Well, sucks to be them. The only thing creepier than a sad clown hunting you down with a machete is a mime with an invisible machete. Or maybe a happy clown. Where's David?"

I chuckle. This is just like Raven. Not flighty, but unafraid to let you know when she's no longer interested.

"He went home a while ago."

"Awwww..."

"Not tonight, Raven. The kid's into elf magic."

She laughs. "You know, for someone who claims not to like him, you're acting a lot like a worried father."

"Whatever."

❋

A misshapen, floating head, about the size of a beach ball and wearing heavy makeup, is taunting me. A mix between a wax statue and a leering clown, it bounces just outside my reach on a field of undulating green. Its marionette bar and strings dangle unused underneath. I ignore it at first. Then it starts singing show tunes in a piercing, high-pitched, digitized warble, but no matter how hard I try or how much I swear I can't get any closer. Anger builds, and I'm about to blast it out of the green sky when my phone alarm sounds. I see small jewels caught and cradled in the strings, like insects in a spider web, then roll out of bed.

I'm much groggier than I'd like to be. In my line of work, dreams like this are sometimes a sign someone's trying to hack you when your defenses are weakest, so I spend the next half hour in meditation, scouring the inside of my mind. The alarm continues to sound at ten minute intervals, preventing me from falling into too deep a trance. I don't find anything, so having paid due diligence to paranoia, I roll out of bed and start my day.

Alerted by the alarm and my motion, the monitor above my bed activates and begins its endless product placement revue. My landlord, Frank, claims the advertising revenue helps keep rent costs low, but I figure him for a fat bastard looking to squeeze out a few extra bucks wherever and whenever he can. It had irritated me endlessly until I found someone who could shut the sound off without tripping the tamper alarm and breaking my lease. Now it's merely annoying and I have to admit it does have its uses. My tiki people collection was the result of a bored night spent watching it, and I've never regretted that purchase.

I step into the shower. The water, pre-soaped, cascades around me, and I plan my day. First a stop at Madame Laveau's, then on to Central Park to check up on some elven activity I'd been following. That should bring me to lunch, after which I'll have more than enough time to chase down the Count's mystery gun.

Adequately clean, I switch the setting to rinse, then turn the shower off completely. Jets of warm air burst from the walls, but I hate that and step through the microfiber curtain instead. I towel myself dry and watch as the tiles wick the dripping water into the corners of the room.

After a quick breakfast of Chocolate Whammy Poofs, I'm ready to go.

❀

Madame Laveau's parlor is tucked away in an artsy district, sandwiched between jewelers, consignment stores, woodcrafters, and a DMV branch office. I push open the faux-wood door and the doorbell rings. It's actually a physical one that hangs from the doorframe. The parlor itself is lined with electronic candles of all shapes and sizes, hugging the walls like Coliseum spectators. Not for the first time, I wonder what they're waiting for. Like all public mambos, she claims nothing but good intentions, but no one's that pure. The candle flames, alerted by the opening door, flicker provocatively. This always disappoints me, that even someone as aboveboard as Laveau still feels the need for petty dramatics.

"Come in, my child, and set yourself down," Madame Laveau calls through the curtain cordoning off the back room. While she's a few years younger than me, I'm okay with her calling me "child" the same way I'm fine with calling a Catholic priest "Father." Some things are just par for the course.

I seat myself at the circular table which takes up most of the room and admire her crystal ball. Pure quartz from Arkansas, it was machined in low-earth orbit and is perfectly spherical to .00001 percent precision. She loves to boast about it. Lasers also engraved the veve of her guiding loa—a wispy, fractal pattern that dances in the right light—into the interior. I think it looks a bit like a labyrinth, myself. The ball rests on a red frilly cushion and, along with the portraits of Catholic saints interspersed between the candles, keeps overwatch on the goings on.

Also on the table, placed dead center, is a flatscreen monitor. It's angled slightly towards me and I lean closer to see what she's been working on. A 3-D model, unfinished, of a balding, middle-aged man floats against a black backdrop. He's got a significant paunch and his arms are outstretched in a pose eerily reminiscent of crucifixion. He's dressed in the rough shapes of clothes, but all his surfaces are smooth and gray.

Madame Laveau sweeps out of the back room, a mass of hoop earrings and authentic African fashion. "I'm sorry for the wait, my child, but—" She stops when she sees me. "You could have told me it was you, Dick."

"And deprive myself of your grand entrances?" I smirk.

Shaking her head, Madame Laveau seats herself opposite me. Due to the construction of the chairs, her eyes are a few inches above mine despite her being shorter than me.

"Is this anyone I know?" I ask, nodding toward the monitor. "Seems like a putz."

She swivels the monitor back toward herself and her eyes flash with indignation. "It does not sit well to mock the newly departed."

I agree. "Yes. You should get in all the mockery you can while they're still alive."

"It was a heart attack," she says in sharp tones, expecting me to show remorse. "He left behind a grieving wife and three kids."

"Nice. How's he doing?"

"Oh, child, he's having the time of his life. It's she who's inconsolable. They weren't too staunch in churchgoing ways and now she's worried sick that he's going to Hell."

I can't help it; I laugh. "She's worried about him going to Hell and she came to a mambo for help?"

"Don't be so smug, child. Grief takes us all in strange ways."

Instead of answering, I reach into my coat pocket and pull out a small red bag held closed with a leather drawstring.

Madame Laveau sighs. "I suppose that's the most I can expect from you, Dick. Where did the little jokers hide it this time?"

"A water main." A group of pixies has decided that stealing her gris-gris bags is the height of fun. Madame Laveau's trying to turn the tables by refusing to get angry or upset, and doesn't even look for them herself. She's right; pixies always get bored, eventually. Until that happens it's easy money for me. Working with Raven's given me an uncanny insight into the way their minds work.

"It's remarkably dry," Madame Laveau says, turning it over in her hands.

"When I found it, it was hermetically sealed in bubble wrap, with gray pixie dust between the layers."

"The little jokers are getting canny."

Gray pixie dust is an integral ingredient in most invisibility potions, and I'd have kept it for further use but it never lasts more than day after it's exposed to air. Madame Laveau places her hands under the table and a moment later my phone vibrates silently. The payment has been made. "Now child," she says, "if you'll excuse me, I have work to do."

The bell above her door marks my passage back into the press of humanity outside. That wife was lucky to stumble into her parlor. Hucksters and frauds abound, sprouting like vampiric mushrooms in the shitpiles of people's hopes and despair, and always find a way to drain them dry. Madame Laveau, on the other hand, will probably just charge her for the contact with the other side, if that, with everything else free. I respect her for standing on principles, even though I don't see the need for that kind of charity myself. People are all too ready to screw themselves over and most of the time pointing that out just pisses them off.

At the parking lot, I head for the public cab station. There are always a few single-occupant cabs available, and I value the privacy despite the cost. Those are queued near the entrance, with the multi-passenger cabs arrayed in grids a few feet further. The single cab fourth in line is rocking slightly.

Despite the blatantly obvious security cameras inside the cabs, or maybe because of them, the more exhibitionist of Tipton's denizens love to use them for quickies. I don't really mind—whatever floats your boat floats your boat—but every now and then a seat turns up slightly sticky and that's just wrong. If you're going to have fun, at least clean up after yourself.

The cabs themselves resemble nothing more than bullets. High speed bullets of commerce aggressively penetrating new markets. Inside, the stark projectile outline is softened a bit by a chair, complete with cup holder, and flat-screen monitor, but corporate presence is undeniable. Embryonic logos incubate on the walls, feeding off the minds of passengers until they grow strong enough to break through the metal shells of their eggs, and if I actually use the on-board computer system I'll be treated to messages from "our gracious sponsors." Raven says I take this way too seriously, but I hate being manipulated.

I sit, placing my right hand on the scanner embedded in the chair's armrest. A quiet beep confirms my identity and fingerprints, making a notation in government systems to raise my taxes for this usage. After I remove my hand, the scanner blinks. A cleaning film sweeps over it, preparing it for the next passenger and surreptitiously collecting samples of my DNA. I speak my destination aloud and off we go, moving smoothly.

I check my messages to fill the downtime, but realize too late I'd forgotten to set my phone to non-interface mode. The monitor flashes on and a female voice erupts from the walls.

"Thank you for choosing Tipton Public Transport. Today's messages have been brought to you by—"

I finally find the right damn button and the announcer fades away. The monitor switches to active standby and I tap its upper right corner. It switches fully to passive. Its glow disappears and the cab picks up speed.

Back to my phone, I have two new messages. One from Raven, one from David.

"Oh, Dick," Raven's says, "Baron Rutgert called. He says the analysis will be ready by tomorrow, but I doubt it. He's shifty; you can see it in his eyes. I'm forwarding the preliminary results. Johnny also called again and still wants your help. And David has something he wants to pass along. I didn't think you'd mind. I'm cutting him in now." The message ends.

I don't know who to be annoyed with more, Johnny or Raven. John Mochasti, or Johnny Mojo as everyone calls him, is a small-time extortionist who makes his living getting paid to stay away. He's become a bit of an urban legend, and his story's actually good for bar conversation, if you don't already know it by heart:

Back in his heyday, at the tender age of sixteen when he was still bursting with hormones and hope, he bought a box of condoms. Unknown to him, that box had been manufactured by a wizard-owned company, and that wizard was into succubae like none other. This particular box was the result of an experiment in refining the essence of sexuality. The experiment itself was successful, but the wizard was taken down by Captain Eight and Chernobyl for using slave labor—this was during their "defenders of human dignity" phase—and so only one box was ever made. Due to a loophole in state regulations, that box made it to the shelves of a local late-night mini-mart, imbued with more than enough magical power to pleasure her past the point of consciousness, if not sanity.

Sadly, no one was interested in an overweight, pimply teen, and the cruel whimsy of fate saw to it that the condom Johnny placed in his wallet languished unused for over a year. When he finally got his chance, the night of his senior prom, the magic had curdled.

The foil wrapper was excitedly torn open by shaking fingers, unleashing the stagnant energy. An unimaginably blue bolt of light struck Johnny square in the balls, launching him into the wall several feet away. The human outline in the drywall has since been plastered over, but that spot is still a minor place of power frequented by fairies.

Johnny's intended conquest got off lucky. The magical field merely flipped the polarity of her sexual orientation and she's now a proud, founding member of a community theater, or so the legend goes. Johnny, on the other hand, was inflicted with a curse painful beyond measure. Not only would he never get laid, ever, but anyone coming within two hundred feet of him would be similarly cock-blocked for at least twenty-four hours.

Some would rail against their fate and turn to Internet forums as their only solace, but Johnny was made of sterner stuff. He turned to internet forums *and* started extorting local night clubs. They were skeptical at first, but Johnny persevered, gracing their establishments nightly with his distinctive cologne and heavy breathing. They continued to lose business month after month, and after a disastrous ladies' night that five fire trucks could barely handle, they saw the error of their ways. In short order, Johnny saved enough money to move out of his parents' apartment and now divides his time between managing his racket, playing online games, and asking me to do things for free. Raven didn't give me his number because I already have it. On my block list.

David, on the other hand, has no business knowing my cell phone number, or even being cut in. Raven should know better. The people I piss off on a regular basis can be quite vengeful and if they hack my phone and find his number, his life could get terminally rough. I haven't pissed anyone off recently but you never know.

His message says, "Greetings, fellow delver into the mysteries of Tipton. Those who shall not speak continue to gather, swelling greatly since last we spoke. I dare not say more."

That's it.

Since last we spoke? I check the timestamp on the message. David left it forty minutes ago. Doesn't the kid go to school? Based on our visit yesterday, I estimate how long it would take him to get back down there. I hope he had the sense to get clear before calling Raven, but as I mentally line the times up, forget school. Doesn't the kid sleep?

I'm worried, a bit, but I don't have the time to play truancy officer. The elf-sign in Central Park indicates something big going down, and the sign never lasts for more than a day after the elves are done meeting. While elves aren't averse to modern technology, old habits die hard and most are more comfortable leaving messages via bark carvings than e-mail. Central Park fits the bill perfectly.

Tipton has vast reservoirs of water, used for everything from drinking to humidity control. Central Park is actually part of the largest water treatment plant. Preliminary stations filter out the real nasty poisons, leaving behind trace organics and chemicals deemed, by leading experts in the fields, unlikely to make plants explode. Next, the water's routed to Central Park, and once there it filters through the roots of the plants and trees being grown hydroponically. Any excess continues down the line to the final processing center. Central Park's succeeded beyond anyone's wildest dreams and is always touted by politicians as a triumph of human ingenuity, when the real reason for its success is elven caretaking.

I step through the giant arch marking the west entrance. About twelve years ago, Central Park had been the site of an exhibition raising funds for a lunar habitat. Most of the props and pavilions are gone, but here and there among the bushes and paths the odd commemorative plaque or foundation sockets remain. The more popular neo-industrial sculptures have also been retained by popular request and add a nice, rough touch to the carefully manicured greenery.

Around me, families enjoy a day out, teens enjoy skipping school, and a few Amishmen tend topiary. My destination is the space gazebo. Defined by futuristic curves and made from a non-iron alloy, it's been claimed by the elves. They've encouraged the surrounding hedge to form a fully enclosing ring and most humans have forgotten it was ever here to begin with. As I approach, I see a familiar face trimming bushes, positioned at just the right angle to keep an eye on this place. The beard has changed, but there's no mistaking Special Agent Ezekiel Kanaghy. He's with the Spiritual Bureau of Investigation, and they often use the Amish for cover, taking advantage of their reputation for craftsmanship and honesty. His presence isn't worth doing anything about, but I still hope the man drowns in a butter churn.

Ignoring him, I step through the seven-foot hedge. There's a spot where the plants will curl away, but you have to know exactly where it is and have complete confidence it will open for you. It's cool and dark inside. Glow-in-the-dark strips embedded into the gazebo itself provide dim illumination, enough to see shapes but not to form real shadows. Six saplings, almost big enough to be called trees, form a ring around the gazebo. Each is accompanied by a miniature monolith bearing a name inscribed into its polished blackness. Jules Verne. H.G. Wells. Isaac Asimov. Arthur C. Clarke. Robert A. Heinlein. George Lucas. This last has a deep scar through the name; at one point, some vandals tried to scratch it out and replace it with Gene Roddenberry. The pettiness of human nature never ceases to amaze me.

I inspect each sapling in turn for elf sign, for the notes each speaker has left behind. I set my phone to flashlight mode and spend the better part of an hour scrutinizing every inch of bark I can see, but there's nothing. Whatever they discussed, they've been careful to leave no trace behind.

Chapter 3

I am not a man accustomed to significant delay," Count Fantabuloso informs me. "However, being a man of business, I am no stranger to exigencies. Please, educate me."

It's been a slow few weeks, with no leads and less progress. It's not that my usual sources know nothing; it's that they know even less than that. I can't even find half of them. Iron Jim, a homeless man who hangs out in Trent, is rumored to have OD'ed but I know he's never used drugs in his life. Billy Millions, who you can always track down by the scent of bullshit surrounding his latest scheme, is nowhere to be found. Janet and Jane, the Wiggs sisters, damn near threw me out of their brothel before I had a chance to step all the way in the door. Even David's been hanging around less than usual. Johnny Mojo's still trying to get a hold of me, and I'm still avoiding him. For good reasons. As for the gun itself, it isn't on any registry, there are no similar designs in production anywhere, and even Raven has no clue where to go from here. We can't even hazard a guess about how it got into the city.

I tell the Count so, and for a moment the only sound in the room is the thump of his feet on the treadmill.

As he often does, the Count's holding this meeting in his private gym. It has everything a baller could want, from weights to treadmills to punching bags and even a small, octagonal cage in the back corner, all in perfect working order and studded with bling. The Count himself is doing his part to fight the obesity epidemic in a pink and purple jogging suit. The word SOUL is outlined in small jewels across the jacket's back. Running up his pant legs, the word PLAYER is embroidered in silver thread. At the moment, he's refining his pimp walk. Every third step, he dips an alternating shoulder as far back as it can go.

"This is vexing fierce," he says. "He confounds not you, but my own trusted agents furthermore." Step-step-lean, step-step-lean. The blue feather in his purple hat flutters like an exotic dancer.

I sneak a look at the treadmill display. The Count's pimping it at the respectable speed of 3.2 miles an hour. Going nowhere, admittedly, but anyone would have to admit he's doing so in consummate style. The Differance Stick, present as always, is propped against the treadmill's side.

The Barons Elmdore and Marcus, a bored, background noise of muscle, are seated on weight benches, silently doing curls. Their reflections in the mirrored walls are equally apathetic. Both are in uniform.

"Whoever's behind this, they have to have an operation," I say.

"I fail to see villains bearing such skill," he replies.

There it is again, that condescending tone of voice that drives me crazy. The barons grin, probably glad it's aimed at someone else for a change.

"Not just skill," I say. "Whoever they are, they're either completely tight-lipped or have enough money and muscle to scare everyone into hiding."

"Phones are ubiquitous. Is that not so?" the Count says.

"Unfortunately, my telecommunications contacts have turned over a new leaf."

"Decided to go straight, huh?" the Baron Marcus says, switching to a heavier dumbbell.

"No. Promotion."

Everyone except the Count chuckles at that. It's a shame, too. Tipton is home to over one hundred million people, but nearly everyone has a phone, and any phone worth its five-year contract not only has a GPS locator but interfaces with Tipton's integrated networks as well, constantly broadcasting its position, status, etc. It's a huge amount of data, and specialized skills are needed to mine it effectively. Unfortunately, my main contact, Rebecca, recently got promoted to Data Security Supervisor. Her paycheck's now big enough that she doesn't need anything else under the table. Her spending will outpace her income again soon and I'll have a way back in, but there's nothing for it right now.

"Regarding life's gayer side," the Count interjects, "Lord British is holding a soiree evenings hence. Unfortunately the Baron Marcus, my premier man, has fallen deathly ill. Recuperation is well deserved, but I still require able-bodied guards."

I don't like where this is heading, and the Baron Marcus's grin confirms it. Great.

The Count continues. "Two days hence, Bamborough's gates sweep open. Dick, you are deputized; I know I need *not* tell you *not* to make a half-assed mess."

With that, he turns the treadmill off and moves to a convoluted machine to work his quads. The esquire posted at the door sees me out as both barons smirk. They hate Lord British as much as I do and apparently it's my turn to get the short end of the stick.

I'm not one to complain, but the Baron Elmdore, head of the Count's intelligence and internal affairs, is the natural choice. This is obviously an opportunity for me to snoop around Lord British's estate, but, well, I hate the man and his minions. Then again, Count Fantabuloso might no longer trust Elmdore—he's admittedly in the best position to hide information from the Count—and his presence at the meeting could have been part of a ploy intended to get the baron to tip his hand. The Count's plans always have wheels within wheels, most complete with spinners. I can handle anything the Count can dish out, but I never appreciate being used as bait. And regardless of what's really going on, I now have to deal with Lord British.

❀

Raven's less than sympathetic when I break her the news. Her face morphs into a slew of emoticons expressing condolences and regret, but she's smirking at me the entire time. I thank her for her support.

"British really isn't that bad," she says. "Not once you get past his callous disregard for the rights and feelings of others. Besides, you can just piss him off like last time."

Yeah. That.

"Did you have to bring that up?" I say.

"Dick, it was the highlight of your week and you know it."

"If you call barely managing to limp out of there in one piece a highlight, then yes, yes it was. It was the highlight of my whole damn month."

"At least you learned a valuable lesson," Raven says, still smirking.

"What?"

"Don't trust Johnny, even if he has the money."

Despite myself I laugh, a short, sharp sound with very little humor behind it.

Johnny Mojo had called with a job. I was going to ignore him as usual, but then Raven told me how much the down payment was. Curious about the novelty of Johnny being willing to pay, I decided to give him a chance. As it turns out, it wasn't even his money; he was approaching me on behalf of anonymous backers. The job, as he described it, was simple. Break into Lord British's estates, get some information about the layout of the place and the progress of the security upgrades, and then let myself out just in time to collect a handsome fee. Most of the systems weren't supposed to be up yet.

Instead, I ran into submachine gun turrets, elven hounds, *and* grounding runestones. What the hell?

Adding insult to injury, not only did Johnny and his backers refuse to pay anything beyond the down payment, but when I called him to bitch him out about the entire situation, all he did was send me a video clip of some fish-headed alien yelling

"It's a trap!" in an infinite loop. Needless to say, that escapade did little to improve my opinion of either Johnny Mojo or Lord British.

"Btw," Raven continues, "Johnny called again. Insists it's important."

"It can wait. Oh, I saw Zeke today, Amish-ing it up in Central Park."

A frown flits across her face. "Really," she says. It's a real frown, not an emoticon, and her hair darkens a few shades. "What was he doing?"

"I'm not sure. I didn't talk to him. I just thought I'd let you know." For some reason, the SBI's taken an unrequited interest in Raven, and they're as subtle about it as a love-struck teenager. "Is everything all right?"

"Thanks," she says, dodging the question. "What are you going to do now?"

While I'm a little worried, I trust her, so I let the subject drop. "Well, since I can't find anyone and Rutgert's report wasn't that helpful, I figure I'll stake out Bamborough."

❃

One of the best places to spy on Bamborough, Lord British's manor, is Perrine Dining Court. Since it's one of the upscale districts and relies on casual tourism, Perrine's designers felt the need to distinguish it. The theme is electronica. Every square inch is festooned with pointless displays, from ads to interactive games to constantly changing fractal art, and fiber-optic cables form an integral part of the décor. It's like my desk on crack. Storefronts glint and glitter and a carbon-market ticker scrolls around the top of a court-wide electronic marquee, connecting environmentally savvy day traders with the pulse of socially responsible capitalism. The walkways light up in primary colors as people walk by, and with a staggered, multi-level series of frosted glass platforms spanning the central open space, Perrine resembles nothing so much as a crystalline 3-D crop circle.

I order a burger and fries from Mighty Munchies, the cheapest joint here, and find a table. The western end of the court, the tourist corner, features real windows looking out onto an impressive vista of other buildings in Tipton. One of these is Eaton Building, of which Bamborough Manor occupies the top five floors. Eaton itself is over one hundred floors shorter than the surrounding buildings, and the result is a thousand-foot cylinder of empty space, a testament to Lord British's arrogance and wealth. He will never be daunted by anyone. No matter how far they might physically rise, he will always consider himself superior. Asshole.

I train my binoculars on Bamborough and see what appear to be gardens manicured into straightjacket respectability. A golf course nestles against a swimming lake and tennis courts are barely visible in the background. The mansion itself, nearly hidden by trees, smirks like a coy streetwalker, and all of it is bullshit. The "windows" are actually giant screens, five whole floors of them, and the bucolic scene—the bastard even has birds flying across the grounds—is purely a tourist show.

Oh, Bamborough actually has a golf course, swimming lake, and the works, but its layout is completely different. As I also learned, there's also a full complement of guards armed with semi-automatics, laser microphone acoustic detection systems, magic sensors, and even roaming elven hounds as guard dogs. Nobody but elves have elven hounds, and Lord British definitely isn't an elf. More likely, his family claims elven blood from back before the Roman invasion of England and his money silences all naysayers one way or another.

I snarl and train my binoculars on the floor below, which handles the routine traffic flowing through the servants' entrance. From my angle I can't see much, mainly a small section of utility road, but this is the best view I can get without actually going skyside.

There isn't much, other than a few trucks presumably ferrying supplies. One passes by every ten minutes or so, more than usual but expected in light of the upcoming party. Failing to impress is definitely high on Lord British's list of cardinal sins, ranking above theft and adultery and equal with unnecessary murder. I snap photos of all the license plates and most of the drivers' faces. After a few hours, I'm ready to pack it in when a black limousine with no plates rolls past.

I keep snapping pictures mainly out of habit; my jaw's grinding in disbelief. The outfits of the two stooges escorting it on foot are unmistakable. The one in front has a black leather trenchcoat held closed by silver clasps along the front. A large, silver ankh is emblazoned on the back, and he carries a short, wooden wand in gloved hands. The other, presumably female, sports a bright purple Mohawk. A black corset wrapped in red string flares out into a black lace skirt. Four belts, too large to be useful, hang from her hips.

It has to be the Goth, the only person in the world I hate more than Lord British, and now they're meeting with each other. My level of interest ratchets up a few notches. I presume there are two more escorts on the other side of the car, but there's no way to get an angle on them.

The car and escorts disappear around a corner and a few seconds later the windows go dark. I zoom out with the binoculars and, sure enough, the band of darkness extends around the entire access floor, a setup that must have cost a fortune. Call me cynical, but even if people value their privacy, no one spends that much money on principle. Still, with the windows dark, there's nothing more I can do. Knowing British, the windows also foil laser microphones.

On my way out, I notice a homeless man on the other side of the court. His bubble of personal space slowly widens as the people around him unconsciously avoid him. True homeless are unusual and hard to distinguish from reality show contestants, so I train my binoculars on him. I might as well. He's scruffy and dirty and wearing two worn trucker caps, one atop the other, but nothing can dilute his look of fierce determination. He stretches his legs, loosens up his arms, carefully leans his pasteboard sign against the wall, then jumps up and down a few times. Satisfied, he drops into a crouch, his back against the sparkling wall, and waits.

Suddenly, he springs into motion, surging against the crowd like a stinky salmon up a river of elbows and swearing. He muscles his way to the Burger Wok counter and snatches a tray a split second ahead of its rightful owner. He holds it triumphantly overhead and, just as shocked looks gave way to anger, offers it back. Unsurprisingly, the customer refuses, and the homeless man absconds before security can converge.

I grin. This can only mean one thing. The Hobolympics, my favorite cultural event, are just around the corner, a truly bright note in a world suffocated by marketing. I nearly skip all the way back to my office but I don't, because I'm a professional.

Chapter 4

As you might have guessed, Lord British is old money, from the stiff-upper-lip school of bribing life like a wealthy man. He's also one of those rare, distinguished people who can walk into a room while reeking of alcohol, realize he's not wearing pants, and then excuse himself without losing any sense of personal dignity. The important thing is that form is maintained, after all.

Like most of his ilk, he believes the most important thing anyone can do is know their place. Then everything you *actually* deserve will come without undue effort. He also believes he has an instinctive and unerring knowledge about everyone else's place as well, and in his retirement considers it his duty to punish those with the presumption to "reach beyond one's standing." Ferreting out his connection to the Goth and nailing both their asses to the wall is something that's been a long time coming.

I arrive at the pre-party security briefing early, in the neighborhood of seven A.M. Several other security contingents, all sporting black suits, earpieces, and sunglasses, are already there. I, too, am wearing such a suit, as is the Esquire Byron, the Baron Marcus' first lieutenant. The two other esquires, wearing their uniforms, stand out like angry, bruised, and swollen thumbs, but they're enjoying the attention. By far the biggest part of visible security at these gigs is scowling and folding your arms in an assertive yet unobtrusive way. They'll be more furniture than anything, and their overstuffed winter coats, sans sleeves, add impressive bulk to their frames.

I'm particularly proud of my tie. Solid black silk, it flares out with just a hint of debonair distinction, marking me as a man of subtle sensibilities and refined judgment, at least according to the catalog, and it's nicely accented by a sterling silver clip with classy gold accents. At least one of the other heads-of-security will have read the same catalog, and if I can intimidate them now they'll be less likely to inquire when I start snooping around.

What I'm most pleased with is the package of peanuts I found in my suit jacket's inside pocket. I buy snacks to keep my blood sugar up during stakeouts and other boring parts of my job. If nothing happens, and it usually doesn't, no problem, but in the excitement of a chase, dodging unfriendly spells, or simply getting shot at, I often forget they're there. I've lost track of how many times my dry cleaner has presented me with the remains of a snack pack in a small plastic bag. Other times, like today, when I forget to buy a snack, I'll check my inside pocket from habit and there they'll be, like little gifts from God. I don't remember how long it's been since I've worn this particular suit, but these are roasted peanuts. What's the worst that can happen?

We're stashed in a conference room that's by no means state of the art, but we're at least important enough to merit complimentary beverages. Four mini-fridges roam the room on autopilot, deftly avoiding the lacquered octagonal tables. Each time one whirs by I grab another can of grape soda. I measure the minutes with peanuts, trying to goad a reaction from the others by creating tableaus on the table in front of me, searching for chinks in their mental armor. No one blinks an eye, even when I have two towers of used cans arranged defensively around clusters of peanut shells.

Giving it up, I scan the room. Booths for private conversations, large enough for four people, are set into the walls. Hints of fully retractable soundproof barriers line the entrances to those alcoves. They might provide adequate cover in a firefight. I think about searching one for the hidden bugs that have to be inside, but there's no reason to be that rude.

Wanda, the head of Lord British's security, arrives predictably late and positions herself at the head of the room. Bored heads swivel dispassionately in her direction and I'm impressed at our coordination. With less than an hour to prepare, we've become a championship-caliber synchronized staring team, specializing in apathy.

Wanda's severe suit only amplifies her angular bust. Given her personality, I wouldn't be surprised to learn she's had a double mastectomy and had the "girls" replaced with anti-personnel mines. I'm never getting close enough to find out; that's for sure. I've never learned her real name, but she looks like a Wanda—her eyes are set so close together they look like they're trying to squeeze a confession out of her nose. That's good enough for me.

"You are here for the briefing," she says sharply, without bothering to introduce herself.

By this time, I'm a little antsy. Several more security contingents have arrived while we've waited, but none are easily tied to the Goth. I'm still expecting his contingent; maybe they're running late.

"You will visibly display your badges at all times whenever you are on the premises," Wanda continues. A few of the security professionals check their badges at the mention of them, marking them as newbies.

"Please program your communications devices with the liaison frequency listed in the briefing." We nod. Of course it's already done, even if we're planning on doing it later.

"You have each been assigned an area, and should the need arise you will use this frequency to contact me." Wanda snaps and the words "1560 MHz" appear briefly in mid-air, courtesy of hidden holographic projectors. I look around, but can't place them. "If there are any questions beyond what's presented in the briefing packets, now is the time," she concludes.

Now it's time for the interactive portion of this morning's entertainment. Regardless of what the briefing packet actually says, everyone's going to try to get as much access to as many areas as possible.

"Mr. Rollinger will not be pleased." This man, seated to my left, looks like a Samoan gangster woke up in a suit one day and decided to just go with it. His companions, cut from the same mold, are actively scowling. An art critic might call it a dynamically intense exploration into active malevolence. I'd say it's clear they're just waiting for a reason to roll up their sleeves and beat someone into a coma.

"Neither will Senator Durbin," another says. This speaker's female, and unlike Wanda, she looks like a Cheryl.

It turns out Mrs. Hancock and Sir Eddings will be similarly upset, which is bullshit. As long as they don't get shot, kidnapped, or publicly embarrassed within view of paparazzi, they won't give a damn.

"Lord British's security services are the best in the world," Wanda replies. Her tone is condescending enough to bring out the best in people.

Letting the vanguard duel it out with her, I mutter a short charm underneath my breath, surreptitiously attuning my eyes. None of the guests mentioned so far are known for moving in esoteric circles, but I'm still certain the Goth will have at least some presence here. At the very least, a go-between.

The Esquire Byron notices what I'm doing and raises his eyebrows. No one except the Count's men is noticeably magical, and theirs is the limited protection enchanted into their undermesh shirts. I shake my head no and he relaxes slightly.

I, on the other hand, am getting more and more wound up. The grape soda I've been chugging is probably caffeinated. To release some tension, I join the negotiations. There's a rumor, I mention, about someone successfully breaking into Bamborough a few months back. Wanda questions the credibility but, like a true professional, I act indignant and refuse to disclose my sources. After some more wrangling, the negotiations end with everyone pissed off about something and we begin the fifty cent tour.

Wanda starts by walking us through the major access and utility corridors, pointing out basic security measures. Magnetically sealed doors, top-of-the-line access panels, cunningly disguised cameras, all standard stuff. Then it's out onto the estate proper, where we're suffered to inspect the manor grounds, just outside the mansion itself, that are being set up for the party.

I have to admit, the area looks a lot different in daytime lighting with no one shooting at me. A long, cobblestone path winds through carefully manicured lawns, flirting with creeks, flower bushes, and wooden benches. It widens as it reaches a large pavilion tent still in the process of being erected. Risers for a band have already been placed underneath. Sound technicians are having a running argument about wiring and brightly colored pennants hang limply from the edges of the tent's roof. A large banner, bearing Lord British's family crest, lies unfolded on the ground.

On the ceiling above, specialty bulbs and LED emitters simulate bright sunlight, and workers on barely-visible scaffolding wrestle the ruffled, plastic sheets used to simulate clouds into place. The manor is a hive of activity, an excellent cover for whatever else Lord British might be doing.

After giving us time to examine this area and issue quiet instructions to subordinates, Wanda takes us around the grounds, highlighting the pool, the polo field, the tennis lawns, and the contemplation pond as if we're tourists. I ignore her, trying to figure out the real layout of the place instead.

Bamborough uses a design strategy common to security-minded estates. In order to maximize the use of vertical space, each location is at a slightly different elevation. The pond floor is the poolhouse ceiling and I'd bet the polo field drains into the tennis lawns. But to create the illusion of an outdoor country manor, lines of sight are strictly controlled, with hedges every thirty yards or so. Where necessary, area ceilings have been coated with LED displays synchronized to the main ceiling. Not only that, but most of the floors slope gently, so people walking from one area to another won't realize they're moving up or down.

The grounds near the manor itself are the only exception. There, the estate opens up into five stories of sheer space, impressive and intimidating to anyone used to Tipton's crowds. In places where the hedges, walls, and privacy screens are temporarily down, the multilevel construction is obvious—it's like looking at a cutaway diagram—but with everything in place the illusion would be nearly seamless.

With a floor plan like this, Lord British could hide anything damn near anywhere. The night I broke in, the first thing I did was stumble into a guardhouse that materialized out of a six-inch rise in one of the lawns. Already on this walkthrough I've spotted dozens of digital cameras and motion sensors, all of which Wanda neglects to mention. I also notice a few of the runestones—magical anchors—which gave me so much trouble. They've been cunningly disguised as waist-high lawn ornaments. They even have plaques nearby falsely proclaiming them to be the work of up-and-coming abstract sculptors.

Wanda finishes the tour by saying, "I will personally be taking care of the areas inside the manor proper. You may station men at the entrances. Your jurisdiction is limited to the pavilion area and surrounding lawns. Do not roam freely during the event, as the automated defenses have not been programmed to recognize you."

And there go my plans of snooping around during the party itself. With runestones draining magic there'll be no way to avoid a bullet enema, and getting shot isn't my idea of a good time. I don't have the time or resources to figure out how to shut down the manor's defenses, so I'll have to work on soft intel instead, pumping guests for information.

The Esquire Byron takes out his phone and starts making preparations while I detach myself from the group and roam. There's a good chance I'll be kicked out soon and I want to make the most of the time I have left. At some point during the morning, cameras will have gotten good videos of us all. Facial- and motion-recognition software would be even now churning through databases, searching for hits. The mask I wore when breaking in would foil facial-recognition software, but the computers will eventually realize that the mystery intruder and I move in an almost identical fashion, as if we might be the same person. Imagine that. Then, I'll be escorted from the premises and Count Fantabuloso will receive a polite message requesting that someone else take over as his chief of security.

Unfortunately for my evening, that never happens. Either I pulled off that infiltration better than I thought or, more likely, Lord British sees no reason to offend the Count. On the other hand, I *had* been limping heavily when I made my escape, and that's been known to fool even high-end systems. Even with top-of-the-line software, gimping around can knock recognition certainty down by about fifteen percent—not enough to risk offending a major player over. The rest of the morning is predictably boring. Every time I get close to an interesting area I'm stopped either by British's security or the not-so-subtle beeps of an automated turret processing through its arming sequence. At least they're playing nice; in stealth mode good turrets are absolutely silent.

After watching the workers for a while, I check back in with Raven. She's searched for anything resembling the style of the Count's mystery gun in the last fifty years, but finding nothing, moved on to looking for possible ties to early twentieth century legends. The mystery gun is too modern to predate that. Or, the thought crosses my mind, it could be something completely new, developed recently. I let her know about the Goth-British connection; she says she'll try that angle but isn't expecting much.

"Oh, btw," she says as I'm about to hang up, "the Baron Rutgert wants to see you."

"About what?" I say.

"I'm not sure, but he sounded pretty excited."

"Great."

I play it like I'm irritated, but that's all the excuse I need to take off for a while. I planned to hit a tuxedo rental place anyway—since I'm going to be hobnobbing with rich assholes instead of skulking around, a tuxedo's a better choice—and I might as well kill some more time.

❀

There's a different nameless esquire manning the counter when I step inside Jimbo's Porn-n-Pawn. Not so surly but much more high strung, he constantly tosses quick glances toward the hyperbolic mirror.

"I have a test coming up," I say.

"We, we don't sell textbooks," he replies, stumbling through the exchange. He looks around as if expecting an ambush.

"Really," I say. "I must have been misinformed."

With another sidelong glance, he reaches under the counter. Being the kind and caring soul that I am, I resist the urge to make his nervousness worse. The door slides aside, and I step through the curtain of air back into the test facility. When I find him, Baron Rutgert is in the high-intensity observation booth, an alcove with a direct video feed to a shielded testing room. The screen's mounted on the far wall and the camera angle gives the impression that you're looking down on the room in question, but it's actually in another part of the city: the Under proper, to be precise, surrounded by yards of concrete and steel. It's also blanketed by a thin layer of water and other protective measures, none of which the Count is willing to discuss. I've had to weasel the specs out of Rutgert, but even he won't give me its location.

On top of all that secrecy, the only people who'd really notice if it blew would be the people stupid enough to be living nearby. There are whole areas of Tipton, mostly the lower floors, that have pretty much been abandoned and forgotten. From what Rutgert's told me, the level of debris, damage, and patchwork fixes is so extreme that the bases of the skyscrapers are propped against each other for support. The connecting skywalks on the upper floors might be the only things keeping everything stable and upright. If the test range blows, the most anyone topside would notice is a slight tremor, if that even makes through their headphones.

Everything in the high-intensity room is automated, and the only way materials get in or out is through a vacuum-sealed pipe, visible near the back. Waldoes of various sizes allow Rutgert to set up any test he can imagine, but without the complication of living things being involved. It looks just like the test range here, but with robotic limbs sprouting from the walls like the tentacles of a dying cyberpunk god.

"That is not dead which can in sleep mode lie, and with strange input even death may die," I mutter to myself.

The room is even creepier after an experiment, when the robotic arms reset themselves, moving with apparent purpose from one contorted pose to another. Currently, they're quiescent.

"This looks serious," I say.

Baron Rutgert, seated as usual in his rolling chair, taps his glasses. His eyes focus on me.

"Quite the setup, isn't it?" he says. "I love to tell the esquires it's downstairs, hence the Ouija board. The new Jimbo hasn't been able to sit still since." He's wearing a plaid, button-up shirt and pale brown slacks. Raven loves to make fun of my dress sense, but even I can tell he doesn't match. His shoes, thoroughly shined, don't help.

"What's happening?" I say.

I'm expecting a new case. Me in the high-intensity room is never good, so I'm pleasantly surprised.

The baron says, "That gun you brought in, something about the initial test results bothered me, so I tested it again, this time in isolation."

When I read through the preliminary report it seemed like standard stuff—steel barrel, wooden parts—but I wait for him to continue.

He reaches under his chair, pulls out a mobile pad, and taps his glasses to synchronize the two. I wait a few seconds for whatever needs to happen to happen.

Rutgert swears and rips off his glasses. From the way he holds his head, it's obvious he's blind.

I draw my handgun and flatten myself against the wall by the door. The Count has many enemies, and those who aren't already dead don't believe in the phrase "innocent bystanders." Not that I'm all that innocent, but plausible deniability is everything in this business. The hiss of the air control system is suddenly very loud and as I reach a hand out to close the door, I try to decide whether it's possible to co-opt the A/C for a chemical attack.

"Get back," I quietly bark at Rutgert. When he doesn't respond, I roll his chair into a corner with my foot.

When we don't immediately pass out, I go through a mental list of the Count's surviving enemies. Who would have the means to attack here? About halfway through, it occurs to me that the ones who are dead could conceivably find a way back and would undoubtedly be very pissed off. I chant a small, protective cantrip, nothing big. A stream of power still rushes through my head and it's damn hard to stop there.

The high-intensity room is tucked away in the back of the complex, and I've already shut the door to the only exit. I could lock it if necessary, but that would be suicide. The same people who'd shoot through the walls when confronted with a locked door will try to open an unlocked door first. It's just something about human nature, and I'd rather have a chance to shoot back.

After several nervous seconds, I tap the panel and bob my head around the frame, taking a quick peek outside.

Nothing but empty corridor.

I relax a bit and lower my sidearm.

Inside, Rutgert's still holding his head. His glasses dangle from his left hand, he doesn't appear to be affected by anything magical. The video screen still shows the unmoving and silently mocking waldoes: absolutely nothing of note. Fluorescent strips in the ceiling cast everything in soft and gentle shadows.

The metal walls start to pulse. I shake my head to clear it. Now is not the time. For all I know the assailants are waiting for us to really drop our guard before attacking.

I force myself to focus on reality, to ignore the siren call of magical power. The room eventually stops smirking, starts behaving the way it should.

As it turns out, this isn't the prelude to an attack. It's a known issue instead.

"Oh, God damn it," Baron Rutgert fumes when he finally recovers himself. "I always forget these pieces of shit do this." He massages his temples and blinks his vision back. "Whenever you multiplex data streams and link speeds exceed two hundred Mbps, God *damn*. Feedback builds and for some Godforsaken reason the glasses shunt it into video memory."

"What?" I ask, more than a little nonplussed and watching for hostiles.

He smacks his forehead with the inside of his fist. "You'd think they'd recall the little bastards but no, you have to tweak the electronics to get them above one-twenty, and it's right there in the damn EULA. 'Unauthorized modification of this equipment may result in physical injury, up to and including seizures, permanent vision loss, coma, and death.'"

With magic still trying to hijack my consciousness, it takes me a bit to interpret what he's saying. When I figure it out, I'm tempted to shoot him.

"I think they leave these kinds of design flaws in on purpose, and ever since Frenetti vs. Antioch, they've been untouchable."

"That's nice to know," I say, feeling a headache build.

"Yeah, the bastards are—" He pauses. "Dick, are you okay?"

"Just give me a moment." I close my eyes, trying to focus.

"Your eyes, they're glowing."

What else is new? I snarl under my breath. "I said give me a moment." That comes out harsh, but I don't care. A song of power and blood still whirls through my mind and, while I appreciate the way it completely obliterates any advertising jingles it comes across, it's still one hell of a mind-fuck to have to deal with just because Rutgert's glasses decided they didn't like being hacked. There's a reason I have a reputation for being an asshole.

"Dick?" Rutgert's voice penetrates the fog, a needless annoyance.

"What?"

"Are you planning on putting the gun away any time soon?"

"What?"

"Could you at least stop pointing it at me?"

I find that funny and that's what actually snaps me out of it. I open my eyes and the world fades back into view, less vibrant than before, less oppressively alive. I take a deep breath and holster my weapon.

"Sorry," I say. "What was it you wanted to show me?"

Baron Rutgert gives me an odd, measuring look. After a few moments he hands over the mobile pad. Two diagrams are displayed. They swim a little, but each holds the black outline of a handgun on a white background, surrounded by colorful lines. It's like the pictures of magnetic fields in physics books, but much more tangled and complex. The only thing I really notice through the dull thumping in my skull is that the one on the right is cleaner, calmer, and has less red and more blue.

"The one on the left is from your test fire," Rutgert says. "The one on the right is from an automated test."

"It looks more subdued," I say. I'm not sure where he's going with this and that headache is really starting to build.

"That's exactly it. The magical potential decreased more than fivefold. That doesn't happen unless magic's draining away."

"Is it?"

"Actually, no. I had an esquire fire it again. Those results are on the next page." I pretend to flick the screen over and Rutgert continues, "The field potentials came back to full strength. Do you know what this means?"

I nod, sarcasm rising. Out of a ten-round clip, one round was missing and three were fired. "We've got six chances left to find out what the rounds actually do."

Rutgert blinks, his train of thought completely derailed. I take pity on him.

"And that the gun feeds off the natural magic inherent in the shooter," I finish.

He wipes his hands on his slacks and, after the gears in his head realign, picks right up where he left off. "Yeah. If we could duplicate that effect, the potential power generated would be enormous, more than enough to..."

I tune out his excited techno babble. Any magic which draws its power from the wielder is dangerous, especially when one of its effects is to make you want to keep using it. Magic is addictive enough on its own without adding true compulsion to the mix. Rutgert continues with his theories and avenues of analysis, but I'm leery. The gun didn't seem intelligent when I fired it, but perhaps it's smart enough to hide itself.

On top of it all, this seems like the Goth's style and that only deepens my suspicions. If only I had something solid to go on. As much as I would love to blame him and British for everything, without more evidence even I have to admit this is just speculation.

Somewhere along the way I realize that Rutgert's been silent for a few seconds and is now excusing himself.

"I'll be right back," he says, probably enraptured by a brilliant idea.

I finish downloading the data from the mobile pad through my phone to my desk/chair, then I message it to Raven as well and see myself out. The esquire at the counter nearly jumps out of his skin when the door slides open and this time I do mutter something ominous.

"Oh don't worry," I say. "The safeties haven't failed in *weeks*."

His eyes go wide and I grunt. If he doesn't calm down he'll stroke out.

Chapter 5

Despite the impressive décor, Lord British's shindig is disappointingly pedestrian. The program does its best, but while the folded sheet of electronic paper charmingly describes every sculpture and point of interest as I draw near, it can't overcome the mind-numbing banality with which rich people amuse themselves in public. In private is a complete different matter, as plenty of Internet videos attest. I'm adrift in an ocean of crap, and the bullshit icebergs floating through it never shut up. The theme of the soiree, the program informs me, is the merging of past and future.

Pedestals with replicas of technology throughout the ages are spaced around the perimeter of the wide pavilion, each backlit in a display case and standing in its own personal spotlight. The apex of the finished pavilion is at least two stories high and if I squint I can barely make out the camera hiding there. Brightly colored pennants hang from the edges. A jazz combo plays old standards and the ice sculpture near an hors-d'oeuvre buffet melts in a dignified manner. At first I think it's an ostrich molesting a goose, but on closer inspection it turns out to be a tree and gear intertwined. The very human scent of people jammed together, along with the perfume, deodorant, and cologne used to keep everything civil, saturates the air.

The program helpfully recommends a route that will take me from the stone axes of the Paleolithic and Cro-Magnon art up through the next-gen solar panels and optical processors currently in use. Most of the distinguished guests, lingering like well-dressed athlete's foot, are audibly enjoying the privileges of wealth.

"And to think," a woman in a sparkling blue evening gown says to another. Her voice can only be described as a stage whisper. "The plebian have to mingle in such close quarters."

Her companion, slightly tipsy, agrees.

Yes, of course. At this party, everyone can stretch out their arms without touching someone else. Jolly good show.

My tuxedo isn't the most comfortable, and though it moves well it feels way too tight. The cummerbund, changing colors in response to ambient lighting, reminds me a bit too much of Raven's hair. I can almost hear her teasing me. Despite myself, I've been hoping for a smoking gun, some magical activity so obvious all I'll have to do is knock Lord British out, drag the Goth from wherever he's hiding, and hand them both over to the Count. Instead, I've spent the last two hours trying to figure out which bon mots were intentional jokes and which were people being assholes.

It's not that I hate them. It's just, inevitably, that they represent the worst of everything humanity can be. Elves, or so the stereotype goes, are haughty and ethereal, bloodthirsty and vicious. Dwarves are finely tuned machines that convert alcohol into swear words, engineering, and more alcohol. Pixies are cracked-out, flying five-year-olds, goblins spawn from masturbation socks that aren't disposed of properly, and gnomes are gnomes. The prevailing racial slur for humans is "wannabes." Trust me, in nonhuman languages, that's much worse than it sounds. It's not because we're younger than the other races. I used to ignore it, writing it off as reciprocal douchebagism, but the more I've thought about it the more it makes sense.

From a nonhuman's perspective, it probably does look like we're trying to copy them and failing miserably. Elven arrogance without the innate grace. Pixie whimsy sans the social reflexes. Dwarven down-to-earthness (and alcoholism) without the inner discipline and dedication to craftsmanship. Goblin deviousness without the capacity to truly enjoy evil. We've picked up all the worst qualities, but even the most assiduous among us are only imitation assholes. It's not just rich people either, but at least the people on the bottom have people above them to keep them in check.

While I'm on the subject, gnomes bother me too. All they do is build more gnomes, and I've never seen any get destroyed. By all rights they should have taken over the earth by now, with gnomes bursting out of every open seam, but they haven't. Where the hell do they go and what do they do?

I take a deep breath and start to wander around. Being around the ridiculously affluent always puts me in a cranky mood, and the smoke from the novelty cigars being handed out by waitstaff is giving me a headache. They act so self-important, but put them in a room with a demon and their blood will boil just like anyone else's. Again, I can hear Raven's teasing voice telling me I'm taking this way too seriously.

If you believe the stories of saints, human beings do have a unique capacity, an ability to transcend. From what Raven says, you hear it whispered in ancient legends about the Shining Lands, legends which all nonhuman cultures share in one form or another. Human beings, the newest creation, the weakest of the weak, are nevertheless the only ones with the chance to reach that storied paradise. Invariably, human failings prevent that from happening, and some of the flameouts are quite hilarious, but those are newer additions to the old stories. Or so Raven tells me. She's big into interspecies anthropology.

After cooling down a bit, I end up inside the mansion proper. Bamborough's foyer, as well as its ballroom, have been opened for the event. The foyer's claim to fame is a series of artfully displayed concept sketches, spanning the gamut from reproductions of the cave art at Lasceaux to the blueprints for the REpeated-Use Space Elevator, acronymed REUSE by bureaucrats convinced they have a sense of humor. DaVinci's sketches figure prominently. My program chirps excitedly as I pass each one, desperate to impart refinement.

Where the foyer is huge and window-filled, the ballroom is even bigger, its walls rising at least twenty-five feet from hardwood floors before culminating in decorative Greek arches. Party-goers mingle throughout and buffet tables line the long edges of the rectangular space. The main stage's curtain, red, is lowered, and golden rope barriers discreetly block off the stairs on either side. Above, chandeliers glow with light, and while it's impossible to see past the fake candles, there have to be cameras perched behind. Background music mingles with the hubbub of people aggressively networking.

There's an esquire posted next to the buffet table and I decide to talk to him. Not only does he look lonely, standing next to the stylized waterfall of cocktail shrimp, but I've been here for over two hours making small talk, and it's about to drive me out of my mind. I'd rather have something to do or someplace to go.

I shoulder my way through the crowd—no one really notices—and when I reach the crustaceous waterfall I pick up a small, chilled plate and stack some shrimp on board, leaving the cocktail sauce alone.

"You want some?" I offer the plate to the esquire.

He stares at the food but replies, "Can't eat while on duty."

"What if I order you to?" I know he's hungry, and depending on how much he's eaten today I might get him to break.

"You're only technically in charge."

Nicely played. I laugh, and he smiles in return.

"How's it going?" I say, leaving the plate just within his reach.

"I've never seen elves before."

As soon as he says it, I could just kick myself. I'm so used to dealing with magical creatures that their presence here hasn't registered as anything unusual. But that kind of oversight is what gets people killed, and it is odd for them to be out in the open, especially among mundane company. They're probably counting on the money distortion field: if they're here, they must be rich; therefore any eccentricities will be automatically excused. Thinking back, I've only seen a few—three elves inspecting the sketches, a dwarf making bedroom eyes at the bottles of Grey Goose displayed behind the bar. That's probably why it didn't register. If nothing else, this is proof that Lord British is expanding his interests.

I'm curious and pissed off at the same time. I'd like him better if he'd stay out of esoteric business, but I'd also enjoy being an even bigger thorn in his side.

"Don't worry," I say to the esquire. "They bleed just like everything else."

He smiles, a little relieved. "Good to know."

"Of course, making them bleed is the hard part."

I leave him with the cocktail shrimp still within reach and head out to the bar. It's outside on the cricket lawn, where the hedges have been retracted to create more open space. That's where the dwarf I saw earlier will probably be, and dwarves are easier to talk to than elves.

The lawn smells overly green, possibly a malfunction in the odorant release systems, and my program chirps to remind me that sunset is only fifteen minutes away.

I take a moment to watch the people congregated around the bar. It's never a good idea to walk into any situation blind if you can help it. As expected, there's a dwarf front and center, dressed in a black tuxedo. Silver thread woven into the jacket glints in the waning light, an effect resembling chain mail. His beard's plaited for the event and though I can't see them, his clan colors will be pinned to his upper left torso like military ribbons. I'd heard that the clans initially considered using ties to indicate affiliation, but even they realized that anyone sporting a plaid bow tie would always be lacking in dignity, regardless of accompanying weaponry.

When the opportunity presents itself, I pick a stool to his left at the bar, order a drink, and wait for him to notice me. Then, losing patience, I initiate the conversation.

"Would you like me to buy you a drink?" I say.

He looks me at me like I've lost my mind. Everyone knows dwarves don't just hold their liquor well. Dwarves walking into biker bars and drinking the keg under the table are the source of some interesting urban legends, especially if they have their battle axes on them at the time.

"I wish I could," he groans, "but it's a religious observance."

I raise my eyebrows. All the dwarven holidays I know of involve more alcohol, not less.

"You mean you don't know?" he says. He slams his hand on the counter and growls at the bartender. "Get some more of, of, what do you call this swill?"

Obviously enjoying every moment, the bartender grins. "Water."

The dwarf spits and fumes quietly to himself. The woman to his right excuses herself and totters off, leaving behind a half-imbibed margarita. The dwarf stares at it like a giant octopus thinking of reasons not to destroy Tokyo.

"You were saying?" I prompt after a few seconds of silence.

"Yes, I was. It's these damn cultural initiatives. After I don't know how many millennia we decide to make nice with the elves, but simply friending each other on SocialWeb isn't enough. Instead, in the fine traditions of *human* civilization," and he says 'human' with more than a touch of disdain, "we each exchange a cultural attaché instead."

This is definitely new. Elves and dwarves get along like wet cats stuffed in a sack. I nod sympathetically. "And that lucky dwarf was you?"

"Of course not. But as it turns out, Thunder Ale makes elves explode and, for some reason, dwarves turn out to be fatally incompetent at balancing on tree branches for hours on end. Who knew?"

The bartender bites her lip and turns around to hide her laughter.

He's tall for a dwarf, looking to be just under five feet. His hair and eyebrows are a deep, burnt red and his face and hands have the milky complexion common to city dwarves.

Knowing the dwarven penchant for tall tales, I wait for him to continue. When he doesn't, I prod him some more. "It looks like you got the blunt pick." That gets him going.

"Damn right I did. In the name of progress, we decided to let bygones be bygones and start over. And that, my friend, is why a deep-blooded dwarf such as myself is observing the elven fast of Ni'Tarian. Five days of no food, nothing to drink but water, and no sleep. Just chanting every two hours about how great ladybugs are." He mournfully gazes at the bottles stacked behind the bar, then motions me in close. "You want to know a secret?" he whispers loudly. "Ladybugs aren't that great."

"Are you sure you don't want me to buy you something," I say.

"Damn it, no. We gave our words and our words we'll keep. Even if they expect someone in my condition to attend a 'gala reception commemorating our historic alliance.' Bah. I'd like a historic alliance between my stomach and some good beer." His wristwatch sounds an alarm and he swears. "Now, if you'll excuse me, I probably have to go seduce a tree." He lurches off his chair and calls out to the party in general. "Don't you believe a word of what that trollop said, baby! You're the only rhododendron for me."

I don't get the dwarf's name, but they're usually testy about that and more talkative if you don't ask at first. Their clan affiliation is much more important. His colors are red, blue, and gold, but the specific pattern on his ribbon eludes me. I make a mental note of it and plan to run it by Raven later.

❀

When I find the elves, they're admiring the ice sculpture in the pavilion. As I approach, sunset hits and they quite literally disappear. One moment they're there, the next there's nothing. I guess they don't want to talk. A simulated sun sinks below the fake horizon, but instead of the afterglow of dusk, fireworks erupt from launchers hidden in the lawn. The jazz combo stops and everyone turns to watch the show. The smell of gunpowder and cinnamon wafts through the air, along with more exotic scents. Designer explosives are coming back into style. The short display concludes with Lord British's family crest glittering through the air, and the PA system beeps demurely before informing everyone that Lord British's salutatory speech is about to begin. I filter back to the ballroom with everyone else. Despite my best efforts, the program remains mum about the true purpose behind this shindig and I have to admit that despite myself I'm a bit curious.

❃

The buffet tables have been whisked away and the red curtain's been drawn back, revealing a rounded podium front and center on the stage. Six chairs, all occupied, form a row behind it. An elf is seated there, as is the reluctant dwarven attaché. The other four are human and look distinctly uncomfortable.

The room fills, and there are hints of movement as security quietly ramps up. The Count arrives with the Baron Elmdore and they seat themselves at the table marked "Fantabuloso." I also take a spot at that table and two esquires unobtrusively flank us. The lights dim and I glance upward, but I still can't see past the chandeliers.

We have a short conversation where I let the Count know my suspicions about the Goth. It's strange that there's still no sign of anything or anyone related to him here tonight, and the Baron Elmdore thinks I'm letting personal feelings interfere with my judgment, but I'm not about to let it go. My gut's been right more times than his brain.

When enough people filter into the room, a spotlight illuminates the podium. Lord British walks onstage from the wings, slightly wobbly but wearing pants, and I lean forward, eager to discover what he's drunk enough to say this time. He sets his martini glass carefully on the podium, taps the microphone twice, and his cultured, upper-class drawl fills the room.

"Today, we commemorate a historic alliance between two peoples traditionally at odds. I know many of you find their presence strange, but I assure you their money is the oldest of all." He chuckles dryly and continues. "The elves and dwarves, long considered to be nothing but legend, have chosen this occasion to make their grand entrance back into civilized society, and have graciously selected the British Estates as worthy of hosting their welcome back party..."

Lord British has to be getting something out of it and I listen to the rest of the speech with half an ear, speculating about various angles. Elves and dwarves only ally together when facing a mutual threat, but why would the Goth be involved? His shtick is building a power base among disaffected teens. Maybe something big *is* about to go down, but surely I'd have heard something. Wouldn't I? Then again, all my usual contacts are suspiciously absent. Try as I might, I just can't make it all fit. I'll have to use the Hobolympics to dig further. Most of the major Under presences will show and it's always a great place to get information.

The Count interrupts my thoughts. "Your visage indicates a pensive cast." It's not so much a statement as a demand for more information. For the evening's festivities he's selected a neon orange suit with glittering silver lapels. The matching hat sports no feathers, surprisingly. Instead, golden writing is embroidered on every surface of the wide brim, tracing such inspirational quotes as "You're only as badass as the last motherfucker you took out" and "Genius is one percent inspiration and ninety-nine percent perspiration." The Differance Stick, menacingly solid, is propped against the table on his left and its capstone brass knob glints dully. The Baron Elmdore and the esquires are, of course, in street uniform.

"This could be big," I say, after waiting long enough that he almost feels the need to repeat himself.

"Could?" The Baron Elmdore laughs dryly. The esquires studiously pretend to be transfixed by the riveting succession of speeches.

"Yes," I say. "Could. Depending on the alliances and their relative strength—"

"The sparks of ancient hate oft flame to war," Count Fantabuloso finishes for me.

"But not necessarily," I say. "Tipton is big enough that, especially with Lord British's backing, they might elude notice for quite a while."

"Do you really believe that?" the Baron Elmdore says.

"Why else would the Goth be involved?"

"You're trippin', Dick. The Goth is not involved."

"So you say."

His elbows propped on the table and fingers interlaced, Count Fantabuloso interrupts again. "Yes, that is the crux of due diligence. Negotiations will proceed apace."

This is cryptic even for him. I take it to mean that if British and the Goth are the ones smuggling in weapons, Count Fantabuloso would have no objection to being belatedly brought into the loop. As long as he thinks it will help keep the peace, he'll be willing to let bygones be bygones. A cut of the profit won't hurt either.

"You plan on speaking with Lord British later?" I ask.

The Count says nothing, just fixes me with a look implying an intelligent person would not have needed to ask that question.

"In that case," I say, standing, "now would be a good time for me to take a further look around."

After having to deal with the upper class all day, I'm in no mood to deal with his condescension. Elmdore can gather information from the speeches. I'll do things my way.

A waiter materializes from nowhere and asks if everything

is satisfactory, and reiterates that he'll be happy to procure whatever refreshments I require. I tell him I need some air. Just before I'm out of earshot, I hear the Baron Elmdore.

"What's his problem?"

❀

Out in the pavilion area, workers are packing things away. Now that there's no one out here cultured enough to fully appreciate how much money must have been spent on special effects, the lighting's reverted to city nighttime standard, a muted glow that will eventually drive you crazy. I wander the grounds, keeping an eye out for anything interesting, but the outside is just as banal as the inside, and I don't feel like testing if the turrets are still playing nice. Just as I'm about to call it a night, though, I notice a familiar, bearded face dismantling a pedestal. Ezekiel Kanaghy, Amish Special Agent.

SBI agents are far from my favorite people. Not only do they view themselves as protectors of Christendom in the same way abortion clinic bombers do, but they always turn up just in time to complicate my life. They aren't fond of nonhumans, and their idea of a civil interspecies discussion is to thump an elf on the back of the head with a Bible and hope it explodes. If he's here, maybe I *am* on to something.

"Hey there..." I say, peering closely at his ID badge, "Ishmael. How long have you been working here?"

He looks up and recognition sparks across his face. He doesn't like me either. "Can I help you," he says darkly. It's not a question.

"I just thought you seemed familiar. You wouldn't happen to know anything about a burglary last month? At the Rivendale?" I know he was there—I watched the entire thing go down from an abandoned storefront across the court. That raid didn't go well. They lost two men and the goblin ringleader still got away. Zeke's eye twitches, but he says nothing.

"No? How about the greenhouse incident a few weeks back?" I wait for more tells.

"I do simple mechanisms," he says slowly. "Now, if you'll excuse me."

"The Brotherhood doesn't take intrusions kindly," I say.

Now something does show in his face. Interest. It's brief and guarded, just a flicker, but it's there. The greenhouse raid is apparently news to him, but if it wasn't the SBI behind that raid, who else would be stupid enough to take on the Brotherhood?

"My brother Yoder does greenhouses," Ezekiel says. "Here's his card. He might be able to help." He reaches into his overalls and pulls out a business card. I take it without looking and slide it into my wallet.

"Thanks, but I have my own guy."

"Suit yourself."

I have a feeling nothing else is going to happen tonight. I check back in with the Count and excuse myself. The barons and esquires can handle things and he has no objection. On the way out, I see a shadow against a tree and hear a gravelly, dwarven voice.

"Oh, you like getting fertilized, don't you, you dirty girl?"

Chapter 6

The first night of the Hobolympics finally arrives and I'm in my office waiting for Raven. We're going to hit the opening ceremonies. It's been a few days since Lord British's soiree, and despite a few new leads since then I still haven't found much of anything. If I didn't know better I'd say they were avoiding me specifically. Rumors of silent disappearances abounded, and everyone else is running scared. The Hobolympics is my best—and probably only, if I'm being honest—shot at this point and I'm actually putting serious thought into contacting Kanaghy.

My office is dark. The silence is a welcome change from the constant advertising. Most days it seems like people aren't dumb enough already; they need corporations flattering and pampering them into indulging every reasonably-priced whim. It gets infuriating after a while. Enough people want to turn me into a zombie already and *they* actually know me. I like to think that the personal connection counts for something.

My office chair is firm but comfortable, and in low power standby doesn't make a sound, not even a hum. It also runs dark. The prizes on my trophy shelves form gloomy shapes and Kanaghy's business card sheds the only light in the room. It's got nothing but a phone number I don't recognize in blocky text. The glow fades and I slip the card back into my pocket.

I've only worked with the SBI once and will never do so again. The case itself wasn't that bad, but the bureaucracy reeked with the overpowering smell of bullshit. There'd been a rash of murders and the mundane media had gotten wind.

As usual, they sensationalized the new serial killer. The SBI wanted to put a stop to it immediately. Cliché of clichés, I was crammed into a small room with five SBI agents, having been hired on as a local expert. Ezekiel Kanaghy was my babysitter.

The area coordinator, Daniel Verkler, activated a monitor and the first frame of an amateur video appeared.

"This video sheds light on the source of the demon." At the word 'demon' you could hear the sneer through his professionalism. The lights dimmed and the video played.

The title of the video, *The Meatspin Curse*, appeared in the default font preferred by amateur videographers worldwide. The words faded, revealing a low coffee table covered in magazines and empty pop cans. A hand dramatically swept it clear, revealing a pentagram in blue lipstick. At that point, I knew this wasn't going to be good.

"Dude, don't fuck this up," an unidentified male voice said.

"Lay off me," another male voice, higher-pitched, replied. "It's a dramatic entrance."

The video spun, revealing the second voice's owner: a Hispanic male with so many piercings his face looked like someone had used it for nail gun target practice. Behind him were others, two males and one female. All looked to be under eighteen. The camera zoomed in on the Hispanic's face. His eyes were bloodshot and he was obviously baked.

"This," he said, "is the Meatspin Curse. An ancient art of the blackest magic, passed down to us through generations of warlocks and the blackest of popes, it can inflict untold pain and humiliation upon your enemies. Use only with the utmost care."

A warning flashed on-screen: "This video is for instructional purposes only."

The wannabe magician next took a hit from a blunt, then placed said blunt carefully in the blue-lipstick pentagram. "Everyone, assume the position," he said.

"As you wish, Grand Magus," they chorused. The girl in the

back giggled. Pentagrams had been drawn on the dirty carpet in front of the coffee table, one for each idiot. They stepped inside.

"May the spirits of vengeance smile upon us," the Grand Magus intoned. "First, you students of the blackest arts," he spoke directly to the camera, "you need to hold the image of those who you hate firmly in mind...are you zoomed in on me?"

"Why?" the camera operator said, off-screen.

"Because it's dramatic."

"Yeah, I'm zoomed in," the camera operator lied.

"Are you sure?"

"Yes, I'm sure. Geez."

"So mote it be. Ye students of the blackest arts, after creating this mental poppet of those to be utterly destroyed, you must... hit it!"

"Watch out here I come!" the song began, painfully loud.

The darkened room lit up like a Christmas tree. Screens embedded in the walls erupted into life and a globe set in the ceiling produced strobe lighting in primary colors. I couldn't believe I was watching this.

For those not in the know, the origins of meatspin are lost to antiquity, but the video resurfaces every generation and will continue to do so for as long as teenagers are retarded. The basic premise, if it can be called that, well, it's not for the easily offended and I feel stupid for even describing it.

Meatspin is nothing more than a close up of two male crotches engaged in anal sex. It's looped so that the penis of the guy on top is swinging around in a perpetual circle. This stunning display of teenage sophistication is always accompanied by some song referencing circular motion. I grew out of this shit after high school.

There've been many variations over the years, but for their training video these budding mages chose the classic version. As the genitalia spun in the background, they spun in place. Their left hands were on their hips and they twirled their right hands in the air, spinning imaginary lassos. In time with the beat, they pivoted on their left legs and their right feet touched each of the points of their pentagrams in turn.

"Warning: Do Not Attempt Without Proper Supervision" appeared briefly on screen.

Verkler paused the video. "The video continues for several more minutes. We don't need to watch it all. The 'curse' itself is harmless enough, but the marijuana they were smoking was laced with true demon weed. As you no doubt know, that's a potent component in summoning spells. At four thirty-eight from the end, you can see it beginning to take form from the smoke." He fast-forwarded to show us. And from such humble beginnings the perverted reefer-demon was born.

When I showed Raven a copy of the video she laughed so hard she cried. "What a way go to," she said. "At least that explains the modus operandi."

"Yeah." The only way to describe the demon's victims was that they were literally fucked to pieces. "What do you think would work against it?"

"Other than the standards," she said, still laughing, "you could try spermicidal condoms. Or Johnny."

"I'm being serious," I said.

"I am too." And she managed a straight face for about five seconds.

We spent five weeks chasing the damn thing through red light districts across the city, with the SBI's self-righteousness causing problems every step of the way. We could have caught the thing in two if they hadn't been so uptight, and six people needlessly died. We finally caught up to it in a private booth at a peep show.

Two bloodshot eyes floating in a cloud of marijuana smoke, it attacked us with spinning male genitalia, which it could apparently generate at will. It wasn't a dignified fight, but with holy water, recorded Southern Baptist rants against alternative lifestyles, and the valiant self-sacrifice of four "borrowed" drug sniffing dogs, we managed to contain it.

The outer door to the office opens, snapping me out of my reverie, and I roll out of my desk/chair, taking cover behind it and drawing my weapon. It's probably just Raven but you never know.

"Dick, it's just us," Raven's voice calls out.

Us?

"Greetings, Mr. Richards. I look forward to these sporting contests."

Ah. David.

Raven turns the lights on. I step out into the front office and cock an eyebrow at her.

"What? I figured he could use a night out," she says.

I take a deep breath. Yeah, he probably could, and it's not like Raven and I were going on a date in the first place. We don't hang out much, but when our interests converge it's always a pleasant evening. Plus, she's several years younger than me. I hadn't expected her to know about the Hobolympics, let alone enjoy them, but she's always full of surprises.

She's wearing a pair of tight jeans and a dark blue sweatshirt with the word "Alfheim" on it in big yellow letters. She's a fan of the elven teams, where I prefer the underdogs myself, whoever they may be. I'm also wearing jeans and a T-shirt, but have a light windbreaker in case the A/C down there is erring on the cold side. My gun's tucked in the back of my pants just in case. David has his hat, of course, this one shiny and golden. Other than that, his shapeless black hoodie almost makes him look like a normal teenager.

"So," I ask him. "You heard of the Hobolympics before?"

"A minor amount," he replies. "If memory serves, these are festivities patronized by His Imperial Majesty, Emperor of the Under himself. Over the course of a fortnight they showcase the best of underworld culture." He sounds like he's quoting from a tour book.

"Just pretend you don't know," Raven says. "Dick loves to clue people in about their ignorance."

She's spared a snappy retort by an incoming phone call. "It's the Count," she says, looking at her caller ID. "Should I answer?"

It's a valid question. The Count knows my personal number, so this might be something that can wait. Then again...

"Just hand me the phone," I say. She does, and I tap *answer*. "This is Dick."

"Forgive this untimely intrusion but," Count Fantabuloso says in his sharp, clipped tone, "arrangements have been made. Lord British is no longer a person of interest."

I take a deep breath. "Is there a reason I should leave him alone?" I word the question that way on purpose.

"No," the Count says and hangs up without ceremony. Excellent. Either he doesn't want to tell me the reason, or there's no reason for me to leave Lord British alone, but I get to pick which. I'm sure Lord British and the Goth are colluding on something. I don't know what, how or why, but it's bound to be worth finding out and I now have carte blanche to do so.

"You're smiling," Raven says.

I look at her. "I do that sometimes."

❀

Official Hobolympics events include the 200m pie snatch, the always-popular hobo rolling, and the panhandling decathlon. Unofficial events include non-refereed cage fighting, extreme prostitution, and semi-public executions. It's a fine example of humanity at its most human, and the nonhumans are happy to contribute to the bedlam. In the old Olympic spirit, clan and gang wars are suspended for the duration of the games so that all qualified athletes can compete. As you might guess, the black market makes a killing.

Leaving my office, David actually pulls his hoodie's hood over his magician's hat. I shake my head. A short subway ride and several elevator layovers later, we reach Udderly platform.

The giant cut-out of a cow from which the platform takes its name still looms ominously, its rusting façade revealing the metal framework underneath. It was once a happy cow from California, but time and abuse have bequeathed it the emaciated grin of a serial killer.

Udderly Platform used to be a transitional station. Two subway lines converged here, as did three major roads. Then it was annexed by the Under and contracted chronic and inflamed criminal activity. Since then, the building materials have been cannibalized to the point where Udderly Platform is just a platform suspended in space from the elevator shaft. The creaking steel wires look way too thin to support all the weight, and two catwalks with flimsy guardrails lead to gutted subway tubes. They were sealed off a few floors up and all that's left of them below are their metal and fiberglass skeletons.

David takes it all in, wide-eyed. Udderly Platform is the official entrance to the domain of the Great Mantato Tuberfruit, self-proclaimed King of the Spuds and Emperor of the Under, but I'm not surprised David's never been here before. You have to know exactly where Udderly is to find it and the only other ways into Tuberfruit world lead through the territory of the more violent gangs. There's no safety railing on the platform itself and looking down past the edge gives a glimpse into steampunk hell. Raven takes David around the platform, pointing out notable sights.

When the lift, a motorized platform large enough to hold twenty people, arrives, it's manned by a man in a lumpy potato costume. He carries a scythe and launches into a scripted speech. It's impressive how much he manages to roll his eyes with just his voice.

"On behalf of the Great Mantato Tuberfruit himself, we'd like to thank you for choosing Tuberfruit Enterprises for your travel needs. This trip may be recorded for quality assurance purposes. Para Español, marque dos." The grim ferryman indicates a number pad chalked onto the lift's metal floor and gives us a don't-you-dare glare. "For service in English," he continues, "please press one or stay on the line. If you happen to speak Russian or French, that's just too damn bad.

"Today, I will be your ferryman into the Under. This service is presented free as a courtesy to you, our valued customer, and use of this service begins your five-day free trial period. If you do not cancel within that time, your account will be charged monthly at the rate of nineteen ninety-nine. Should you renege, we *will* come for you. Remember, potatoes have eyes everywhere and the Great Mantato Tuberfruit is no exception." He brandishes his scythe, if it could be called brandishing. 'Waves it around without caring if he hits somebody' would be more accurate. "Do you agree to the terms and conditions?" he concludes.

"We've got these," I say, and hand him three lifetime passes, signed by the Great Tuberfruit himself.

If looks could kill, the ferryman would be wanted for assault with a foam weapon. It's the potato suit. I just can't take him seriously.

"You could have said so," he mutters, inspecting the passes. "I don't get paid by the word."

David steps in. "I apologize for any inconvenience. That was an eloquent speech, sure to earn you much recompense."

Still miffed and now a little confused, the ferryman grudgingly thanks him. I can't help but feel I've just been shown up by a teenager, and Raven's smirk doesn't help matters. Satisfied, the ferryman hands the passes back and pulls a large lever. The lift jerks to a start.

The trip takes about twenty minutes and I figure I have worse things to do than play tour guide for David. I point out the sign which reads "Abandon all hope, ye who enter her." An arrow under the words points to a life-size poster of a reality TV star known for her endless paternity suits. Then there's the water main with the word "Styx" stenciled onto it. Funhouse mirror reflections, frozen in steel, erupt from exposed surfaces. As we go deeper a red glow, but no heat, emanates from lights hidden in the gutted wreckage, and the metal surfaces shimmer until they almost look alive.

"Why does he do this?" David asks me.

I glance at Raven, who's quite clearly not paying any attention to us.

"Do you want the Emperor's own words, or what I think?" I reply.

"Both?"

"Well, the Emperor claims that potatoes, being born in darkness, living in darkness, and only emerging from darkness in order to sate animal appetites, are more demonic than demons. The irony of having eyes everywhere but no sight makes them even more suited to be the rulers of Hell."

"An...interesting point."

"I think he's just nuts, myself."

❀

As the name suggests, Truck Stop Stadium used to be a truck stop, but the Great Mantato Tuberfruit's architectural brilliance transformed it into what Raven once called an ant-farm auditorium designed by M.C. Escher. Twisting tunnels open onto balconies facing the stadium floor, but there's no real way to tell how to quickly get from one section to another, and that always annoys me. Lights set in the floor and ceiling emit primary colors, washing everything out. People say that if you learn the code of colors you can effortlessly find your way through the Tuberfruit's empire, but I doubt it. He probably started that as a rumor to taunt people. Despite it all, the three of us eventually find good seats.

About twenty minutes later, the Emperor himself strides to a podium on the stadium floor. Everyone hushes immediately. This is Truck Stop Stadium, after all, and these are the opening ceremonies of the Hobolympics.

"Greetings," he says. Echoes hiss and sputter as they fight their way free of the PA system. "I, the Great Mantato Tuberfruit, hereby welcome you to the opening ceremonies of the...fifty-third. Ish. Hobolympics." A cheer erupts from the stadium. "As you all know, the Hobolympics are a time of peace and celebration, a retreat from the drudgery of daily life so we can appreciate the desperation and violence that have brought us where we are today. To those no longer with us, I salute you."

The lights flicker and dim. The show begins.

"At the beginning of time, humanity did little more than huddle around campfires, seeking warmth and escape from the terrors of the night."

Red spotlights reveal shadowy figures clustered around a dark mound. One makes a sudden movement and blinding fireworks assault our eyes. When sight returns, the figures are revealed as hobos, the dark mound a now functional trashcan fire.

"Little memory remains of those dark times," the Emperor's voice narrates, "but those who seek warmth and companionship will always remember in their bones. Out of the struggle for survival the first competitions were held. A scuffle over a silver dollar. Jostling for place in a bread line."

The hobos brawl. They don't appear to be acting. Possibly drugged-out, but not acting.

"Those in power sought to stamp us out, to piss on the flames of our desire, but we endured. The memory of that first flame survives in every small and hard-earned comfort."

Men in grimy police uniforms upturn the trashcan fire and stamp it out, pausing occasionally to beat hobos with nightsticks, but one of the transients, unnoticed in the melee, lights a cigarette with the flickering embers before they die. He takes a long drag. The Hobolympic flame lives on.

"Cunning, deception, and force were the hallmarks of life, ever more necessary as our enemies became ever more determined."

The cigarette-smoking hobo is spotlighted, and dogs bark and bay in the distance.

"At first, it was all we could do to avoid extermination, but through the years, determination bred strength, exile bred cunning, and STDs bred endurance."

Panicky at first, the spotlighted hobo finds a metal pipe on the ground and brandishes it drunkenly, ready to take on the world. He gestures to his crotch with a suck-on-this motion and narrowly avoids racking himself with the pipe. The crowd goes wild.

"While experience has taught us all too plainly that we are mortal, we stand and fall, if not with dignity, at least with fervor."

The spotlight widens and a blur of menacing black clotheslines the hobo. He flies backward, spinning in the air, and lands like a rag doll against the corner of a building.

"But we have friends, old and new, ready to pick us up when we fall."

An elf, a dwarf, a goblin, and a pixie enter the spotlight. They ease the hobo up and stand protectively over him while he gingerly makes sure his head is still attached. The elf returns the cigarette to the hobo, who smokes it gratefully.

"For the next two weeks, there is no struggle, no poverty. All there is, is brotherhood and companionship, and the best our world has to offer!"

The spotlight widens further, fading into rising house lights, and hundreds of carousers materialize out of the darkness. Hobos, grimy policemen, lightly armed nonhumans, people in every state of wobbly uprightness--all drunkenly preen over a giant Chinese buffet.

On his podium, hair flying in some unseen wind, the Great Mantato Tuberfruit raises his arms and is enveloped in a golden glow. "Welcome," he shouts, "to the Hobolympics!"

As one, the balconies empty and there's bedlam in the tunnels. Everyone wants to be first in line or, failing that, to get to the buffet before all the food is eaten.

❀

After dinner, the ceremonies continue. About halfway through the athletes' parade David turns to me. "Why are people throwing things at them?" He's surprised enough to almost speak normally.

"Entertainment," I say.

Raven stops cheering for the elven teams long enough to add, "It's like trolling on the Internet. These people know their opinions don't really matter, but they'll jump on the chance to express them anyway. It's a more personal form of blogging." She laughs.

Even I have to admit that's cold. Raven does that occasionally: viciously skewers something, then laughs light-heartedly as if what she just criticized was the most wonderful part of the world and she couldn't imagine living without it. Sometimes I think she really means it. All of it.

"Don't the athletes care?" David asks.

"Compared to what they're used to," I say, "this is cake. You see them?" I point to a band of hobgoblins just entering the arena. "They've been involved in a twenty-year guerrilla war against a neighboring tribe of pixies. They're used to people trying to kill them."

"And they've ceased hostilities to participate? How noble."

"Actually," I say, "both sides have gotten tired of fighting. After the parade is the Declaration of Intent to Kill and the Ceremonial Exchange of Death Threats. Then the two squads will face off in a dueling room. When the dust settles, both sides will consider the war over."

The look on David's face comes close to sheer horror, and he sits there, staring at me.

"I'm going to nip back down to the buffet," Raven says. "It looks like there's still some coconut flan and I want to beat the dessert rush."

I have no idea what I'm supposed to say, and thinking fast I come up with, "The world's not a nice place, David. Sometimes the best you can do is force all the assholes into the same room, convince them to follow some rules, and let them beat the shit out of each other so no one else gets hurt."

I might as well have told him I'm an exiled Nigerian banker who needs his help recovering frozen assets, but he nods slowly. "That's why you're a detective?"

Again, I'm at a loss. What does being a detective have to do with that at all? I could be honest and say I'm nosy and love poking around in other people's business, or that I love the thrill of the chase and knowing you're just far enough ahead of the other guy to not get hurt. Plus, the looks on their faces when they realize their precious secrets aren't so secret anymore are always priceless. That was why I started, and I stay because I'm the best at what I do. But I doubt that's what David needs to hear.

"Yeah," I lie. "This way I can keep tabs on them. If you'll excuse me, I need to check out the market. It should be open by now and I need to check on some business."

A feeling in the back of my mind nags me that I shouldn't leave him there, but he's lived through worse and knows enough magic to keep himself safe. Plus, Raven will be back soon with coconut flan and she'll know what to say better than I would. David nods, deep in thought.

❋

Merchant stalls spring up during the Hobolympics like pop-ups on porn sites. The black market bazaar, offering everything from previously-owned grimoires to illegal spell components, is like a class reunion, with chances for old friends to see how everyone else is getting along, settle old scores, and discreetly forge business partnerships. Most of the stalls are set up on the main floor, tent mushrooms on metallic loam. Side corridors lead to ledges for specialty shops. There aren't many customers yet—most are still enjoying the opening ceremonies—but enterprising businessmen always try to get the jump on each other and I see some familiar faces moving about. Johnny Mojo. Squee Dave. Little Benjamin. Mr. Chips. The last three are respectable businessmen, veritable pillars of the community, but Johnny's fair game. Rather than avoid him I take the initiative.

He's 5'8", 210 pounds, and wearing a dark green T-shirt that advertises one of the millions of online games he plays in his spare time. His hair looks like he woke up on someone's couch fully clothed and, in the interest of respectability, ran his hand through it oblivious to the nacho crumbs still on his fingers.

"Hey Johnny!" I yell from three tents away. "I hear you've been trying to reach me."

He looks up, sees me, and bolts in the other direction. That surprises me. I figured he'd want to tell me about his newest scheme and offer me a percentage if I only do him a small favor. I don't like him, but I can't just let him go. He's been harassing Raven for a few weeks now and it's time to return the favor.

I catch up with him outside a stall hawking cheaply-made silver bullets. He tries to dodge into a tunnel leading to a specialty ledge, but it turns out to be a dead end.

"What's up, Johnny?" I say as cheerfully as possible.

"What do you want, Dick?" He's a bit more high-strung than normal. His favorite character probably hit the level cap or something.

"I just wanted to catch up with you. You've been bothering Raven for weeks now and it's been just ages since we talked. Have you reached level five hundred yet?"

He scratches a splotchy face. He opens his mouth to talk, then closes it again. Finally, he explodes. "Yes, I have. In fact, I've reached it ten times. Are you happy now?"

"Congrats! You know, Johnny," I say, acting like I'm about to put a friendly arm around his shoulder, "magical research has come a long way, even in the last five years." I've never been intimidated by his curse, never try to avoid him in person, and that always puts him on edge. "I picked up a brochure from the Wanderlei Institute. They specialize in removing curses like yours and might be able to help." I reach inside my windbreaker as if to pull it out and he backs away.

"Fuck you, Dick. Fuck you." He shoulders his way past me and storms down the tunnel. The green lighting makes him look like a tall, fat, sexually-frustrated goblin.

"There's no shame in seeking help!" I call after him.

His behavior's strange, even for Johnny, I think to myself as I head back down to the main floor of the bazaar. After spending most of the last month trying to contact me, he just avoided me like *I* was cursed. He's probably up to something; the question is whether it's worth my time to figure out what.

❀

There's a firm tug on my arm. I whirl, ready to put my fist through someone's skull. I've seen a few faces here who'd be happy to see me dead, and now that the bazaar's crowded with shoppers they might be bold enough to try. In the ancient Greek tradition the Hobolympics are supposed to be a time of peace, but I have this talent for getting under people's skin.

"Excuse me? Sir?" the owner of the hand says. I relax. It's just a magic junkie, blinking rapidly as if to clear reality out of his eyes. Runic tattoos on his eyelids proclaim his affiliation with some school of the arcane. "I have a pregnant wife laid up in a hotel. Can you spare a quartz crystal? A small lodestone for a simple healing enchantment? No? How about just a magic diagram—it doesn't even have to be complete."

I not-so-kindly release his grip for him and walk off.

This, more than anything, is why I use magic as sparingly as possible. Not just because it pushes me close to the edge, but because this guy is a prime example of what happens to people it uses up.

"How about pixie droppings?" he cries, trying to catch up. "I'll even take pixie shit!" He's probably reached his breaking point, but I ignore him anyway.

While magic itself isn't addictive, using it is. That sounds like an addict's joke so I'd better explain. Quite simply, people like having control over their lives. Magic increases that power, and people continually want more—to be in charge, to be masters of their own destinies. Then, quite suddenly, people run into their limits. It's like crashing into a brick wall and most people can't take it. That's bad enough as it is, but if I'd start using it heavily on the job, my life would turn into an arms race. I'd scry, they'd screen. I'd translocate, they'd shield. And so on ad nauseum.

Eventually, when it counted, I'd need to magic myself to safety and it simply wouldn't work. I'd be too tired or their magic would be too strong. Then I'd get the Deal. Power for my soul. It's damn hard to say no if your life's on the line, and when the demons finally collect it's a bitch. Or so I've heard.

Some say that the pure of heart can resist, but I doubt that's anything more than an urban legend inculcated by the demons themselves. "Oh yeah, those other assholes will screw themselves over eventually, but I can tell *you* are a pillar of uncommon strength and virtue, misunderstood and spat upon in a cynical world. Just sign on the dotted line, never mind the fine print, and you'll finally have all the power you need to get the life you deserve."

The junkie falls behind and latches onto someone else. I'd rather die than end up like that.

As usual, there are rumors everywhere. Elves are buying suspiciously large amounts of silver-doped metal dust, which is frustrating the pixies. A tribe of goblins has a bone to pick with Count Fantabuloso, and the odds are 150:1 against them. About two weeks ago, a stoned hippie wandered down here and was last seen licking the walls, never a good idea. Nobody's heard from the dwarfs recently, but if they get going on a big, multi-clan project they can disappear for decades. That last might have something to do with the alliance.

There have also been dragon sightings, but there are always dragon sightings. For nonhumans, they're a cross between Jesus, Elvis, and Tupac, with the accompanying divine abilities. My favorite is the one where they walk among us, but aren't seen because they change themselves into humanoids *and* make themselves invisible at the same time.

I figure the opening ceremonies should be nearly over, so I head back to Truck Stop Stadium proper. Hopefully Raven's kept David entertained for these few hours and he's had a good night away from his family. Maybe I'll see if they want to get something to eat before breaking for home. But whatever my plans actually are, they fly right out of my head when I round a bend in a tunnel and see David "talking" to two mimes.

They're on the bazaar's main floor, off to the side, and I excuse myself right into their conversation. One of the mimes crosses her arms in an exaggerated fashion.

"Sorry about the interruption," I say, "but the opening ceremonies are over and David and I need to be going." I glare at David, willing him to play along.

"If you would permit me an excuse," he says, bowing.

I wait until we're out of earshot before demanding, "David, what the hell do you think you're doing?"

"We were simply engaged in conversation," he responds defensively.

"Why?" I say. For that matter, I think, *How?*

"I find the Brotherhood fascinating."

That's not good enough.

"Look, David," I say, grabbing his shoulders, "drop the act. You can't handle this and the Brotherhood aren't people you want to hang around anyway."

He looks me in the eyes. "Fear and ignorance often masquerade as humility."

"What?" I resist the urge to shake him. "Look, David, nobody knows what they're up to. *Nobody*. Even I have no clue most of the time. It's just common sense. You don't poke something unless you're sure you can outrun it."

Almost on cue, Raven appears to make me look even more like an idiot.

"What's this?" she says, holding a grilled turkey leg in each hand. She's acquired a visor sporting the Hobolympics logo and looks every inch the tourist.

"David's been talking to the Brotherhood. He doesn't believe that they're dangerous." I turn back to David. "It's best to stay away."

"How dare you," she scolds him from behind me. "You should listen to your father." I'm sure she winks because David breaks into a grin.

Me, I let go and stand there with my mouth open, trying to remember what I was going to say. Raven's right. I don't have the right to tell him who he can and can't talk to. But at the same time, David has no idea what he's getting into. It's far too easy to get in over your head down in the Under.

"How about something to eat?" Raven's voice prods me out of my thoughts. "These turkey legs don't taste too fresh."

"What?" I say.

"You know, dinner or something." In a stage whisper to David, she adds, "Sometimes you have to repeat yourself. He can be kind of slow."

I don't need that, but dinner does sound good.

"Yeah, sure," I say, and David agrees.

"How about Swanky's?"

❀

Swanky's, quite frankly, is an independently owned diner that's been ambushed by bling. Stepping inside, I'm positive the owner took out his passive aggression by covering absolutely every spare surface with every imaginable kind of fake jewelry. *If I can't get what* I *want, at least* you'll *go blind.* Even the tables are covered, with a thin glass pane laid on top to provide a level eating surface.

We sit near the restrooms, directly underneath a ceiling fan. This is one of Raven's favorite dives, but I've never been here before. Unless the food is out of this world, I doubt I'll be back.

Gilded foil traces spiral patterns on the laminated menus. On the front cover, an overweight man in Aviator sunglasses and bright blue bell bottoms gives me a thumbs up. His speech balloon informs me that I'm "never too broke to be tasteless, so come on in and eat like a celebrity!" The menu items are standard diner food, hamburgers, fries, breakfast all the time, but printed in glittering ink.

I go with the mushroom-Swiss burger and a soda, one of my mainstays. Raven orders a pancake platter and David chooses a chicken dumpling skillet. As it turns out, the cast iron skillet is also covered with flashing LEDs and every time David's fork touches the side it plays a sci-fi sound effect.

Our conversation is mild, mostly Raven asking David questions and David answering between bites. I learn he's actually seventeen, goes to Rimbaud North High School, and got started in ceremonial magic when he found a copy of *The Golden Dawn* at a used bookstore's going-out-of-business sale. I stay out of the conversation for the most part, not wanting to bring up the Brotherhood again. I'm not the kid's father, but a part of me still wants to drive the message home. The world is dangerous, the Under even more so. Magic's not as important as common sense and one of the rules of common sense is that you don't get mixed up in anything when you have no idea what's going on.

I think about that for a moment, then add: unless you're getting paid.

Nevertheless, I refrain from saying anything.

Something about this is really getting under my skin, and after we pay the check and leave, I almost don't notice the smell. It's light and crispy at the same time, like someone made a soufflé out of cinders and ash. It reaches us just as we cross the threshold into the dilapidated, New Las Vegas-style court that Swanky's calls home, and my hands cast a protective spell almost by themselves. Just in time, too.

A blast of energy hits my newly erected shields and the world becomes a nightmare outlined in bright green. I brace my back against a wall and wait for it to clear, ignoring the sensation of a giant Venus flytrap lurking in wait. Elven magic is as much about messing with your mind as it is about knocking you into the next life.

When the air clears, I see Raven on the other side of Swanky's entrance, enveloped in a purple cocoon. I don't see David and the next salvo hits before I can find him. Another neon nightmare leaves me with the beginnings of a migraine, and that tells me how close I just came to punching a one-way ticket into an assisted-living facility. First things first: I need to make sure *I* survive.

I belatedly hit the deck, dismiss the shields, and cast a quick-and-dirty misdirection. The siren song of power rises again but there's nothing for it. With any luck, the majority of the next blast will cruise by while I reestablish my protection. I might lose some hair and skin, but at least I'll be ready to fight back.

My stomach sinks and my eyeballs feel like they're being stretched thin. I hope to God that's a side effect of Raven's magic.

The third blast doesn't come, so after finishing the hand gestures for my triple ward I raise my head slightly. I don't give in to the building rush, but I give it some room to breathe. The court is completely deserted. Everyone else must have fled the scene or, more likely, we've been shunted. Either way, the tabloids will have a field day with this.

Gingerly I raise myself higher, to my hands and knees, and then the third blast comes, aimed right for my chest. The bastard was waiting for me. I feel it a split second before I see it and am able to redirect the brunt into the safety railing. The metal melts and the sound-absorbing foam explodes into sizzling, ball-bearing sized chunks. I hit the deck again.

I have no idea where they are, but staying put isn't an option. I belly-crawl a few feet, trying to angle the surviving railing between me and where I think they might be, and a glowing purple arrow appears in front of me, followed by the words "I'm over here. Raven." The words stay active, waiting for a response.

"I don't know where they are," I whisper.

The words reform themselves. "Two levels down. Bouncing."

I swear under my breath. Whoever it is found something magically reflective and now doesn't even need line of sight. "And David?" I whisper.

"Safe. I'll cover you."

A few seconds later, black mist condenses from thin air. Though it covers the court, I can still see everything in perfect outline. I sprint for a corridor I hope contains an emergency stairwell and make it without being attacked again. So far, so good. Not so good is the corridor being a dead end, holding only back doors into restaurants and clubs. All are immovable. We've definitely been shunted.

I reach behind me for my gun, then think better of it. Magic will be contained within the shunt, but projectiles won't. I don't want to get arrested for homicide.

I edge back to where the corridor opens onto the court. Small, pink blobs of light explode soundlessly into rainbow sparks. The bastard's trying to nail me with faerie fire, making any kind of concealment or invisibility useless, and this is obviously a search pattern.

Not knowing how long Raven can keep up the covering mist, I only wait a few seconds before dashing for the next corridor. My timing's off and my arm is clipped, starts to glow. I hustle my windbreaker off before the glow can spread to my body and, reaching the next side corridor, toss it on the floor. After a few anxious seconds, the pattern's still running so I can only assume I wasn't seen.

With a deep breath I take stock of the situation. I don't see either Raven or David, but they're presumably both safe. My windbreaker's glowing like a Christmas tree, and there's an unknown assailant out there trying to kill me. Waiting here won't do me any good so I have to press the attack somehow.

I think of a trick I learned from Old Jed, my one-time mentor.

It's a good distraction, not much else, but right now it might give me the edge I need. It creates a ball of condensed air used to float something light. While Old Jed was a master at it and could make clothes dance a jig, I'm nowhere as proficient. But right now, I don't need much. I throw my glowing coat over the ball and visualize a course for it to run: wait twenty seconds, then zig-zag across the court like a man taking evasive action.

I book it down the stairwell as stealthily as possible. Awakened by the magic, a glorious song of power threatens to hijack my thoughts. I hate using this much magic, especially because the world starts to bend in strange ways, but I have no choice.

I'm almost at the bottom landing when I see a flash of green and smell a cinder soufflé. Cautiously, I edge myself off the landing and creep forward until I have a good view. My windbreaker is still up there, bobbing and weaving unsteadily. The unknown assailant strikes again. A bolt of green energy leaps from a storefront window, ricochets off the far wall, and rushes toward my windbreaker like an offensive tackle on PCP. On impact, it explodes into a glowing sphere seven feet across. No wonder I'd had no idea where it was coming from.

I focus on the point of origin and, sure enough, there's a figure crouched just in front of the window. Grinning to myself, I sneak closer. There doesn't appear to be anyone else around. Cocky bastard, attacking alone. He attacks again, more powerfully this time, and the green bolt lights the court like eldritch lightning. It nails my windbreaker and its remains flutter to the ground. When I'm about halfway to him, he stands up and walks to the railing to peer upward, his back to me. I have him now.

I could draw my handgun—I feel its reassuring weight at my back and at close range I'd stand no chance of injuring innocent bystanders—but this has quickly become personal. Not only has he blindsided me, but he attacked without consideration for anyone else that might have been with me. Muttering the words to an incapacitation spell under my breath, I inch closer.

He's still clueless. Spell complete, I grab his shoulder and spin him around.

"I think you missed, asshole," I say.

His eyes register surprise as my other hand, charged with the spell and balled into a fist, nails him in the face.

Most magical shielding doesn't protect against physical contact, but my spell arcs around him like an angry rainbow. The last things I see before he—correct that, she—teleports away like a starship jumping to warp speed, are her lithe features and pointed ears. They actually are elves, and not crazy human wannabes. I swear. I should have used my gun in the first place.

My bout of silent swearing is cut short by a burst of non-silent swearing as a bolt of concussive force hits me from behind. The jackass has a spotter.

❁

I wake up face down on a moving walkway, among unconcerned citizens going about their late-night business. The walking surface, its metallic links held together by electrostatic wizardry, bites into my face and my left hand is stepped on. You have to love humanity's ability to decide something's not their problem; they probably figure me for a drunk. My eyes throbbing and ears ringing, I wobble to my feet and stumble through the crowd. It parts reluctantly. I find a public bench and nearly collapse. My phone's clock says two forty-eight A.M. and I stare at it for a while, fighting the urge to use it as a focus for a location spell so I can pursue those elves. I'm worn out enough as it is, and dimly aware that more magic would not be a good idea, but with the last traces of a hymn of power still echoing through my brain everything I think of doing involves magic. I do, however, have the presence of mind to notice that the walkway railing the elves destroyed is still completely intact, thanks to the shunt.

After a few minutes, comprehension dawns. Phones are used to call people and I want to talk to Raven. It takes a while to navigate the address book, but after three rings she answers.

"I see you made it," she says.

"Yeah. Where...?"

"After the smoke, I took David. We're heading for his home right now."

Inside my brain, "Is he all right?" wars with "You left me?!" but all that actually comes out is "David."

"Yeah," she says. "When it started, he used his Cloak and Shield. Since he wasn't a target, they didn't pay attention to him and he wasn't sucked into the shunt."

"Oh."

"Plus, I knew you could handle yourself. Do you need help getting home?"

Of course not, I'm perfectly fine. "No."

"You sure?"

"Bye."

I have trouble stowing my phone; my hands are still shaking and my pockets are quite elusive. I nearly bowl over a woman who shouts at me to have some respect, but I make it back to my apartment and down ten prescription painkillers before wriggling out of my clothes and into bed. As I close my eyes, pain rockets through the inside of my skull like a ferret on crack and I taste metal.

Chapter 7

When I wake up I don't even try to make it to the office. It takes most of what I have left to even raise my head off the pillow, and I deserve a day off anyway. A dull, grinding ache accompanies every movement, and since it's either think or watch the advertising screen loop through its endless infomercials, I think. Jerome, my least favorite tiki person, grins at me from his perch in the bedroom corner.

I must be drifting in and out because the show tune-singing clown makes several visits. Big and bulbous, its disembodied head warbles campy songs while I try to concentrate. If elven mages are skilled enough, they can contaminate you with a mind virus and meditation helps uncover those. This clown, however, isn't their normal style. It should be something more natural and wispy, something with physical and mental camouflage. That still begs the question: where the hell does this clown delusion come from? I wasn't particularly afraid of clowns as a child, and haven't encountered any recently.

As best as I can given my condition, I wait in mental ambush. When the clown switches songs, I imagine a giant hand reaching out to grab it. At first I try to cover its mouth but it skitters away like dirt from a soap bubble. I try to grab it from behind, which works a little better, but I can't keep a firm mental grasp. Before I can try anything else, it disappears.

I sigh and open my eyes. Jerome's still grinning in the corner.

"The clown's your doing, isn't it?" I accuse him. There's no response, and I don't see myself getting up any time soon, so

I ruminate on the past month, keeping an eye out for clowns.

Fact: I've been attacked by elves, and certain factions in the elven and dwarven world are allying. Does a group of elves think I'm taking sides? It would be an understandable assumption on their part, but I haven't taken any jobs from either race in a while, so maybe it's grudge-related.

Fact: Lord British and the Goth are getting in bed over something. I haven't had much time to snoop around, since investigating either of them requires a hell of a lot of prep work to do safely, but if this drought of information continues, I might just have to.

Fact: Count Fantabuloso's mystery gun is both technologically and magically sophisticated, not to mention untraceable thus far. This limits the groups with the knowledge and resources and there's that damn clown again, gearing up for round two. I can hear his squeaky nose and smell his makeup.

I get him this time with a viselike mental grip, and switch to another visualization. The clown's bobbing on a string like a helium balloon with a mind of its own, and I follow the string back to its source. The background, of its own volition, takes on an electronic character, reminiscent of circuit boards. The string eventually merges with one of the pathways, but the lines are too small for me to trace and the pattern starts to give me vertigo. The clown's song gets louder and out of frustration I just yank on the string. It doesn't come free, but the background starts to unravel like a sweater with a loose thread. Sensing imminent victory, I continue pulling until the circuit board falls away, revealing a table covered in a green tablecloth. A bowl of fruit lies near the edge, and the string leads right to it.

"I've got you now," I tell the head, which floats behind me. It swivels slowly in midair.

I focus on the bowl of fruit, slowly drawing closer. The string disappears into the depths of the bowl, but before I can figure out where it goes, the fruit floats out of the bowl and makes a face, which then informs me of the nearest escape routes in case of catastrophe.

That blindsides me out of my trance. The screen in my bedroom is broadcasting the monthly test of Tipton's Emergency Information System, and you can't shut that off without tripping federal alarms. I wait to for it end and then decide: Screw it. I'm going back to sleep. If I've picked up a mind virus and wake up a zombie love slave, my new mistress will just have to live with being disappointed.

❋

Raven calls the next day to ask if I plan on dying, her grinning face plastered on my bedroom wall. When I tell her I don't, she acts disappointed.

"Well, if you do, leave a message with Mrs. Marple so I can start looking for a new job."

I'm not exactly the happiest of campers at this point. My limbs ache, a migraine's driven a flagpole through my temples to claim by brain for Spain, and I'm getting sore from lying in bed too long. "You know, you could show some sympathy instead of sounding like you had to cancel reservations at an exclusive funeral home," I say.

Raven laughs. "And do you know how long it took me to get those? Now I'll be bumped to the back of the line."

And people call *me* an asshole.

"How's David doing?" I say.

"Better than you." Her eyes light up and her hair turns light brown, almost orange. "He knows when to keep his head down."

"Is Kaitas still in Little Greece?" I ask, changing the subject.

"As far as I know. Why?"

"We have business to discuss."

"If she kills you this time, remember. It's Mrs. *Elvira* Marple. Her sister June charges too much."

❀

As soon as I feel up to it, I get my ass out of bed and head for the International Building. Kaitas Maerenar, warleader of the Sun Elves, is headquartered there. Apparently elves and Greeks get along famously, bonding over philosophy and feta cheese.

The quickest way to her turf is the back entrance. Connecting the International Quadrant with the Guggenheim Complex, Via Dolorosa isn't well known. Anyone using it automatically gets Kaitas' attention.

The skyway is called the Via Dolorosa because an unknown graffiti artist tagged it with the Stations of the Cross. Each aspect of Jesus' suffering is linked by flowering vines. Instinctive art lovers, the Sun Elves added real plants, careful to keep the stations themselves unobscured. Walking through it is like a glimpse into a distant future, when all that's left of Catholicism are the stone cathedrals, repurposed for a new religion.

Two elves dressed in the latest hip-hop style guard the International end. They lean on longspears and each bears a bow and quiver on their back. With an air of bored arrogance one asks me my business in Elven, then repeats the question disdainfully in English.

"I'm here to see Kaitas," I say, also in Elven.

"So is everyone else."

"It's a debt of honor."

Without a word, the other one leaves.

Normal Sun Elf policy is that, as long as elves aren't beating up other elves, it's not worth getting involved. They're policemen, in a sense. However, a debt of honor is a serious matter in traditional elven culture. Invoking one is never taken lightly. It's a gamble on my part, but after the week I've had I'm not interested in tap dancing around through diplomatic channels. If things go bad, I figure I have a good chance of fighting my way out of here alive.

Fifteen minutes later, the other elf is still looking at me like I'm an insect and I start to fume. I've been pissed off since I woke up and the delay isn't helping. Jesus, crowned in thorns and shedding bloody tears, gazes at me through a thicket of vegetation.

"What?" I growl at him at under my breath.

I'm still waiting when eleven rolls past, but am starting to calm down. Something Old Jed, my one-time mentor, once told me floats back to mind: The universe is littered with the corpses of those who let emotions overrule common sense. I'll need all my wits about me to navigate this minefield and come out with more information. Despite my pride, I have to admit I'm stumped and Kaitas' diviners are top notch.

My instincts gnaw at me. The unknown weapon, everyone disappearing, the Goth and Lord British, the attempt on my life...it all feels related. Damned if I know how, but that sense is there. The elf finally returns; Kaitas is ready to see me. I take a deep breath to collect myself, game plan firmly in mind. Damn this headache.

❀

If there's one thing I like about elves, it's that their decoration isn't tasteless. It's always a bit jarring to see an eldritch forest growing inside what you know is a skyscraper, but the forest is tasteful nonetheless. For one thing, there are no celebrities trying to sell me anything. More importantly, without screens there are no shock jockey advertizing gurus trying to create buzz around their latest idiocy. The ephemeral glow emanating from mushrooms growing in bark is a little off-putting for some, but I prefer to think of it as elven emergency lighting.

My escort leads me to an elevator embedded in the trunk of a tree, and hesitates slightly before joining me inside. Being enclosed in a metal box is no elf's idea of a good time. The elevator is mainly a courtesy for those who can't run up tree trunks, and elves are as big on formality as aristocrats are. A short ride later we exit onto the landing that serves as Kaitas's council room.

It's a wooden platform in the elven style overlooking the floors below. They've hollowed out this part of the building so that anyone here has an unobstructed view of the forest. At first, the council chairs appear high backed, almost seven feet tall, but as you get closer you see those backs are actually a screen of moss growing on fine mesh. Anyone leaning back will fall through. Luckily the seats, made of woven reed slats, are a little sturdier. Vines descend from the tree branches above, framing the chairs and giving just a hint of walls. For some reason, a red EXIT sign hovers in the foliage, washing everything in a dull, red glow.

Kaitas is perched on a central chair, wearing flowing robes and flanked by two advisors. They, in turn, are flanked by two honor guards. I'm guessing she concluded her normal business before seeing me. Like the Count, she likes to give people her undivided attention in case it makes them nervous.

She gestures me forward and dismisses my escort with a slight nod.

"You claim the Maerenar owe you honor debt," she says in English. Her voice is measured and soft, a little lilting.

I perform the expected bow and watch my words. If I don't prove my case well, she might order my execution. Like I said, elves take honor debt seriously and a false accusation of such debt has ignited blood feuds. "Two days ago, warleader, I was attacked by elves."

"Were you on elven ground?"

"No, warleader."

"Were they unveiled?" Meaning out in the open, where everyone could see them.

"No, warleader."

Her voice acquires just the hint of an obsidian edge. "Then what business is it of the Maerenar?"

"I have performed services for the Maerenar in times past, and had hoped I could count on their friendship. I was attending to my own affairs when attacked. Unless they marked me, they could not know I move under the veil."

Kaitas nods. The elves take the veil of secrecy seriously. The memory of the human hatred and persecution which first drove them away runs deep.

"If they did mark you, again, what business is it of the Maerenar?"

"Any elves who may mark me are enemies I made in service of the Maerenar." It's not completely true, but true enough.

She nods again. "Have you anything else to say?"

I raise my hands and give the traditional closing in elven. Roughly translated, it means, "I lay my fate on your judgment."

My escort reappears with that eerie elven sense of timing, ushers me back into the elevator and from there across a thick bough to a waiting room. It's been hollowed from another tree trunk and, apart from a blue canvas chair, is completely bare. When keeping a guest waiting, it's considered polite to offer a secluded area with minimal distractions in case said guest wishes to commune with the spirits. The canvas chair has probably been added for my benefit. That's a good sign. Kaitas is at least considering my request.

Luckily for my sanity, I'm brought back to the council platform before more than an hour passes. That's a quick decision for elves.

"We have searched the lore and found your claim with merit. Please, ask recompense," Kaitas says.

Despite her utterly calm demeanor and poise, I know the danger's not over yet. Ask for too much and I run the risk of getting myself branded a cutter-charlatan, after the humans who first negotiated humanity's right to use the elven forests, and whose agreements subsequent generations of humanity simply ignored. Ask for too little and I imply that Sun Elf honor is worth very little.

I regret not bringing Raven along. She's the expert in non-human cultures and genuinely seems to enjoy negotiations like this. But I can't stall too much either, because then it might seem like I'm calculating just how much I can milk the Maerenar for. Did I mention I hate politics?

"I seek information, a divination."

"Mere knowledge for honor debt?" she says. "That seems an unfavorable trade."

Crap. I'd aimed too low.

"Many sages would disagree," I reply, trying to recover. "Information is my livelihood."

At an unseen signal, Kaitas tilts her tiara-ed head toward an advisor who whispers something in her ear. A cool smile flits across her face.

"While you are but a child compared to even the greenest elven sage, the Maerenar understand that human importance is not the same as importance to the kin. What would you know?"

Biting my tongue against the casual arrogance, I explain the situation and ask for information regarding the gun and how it entered the city. Knowing I've just dodged a bullet, I get my answer and head home.

❀

Even though the singing clown head doesn't make a repeat appearance, that headache really starts kicking my ass so I rest for the next few days. With nothing to do but watch reruns of SyFy Original Movies and bounce stupid ideas off my tiki people, boredom sets in quickly. The worst part about recuperating from a magical fight is that the pounding in your head isn't just a headache. It's your brain trying to find all of its bits and pieces and weld them back together.

Raven calls a few times, mostly to tease me about being too old for this. After griping at her, I pass on the information from the elves. Apparently, a hippie did it. Strangely enough, I'm not surprised. The description—shaggy, light brown hair, tie-dyed shirt, thick glasses, and open air sandals—is generic enough to be nearly useless, but I hadn't wanted to try Kaitas' goodwill or her patience. She might look demure, but it's the grace of a predator. Rumor has it last time things got ugly in the elven nations, Kaitas restored order by killing the six troublemaking lords. Personally. At the same time.

Other than that, not much happens except that my fridge empties surprisingly quickly. I'm hesitant to leave before I can fully defend myself, but the thought of having groceries and/or fast food delivered for the next few days overcomes that. With the recent attack I'm more paranoid than normal and those would be far too easy to poison.

With a groan, I roll out of bed and don pants. The headache is strident but manageable. After more thought than the situation requires, I also fish out a pair of noise cancelling ear plugs from somewhere in my underwear drawer. "Quiet" is not a word used to describe Tipton and I'm in no mood to deal with it. Grocery shopping goes quickly and with a minimum of frustration. I take the express walkways as much as possible.

Theoretically they're four-laners, but the designers were Chinese, where the healthy weight for a 5'10" individual is considerably less than 250 pounds. They weren't used to designing for such big bones, and given general commuter temperament the sidewalks only hold about two-and-a-half lanes, and one of those lanes is always centered on wherever the loudest asshole happens to be standing. The ads on the walls alternate with public service announcements warning against "ride rage." Apparently the public needs reminding that punching someone in the back of the head because you were late getting out of the house that morning isn't actually okay.

Other than the cabs, the express walks are the quickest way to move between districts, and I don't want to be that surrounded by people. At big interchanges, it's possible to look down on several floors of people switching between walkways, escalators, and public transportation. I've always thought it looks a bit organic--people streaming back and forth like blood cells, keeping the city alive.

Of course, since this is Tipton, the arteries regularly get fouled up with self-important clogs who start a fifteen minute yelling match over who was first in line.

After squaring everything away at the apartment I decide to stop by the office. I might as well check in. The door to Raven's office is cracked open when I arrive, not a good sign. I draw my handgun and creep closer. There are raised voices inside. I pause to listen. Jumping into things gets people killed. Besides, the only people who can get inside peacefully are the ones Raven and I let in, and the doors don't seem like they've been forced.

"Miss Alleghany, I'm not sure you appreciate the implications of your decision."

I recognize the voice. Of all people, why would Raven let Kanaghy in?

"How many times do I have to say no before you understand it?" Raven replies.

"The Agency does not appreciate being stonewalled."

"I guess that makes the stick more uncomfortable."

Way to go, Raven. I wonder what gambit Zeke will try next. Intimidation? I'm really your friend?

"Miss Alleghany, the Davenport Irregularity is potentially the most dangerous emergence this decade. Possibly this century."

Ah. Good old danger and responsibility.

"I'm potentially pregnant too," she shoots back.

There's a pause. "Ma'am, if you've engaged in intimate contact with this entity, it's imperative that you return with me."

I smile. He has no idea he's being messed with.

"My answer is still no," Raven says.

"If you reconsider—"

"Don't make me throw you out."

"—you know where to find me. Good day."

I back up a bit, so as not to appear like I was eavesdropping. The door opens and I grin. "Special Agent Ezekiel Kanaghy. What a surprise."

He steps stiffly into the hall. "...Mr. Richards. I should have known."

"Don't you have better things to do than harass people smarter than you?" I say.

He walks away without a word.

Inside, Raven is almost as Raven as usual. She blows a few strands of pink hair out of her eyes and they forget about gravity, sticking straight out like antennae. Other than that, she tries to act like nothing's happened.

"What was that all about?" I ask.

She goes to her desk, messes with her computer, then looks up and stares off into space.

"Raven?"

"Oh, it's nothing. Ever since I wrote that paper they've been all over me."

"Must have been a pretty impressive paper."

"Well, a girl's got to have *some* secrets." She winks mischievously, but there isn't much of her usual humor behind it. I probe a bit further, but she stays mum. I'll have to look up the Davenport Irregularity for myself. Catchy name.

I ask if anything new happened and she tells me she's started on my cover for the Ablesoft investigation.

"What investigation?" I say. Sometimes Raven gets a few steps ahead of me and doesn't always keep me in the loop.

"Well, you were telling me about the elves and dwarves allying, so I did some digging. Ablesoft's a relatively new tech company and they're owned entirely by dwarves. They're rumored to be extremely progressive—the old clans don't like them—and I figured that if anyone would be in the alliance, it would be them."

"Were you planning on telling me?" I ask.

"Sorry. It kinda slipped my mind." This forthright apology is also unlike Raven. "Their main focus is materials science and the corresponding engineering applications," she concludes.

"How long will it take?"

"Maybe a few days, a week and a half tops."

She seems like she needs some time alone to think, and I don't want to head back to my apartment, so I figure I'll go hunt that hippie before my headache has a chance to get worse. He shouldn't be that hard to find.

There's a popular hostel over in Alcaz District, and hostels attract hippies like campaign donors attract politicians. Even if he isn't there himself, someone will know him. Kaitas has given me one solid piece of information to work with: the guy has a scar running across his forehead.

Along the way I stop by a newsstand to look through the tabloids. As expected, crazy theories about the events outside of Swanky's are on most of the cover pages. It's mindless entertainment, but I pick up a few copies anyway. There's a stack of them back at my apartment, a slightly loony record of my escapades.

I also pick up a package of peach rings and stash them inside my jacket.

After consulting with the neighborhood pot dealers, I find the hippie with the scar blissing out on a commuter park bench. I sit down next to him and strike up a conversation. The way my luck is going, I'm a little surprised he was so easy to find.

"Nice day," I say.

"Dude," he replies.

"What's up?" I try again.

"I. Am. So. Cosmic. Right now."

Resisting the urge to smack him with rolled-up tabloids, I say, "I need to talk to you about a weapon you brought into the city."

"Everything...So beautiful."

I sigh. This is going to be fun.

"It sure is," I say, playing along. "Have you seen any beautiful guns lately?"

"No." He looks at me, his eyes widening, as if he's going to say something else, then tilts his head back and resumes staring upward.

"What about crystals?" Maybe the gun's clip will spark some recollection.

"Right on. Raise that vibration with love." As spaced as he is, he can tell I'm getting impatient because he continues, "Dude, slow down. The monkeys go away. *If* you ignore them."

I'd be lying if I said I hate to do this to him, but I'm in no mood to play around. There's a spell that can completely sober people up for about five minutes. I'll end up with a huge headache, again, because I'm not fully recovered from the attack, but this is the first solid lead I've had in weeks.

Basically, drugs help people jump free of their bodies. It's the fast lane to astral travel, if you hate mental seatbelts. Wherever their minds happen to be, this spell lassos them back less than tenderly. For most people, it's a short stint in migraine hell.

I cast the spell and his body jerks forward like he's been hit with a hammer. His oversized sunglasses fly off his head, fully revealing the scar.

"What the fuck?" he says.

I wait until he notices me. "Hi. Welcome back."

"It feels like my eyes are made out of lead and my brain's on fire. What the fuck did you do to me, dude?"

"It'll wear off. Now, let's talk."

"I don't have to talk to you, man. It's a free country."

"No, you don't. But when this does wear off, your mind will rocket back into outer space. Depending on what you took, it might tear itself apart getting there. On the other hand, I can smooth the process along." I hope he doesn't call my bluff. With the mood I'm in, I might just say fuck it and punch him in the face.

"Okay, okay, get off my balls. What do you want to know?"

It's amazing how hippies are all about peace and love until you take their drugs away. The headache's already starting to build and I'm getting cranky.

"A few weeks ago you brought a magical weapon into this city. It's a handgun, and it fires shaped-crystal rounds. Who asked you to do it?"

"You mean it's a real gun? I thought it was some kind of toy. The guy paid well, though."

I lean forward menacingly. "Who? You don't have much time left."

"I don't—I don't know. He had this shirt on and smelled like Funyuns. Told me to make it quick because he was botting."

Johnny Mojo? That makes even less sense than before.

"That's what you wanted to know, right?" the hippie says. "We're good now?"

I mutter some nonsense syllables and wave my hands. "Yeah."

Next stop: Johnny's place.

❀

I know exactly where Johnny's apartment is. I have a pretty good idea of his schedule. But the last thing I'm going to do is waltz over there and knock on the door. I might push him around whenever I see him in person, just to remind him I have a long memory, but I'm under no illusions that I can bully him into revealing the truth. More than likely, he'd just try to bluff his way past me and then run straight to his boss. Gunrunning isn't Johnny's game. There has to be someone else involved.

His apartment complex, the Wraithmore, sports a post-modernist touch and looks like a bunch of metallic blocks floating in space. One of the clubhouse windows offers great line-of-sight to Johnny's front door and I sit at a mahogany table, ignoring the inlaid chess board with holographic pieces. Needless to say, this is a high-end neighborhood; it must be, to have the money to deviate from standard architecture this much. Not for the first time, I wonder how he manages to pull in so much dough as a small-time extortionist. He might have branched out, but I'm sure I'd have heard about it.

One of the complex staff stops by to ask me what I'm doing. I tell him I'm celebrity watching. A few D-listers live here so it's not unheard of.

I train my binoculars on Johnny's apartment and it explodes.

The firebomb blossoms like a napalm flower, blue-green flames completely engulfing the place. The cubes comprising Johnny's apartment sag like they're melting from the inside out. The automated sprinklers activate but don't do much. That some unknown arms dealer is willing to not only take out Johnny, but half of Wraithmore along with him, tells me just how big this is. The Under has a code of silence. Anything and everything is fair game as long as you don't attract the attention of the human world above. Breaches are punishable by instant execution, so these guys are either extremely confident or extremely worried about what Johnny might let slip. Possibly both.

Anticipation rises in my stomach. While the Under might be magical, nonhumans also live everyday lives and most of my jobs are simply routine. Get proof of someone's infidelity. Find out who's selling black-market pixie dust. All those variations of "the butler did it" can get old, but something this big is bound to be exciting. Despite the slow start, despite the attempt on my life, I'm actually looking forward to seeing this out.

Chapter 8

Apparently, my name for the day is Charles Darwin (no relation), and I'm the CEO of Sensoria, a company in the manufacturing sector. Raven won't tell me exactly what it's supposed to manufacture, only that my company would benefit from Ablesoft's expertise with plastics and advanced polymers. Apparently, a man with my "expert social skills" could easily roll with the punches. I figure it has something to do with electronic noses or other biochemical detection systems, and I tailor answers to possible questions accordingly. My market capitalization weighs in at just over $750 million, whatever that means, but I trust Raven to choose a number that impresses. She's rented a snazzy business suit on my dime—one of the speed skating inspired ones I swore I'd never wear—and last but not least makes a point of asking me not to be an asshole.

"Is that really necessary," I say, "given my obviously expert social skills?"

She hands me a fake briefcase. Well, a real briefcase, but one filled with lies. "You've been grumpier than usual recently. Even David's noticed."

"How? He's never here anymore."

"Do I detect just the hint of a complaint?" she teases.

"You think he's staying out of trouble?"

"Nice try, Dick. Don't change the subject."

"You know, I don't have to put up with this."

When I arrive at Ablesoft Court, security's already been informed of my appointment and I'm ushered into a plush waiting room, much nicer than the ones I usually see. Abstract art clings to the walls and a widescreen TV loops through a marketing reel of Ablesoft's accomplishments. After about twenty minutes, a young woman enters, apologizes for the delay, and shows me to a conference room where Mr. Damien Bosch, Executive Vice President of Product Applications, is already seated. We exchange pleasantries.

"I have to tell you that your proposal caught us by surprise, but its uniqueness convinced us to give it a second look," he begins, jumping right to business. "It's not often that we partner with small companies."

"As I often say, quality often comes in small packages," I reply, playing along.

He gives me a strange look, like he's trying to decide whether that was a joke, then continues. "Uh...yes. We're looking forward to negotiations. Your growth forecast is quite startling, but our analysts can find no fault with it."

"I'm glad we impressed you. Sensoria often surprises in, and over, multiple quarters."

He gives me that look again and I start to wonder whether I'm getting the business-speak right.

"Yes, well. Our accounting department is still crunching the numbers, but we should have a response to your proposal by the end of next week. I understand you wanted to view our production facilities."

❀

Ablesoft's layout mimics a corporate park. Their main floor's designed to resemble a field dotted with modest buildings. Bosch labels each in turn, and mentions that they're all connected in a more traditional fashion underneath: a maze of interconnected rooms and corridors. The tour finishes in front of a tall, glass arch housing double doors. Bosch says their production head is just inside, then excuses himself to other duties with no further instructions. Is this a test?

The doors are carved from granite veined with mica. Symbols and pictographs glitter in the overhead lights. Some I recognize as dwarven. Others appears more secular, like the periodic table at head height. Flowing, curvilinear designs are interwoven throughout and feel distinctly elven. Raven's instincts were on the money once again. Whichever dwarves had made these doors might not only ally with elves, but could quite easily have made the Count's mystery gun. The glass arch is over four feet thick, front to back, but it and the doors stand alone atop a gently sculpted hill.

I guess the doors retract somehow, revealing an elevator. I'm half right. There's indeed an elevator hidden in the arch, but the doors aren't real. When I run my hands over them in search of a control panel, I pass right though. Clever. These are the most realistic holograms I've ever seen.

Walking through the doors, I see nothing but a circle glowing in darkness. I step inside and a glowing panel appears in front of me, a list of floors in gold lettering, lighting up as I point to each in turn. I see "Main Offices" and, in the spirit of experimentation, reach toward it. As my hand passes through, a gentle ping sounds and there's a slight sensation of movement.

When the elevator stops, the list of floors disappears and a line of light becomes a portal into a modern office complex. Important information scrolls across integrated screens as dwarves in business casual shuttle back and forth. The lights are a soft blue and dimmer than normal, but my presence is noted by the environmental computers and the illumination in my area increases.

I request directions from the information kiosk on the landing. Unlike the elevator, it uses tried-and-true touch screen technology. A green line appears on the floor, leading right to the Chief Production Officer's office, who turns out to be the dwarf I'd met at Lord British's soiree. He doesn't seem to recognize me. Dwarves deprived of alcohol for extended periods of time tend to go a little weird.

"Welcome, Mr. Darwin," he says. "I trust you've been so far impressed by our facilities?"

"I have," I say. "I'm afraid Mr. Bosch didn't give me your name."

The dwarf smiles. "He's still a little unnerved by us, actually. You'll have to forgive him. Evanek Falling Rock, at your service." He holds out his hand.

This polished, debonair businessdwarf is a far cry from the far-too-sober one I'd met, so I decide to rustle him a little. I shake his hand. "A pleasure to meet you again. I hope you've recovered from the fast of Ni'Tarian?"

For a moment, he has the deer-in-headlights look of someone who only remembers enough of a bad night to know what he doesn't remember is probably a lot worse.

"It was an entertaining conversation," I say, letting him off the hook, "and most informative. In fact, it's why I decided to propose a partnership in the first place."

He looks relieved, but still nervous. As it turns out, he's a nervous talker and I end up getting a bigger tour than I hoped for.

"Yes, well," he says. "I do want to say that your proposal caught us by surprise. While there is certainly a market for nonhuman prophylactics, and no one's thought to fill that niche before, it was still rather startling. Especially the market analysis of the pixie and hobgoblin sectors."

I shouldn't have been surprised that Raven had set me up as a condom salesman, but I still feel awkward. Recovering nicely, if I do say so myself, I reply, "Given the unique nature of our customer base, I felt that Ablesoft's experience with plastics and polymers would be a perfect fit. Not to mention the dwarven reputation for craftsmanship."

He preens with pride. "And you couldn't have made a better choice, I assure you. Before we begin the production tour, is there anything you'd like to know?"

"Some of the symbols on your clanhold doors, they seem almost elven."

Evanek chuckles. "That's what they said too. But the main doors of a clanhold should show the spirit of the dwarves within. Ours is progress."

Ah. That explains the alliance.

"And what clan do you hail from? I didn't recognize any symbols on the door."

He casts me a suspicious glance and I do my best to look like an ignorant human. An old-school dwarf would have been offended by me asking that question that bluntly, but I've heard the newer ones don't mind as much. Evanek turns out to be the latter.

"Actually," Evanek begins, and his story is odd, even for a dwarf. He and some of his friends had become enamored with modern technology. They saw writing and debugging millions of lines of computer code as no different from slaving away in a jeweler's workshop, painstakingly creating masterpieces from strands of gold and silver. As they learned more, they realized that the full potential of human technology was amazing, and dwarves apparently take to physics and engineering as easily as they do to mining and smithing. However, their efforts were berated by older dwarves as too strange and non-traditional.

So Evanek, along with his friends, decided to strike out on their own. They gathered like-minded colleagues from other clans and founded Ablesoft as an umbrella company for all their activities and thus, a new clanhold was born. In dwarven culture, the existing clans have one hundred years to declare war on a new clan in order to knock some sense into the upstarts. If they wait too long, or lose the war, the new clan gains official diplomatic recognition.

Evanek and his friends never intended for any of this to happen. They seem like college dropouts founding a company out of adolescent rebellion and overconfidence, and are still amazed and slightly embarrassed at their own success. After figuring out he's still looking for an authority figure's approval it's easy to pry more information out of him.

"The final straw, though," he finishes, "was when we partnered with similarly progressive elves."

"Elves?"

"A lot of new technology can create distinctly elven effects, especially when you consider that the cutting edge lies in working with the environment rather than against it. Our magic is the bones of the earth. Theirs is the spirit of the wind. It's an obvious synergy, if you know how to look."

I probe a bit more about the alliance. He hesitates but continues. I note that, now that he's had a chance to put alcohol in his system, he's much more positive about the benefit of exchanging culture and ideas with the elves.

"I bet that infuriates the older dwarves," I say.

"Yeah." He smirks. "They wanted to declare war, but we're in a unique situation. Our new 'clan' has no name, and it's impossible to judge what you can't name. They're still meeting to figure out what to do."

"'Ablesoft' doesn't work?"

"That's a human name, only for use with humans."

"Nice," I say appreciatively, appealing to his ego. "That's some clever legal maneuvering."

"I just hope it lasts." He looks like he realizes he might have said too much, then rallies. "Shall we begin the tour?"

We start at the enzyme factories, large vats of microbes genetically engineered to produce plastics and rubber polymers. Each gleaming cylinder is covered in runes and smells faintly of Porta-Potty. Technicians move between grated catwalks and access ladders, responding to digitized displays and gentle pings.

"This is our main production floor," Evanek says. "Once you give us your specifications, our research department will begin engineering microbes to suit your needs."

"Does the plastic come out as a finished product?" I ask, still pretending to be an interested businessman.

"Oh, no. The bacteria create the basic building blocks, which are distilled and refined later."

Something about the vats' sheen catches my eyes. "These vats, are they mithril?" If they are, it would be fortune in magical metal, almost worth going to war over by itself.

Evanek grins. "Actually, yes. We've found that enchantment is sometimes the only way to create the necessary epigenetic modifications, and mithril is over ten times more efficient than gold at maintaining a magical charge. The runes are tailor-made for each process, sustaining the precise magical frequencies necessary."

"Are you able to reuse the vats?"

"As you may already know, if you re-smelt rune-carved metal, each subsequent enchantment is less powerful." His expression turns smug. "However, we've recently developed a patent-pending technology which allows us to construct equipment out of inscribed tiles, which we can then rearrange as needed. Let me show you our advanced prototype."

He's so confident no one could duplicate this work that I haven't seen an NDA all day. He's probably right.

We head through utilitarian corridors to a section marked Research and Development—Advanced Experimental Division. Evanek is introducing me to a dwarf named Jonkar "Robert" Cunning Anvil when his pager buzzes. He excuses himself while Robert takes me to the main laboratory.

It definitely feels like a dwarven workshop. Scientific journals lie in haphazard piles between electronic components and other tools of the trade. Blinking lights blink and portable processors lie connected in arcane patterns, but in the corner is the traditional steel anvil. No dwarf worth his beard would ever have a workshop without one.

"Sorry about the mess," Robert says. "I wasn't expecting company and—" Something small dashes across the floor, disappearing into the back room. "Blasted gnomes! Always underfoot."

"Why don't you just get rid of them?" I say. I know I'd enjoy the hunt.

"I'd like to," he grumbles, "but the junior engineers keep them as pets. They're trying to evolve a supergnome. In the meantime, they hold fighting tournaments and even have gyms and badges. Can you believe that?" He shuffles between the tables, tidying up. "All they are is bloody retarded von Neumann machines."

"Junior" engineers? Robert doesn't look older than two hundred.

A voice pipes up from the back room. "You're wrong," it says. "Gnomes might live forever, but they're easily destroyed. Those that survive long enough make more gnomes than those which die quickly. That's a textbook case of natural selection."

"You can't have natural selection without some kind of generational continuity. Gnomes will make more gnomes out of any damn thing they come across. There's simply no heritability," Robert shoots back, apparently forgetting me. He and the Baron Rutgert would probably get along great.

"No heritability?" the voice replies. "They stay true to type over 95% of the time."

"Selection bias," Robert scoffs. "In any case, there's no need to prance them about like gladiators."

The source of the voice emerges from the other room. It's the first noticeably female dwarf I've ever seen. Her hair is smoothed and even her clothes have a feminine cast, though it's hard to do much with shoulders as broad as a linebacker's. I don't say anything out of politeness, but I guess the old clans are furious about more than just modern technology and elves.

"Oh, hi," she says. "I didn't realize you were here. I'm Maria. Robert and I like to argue about things we know nothing about."

"Speak for yourself," Robert harrumphs.

She smiles and I sense a setup. "I stand corrected," she says.

"Thank you," Robert says.

"Robert likes to argue about things *he* knows nothing about and it's all I can do to correct him."

"The man's not here to listen to our squabbles, Maria. He's here to see the prototype."

"Ah, an investor." Maria grins. "Right this way." When she turns, I notice a circular patch ironed onto the right shoulder of her lab coat. Inside the red outline, three solid purple circles, barely touching each other, are arranged around a central blue circle like a stylized flower. I read the words underneath.

"The Unified Field Gym?" I say.

"Bloody slavers is what they are," Robert mutters.

"When two gnomes both want a common resource, they fight," Maria explains, "and we think the winner becomes slightly more intelligent. By accelerating the process, we hope to speed their evolution to true sentience."

"And win a few bets along the way," Robert adds, darkly.

Maria ignores him. "Anyway, this is it."

The advanced prototype looks like a mad scientist covered a pack of Tarot cards with aluminum foil and tried to bring them to life. Each mithril card has a rune carved on it, and is connected to at least two others via thin wires. They form a bowl shape and unused cards lie stacked off to the side.

"Right now it's set to levitate anything placed inside it," Robert says. He places a pen from his lab coat's front pocket inside and it begins to float, rotating slowly. "Now, if we rearrange these two components like this..." Robert retrieves the pen and swaps two cards, careful not to disturb the wiring. "...the pen will launch itself like a bottle rocket." Sure enough, he places the pen in the bowl and it twangs off the ceiling.

"Fascinating," I say. "Does Ablesoft also perform weapons research?" He's talking, so now's as good a time as any to probe for information.

Maria groans and rolls her eyes. Robert explodes.

"Weapons research? I told them once and I'll tell them again, if they try to weaponize my life's work I'll bloody hang them with their own entrails. Progress is one thing, but anyone who's lost respect for the bones of the earth has lost their bloody soul!"

I get kicked out the lab and am still trying to figure out how to salvage this when Evanek returns.

"Maria called," he says and sighs. "Robert threw a tantrum again, didn't he?" Apparently this isn't uncommon.

"I asked about weapons research and he lost it."

"I do apologize. That's one of his sore spots. If you'd care to follow me, I'll explain on the way out."

❃

The story's interesting. Dwarves have recently discovered that adamantium emits magical radiation. Unlike mithril, which absorbs and reflects magic, adamantium projects it. That's why the noble families given dwarven gifts often developed magical abilities. Constant exposure to low level radiation mutated their DNA. Robert discovered this and via analogy with uranium, he created the world's first adamantium reactor. It was only a prototype but its power was awe-inspiring. An eldritch purple glow flooded the room and the ambient magical field outside the shielded chamber was powerful enough to have forged the artifacts from the Age of Legends. Just bringing magical items into the room charged them to full capacity.

And if that wasn't enough, the adamantium fuel wafers decayed into an entirely new metal: nihilium. It's completely impervious to magic. Obsidian black in large quantities, but nearly transparent in thin slices, it has a nearly unlimited range of applications.

Everyone was excited and overjoyed, but then some idiot suggested the possibility of an adamantium and/or nihilium bomb. Before anyone could stop him, Robert destroyed the prototype, literally ate the schematics and his research notes, and hid the nihilium somewhere they haven't been able to find.

During the conversation, I probe to see if Ablesoft is involved in handgun manufacturing but Evanek responds that they are solely concerned with productive applications, if they could just get Robert to see that.

I know bullshit when I smell it and side with Robert. I'm not happy with the prospect of a new superweapon in Tipton.

"Does the Count know about these potential weapons applications?" I ask.

"Who?" says Evanek.

That's not good.

❀

Back at the office, I avoid Raven's smirk and sink into my desk/chair. I darken the lights and close my eyes for some brainstorming. I envision a whiteboard inside my head, create an oval, and write "gun" inside. For visualizations it's pretty basic, but it suits my purpose.

From there, I create a line to another oval: Johnny Mojo, FUBAR'd. He'd been in his apartment when the firestorm hit, and he wouldn't have been able to survive that. Whoever killed him obviously has no compunctions about breaking the veil, nor did the elves who attacked me outside of Swanky's. The two are possibly related and I link both facts with a dotted line.

On another front, Ablesoft is performing advanced research, and connected to both Lord British and the Goth. I pause for a moment to reflect on how much I hate that pasty-faced bastard.

Basically, the Goth's recruiters hang out at high schools and nightclubs, looking for alienated teenagers and young twenty-somethings of the goth persuasion. Most of these kids, especially the ones with real issues, just want attention and approval, and the recruiters give them that in spades. After softening them up, they entice them with the promise of magic that's just as dark and misunderstood as they are.

That magic works, and works well, and these kids suddenly have real power over their lives. Unfortunately, there's a catch. The talismans and charms he gives them dole out magic in exchange for pieces of their souls. By the time these kids realize what's happening there's so little left of them that they're too numb to care.

Everyone in the Under knows about his operation, but most shrug it off as what happens when you make stupid choices. I, on the other hand, think that even if these kids are probably going to turn into the same kind of idiots their parents are, they deserve to do it on their own terms and not because some asshole in liquid-paper makeup has a hard-on for building a zombie army.

I spend a few minutes arranging all my thoughts, then let the intricate diagram spin inside my mind. As always happens when I do this, I hear music and smell unidentifiable scents. The whirring mobile picks up speed and I watch it go. It's a lot like reading Tarot cards. Even if you have no idea what they're trying to say, your subconscious often sees things you don't, and is much more accurate than the rational mind.

What surfaces is this:

At Ablesoft, elves and dwarves are forming a new alliance. When the old-school elves and dwarves finally realize how big a potential threat this poses, they'll go to war to stop it. Ablesoft can't withstand the fury of both races, so they've turned to other powers for protection. This is where Lord British comes in.

As long as Ablesoft stays firmly in the human realm, open war can't be declared due to the veil. For his part, Lord British is always on the lookout for opportunities to stick his dick in a different financial market. He's contracted the Goth to provide additional protection. As part of those efforts, they're importing magical weapons, using Johnny Mojo as a (former) contact.

However, now that Count Fantabuloso and Lord British have apparently come to an understanding, the case is effectively moot. The Count will still want a patsy he can use as a public warning, but since Johnny already bit the dust, all the Count has to do is claim responsibility and his reputation will remain intact.

The attempt on my life seems only tangentially related, but could still fit. There's no love lost between me and the Goth, and I'm a potential threat. Even if it's not him, it's a sign that a great many people are getting rather nervous.

I open my eyes, satisfied. Even if I'm wrong, it still gives me a good place to focus further investigation.

Chapter 9

The next day, I get to my office early, planning on writing a preliminary report for the Count now that I have some solid leads. David's already there. Raven really needs to stop giving him the code to the door. Instead of his normal ostentatious headgear he's wearing a black beret. And a black shirt and black pants. As the door closes behind me, he steps closer. Instead of his usual clumsy, exaggerated motions, he uses the exaggerated motions of clumsy pantomime. I'm forced to remind myself, yet again, that I'm not his father.

"Hi, David," I say. "Long time no see."

"I've been busy," he says. He picks his words carefully, like they're the only safe path through a minefield.

It's obvious he's been hanging around the Brotherhood, but this turn to simple, understandable English might do him some good, not that it outweighs everything else.

"Is Raven in?" I say.

"She said she'd be back later but that I could wait for you."

"Are you feeling okay?" I ask him after a moment.

"Yes," he says. "Every word is precious."

"I thought I asked you to stay away from the Brotherhood."

He shrugs apathetically.

That's not good. I've seen it happen with new converts, whether to a cause, gang, or religion. People finally feel like they belong so they swallow the dogma hook, line, and sinker.

"I thought I told you not to—" I start, but catch myself. "I mean, are you sure about the Brotherhood?"

"They're..." He pauses uncomfortably, searching for words. All of his obvious effort makes my brain itch. "...admirable once you get acquainted," he finishes.

Like I haven't heard that before. I try to figure out what to say next, but let it slide for now because, like I said, I'm not his father.

"Are you sure about this?" I ask.

"Yes. They also want to hire you."

That stops me in my tracks. "...You're serious?"

He starts to say something, but doesn't. Apparently saying yes would be a waste of words. My gut tells me accepting their job would be a horrible idea, but I can at least hear them out, however that would work, and see what David's gotten himself into. If worse comes to worst, at least I'll have an idea of how to break myself in and David out.

"What's the scoop?" I say.

"They wish to discuss it personally."

I roll my eyes. Everyone always does.

❀

I half expect to be taken back to the greenhouse but instead we head to a rundown commercial district that's modeled after a small town cultural oasis. Brick storefronts, some with broken windows, are edged with benches for passersby and alcoves for street musicians. A thin crowd of suspicious, downcast people ignores the graffiti and vestigial ads for last year's celebrity fad. We pass a dilapidated community theater and duck into the next alley. Two mimes, seated in midair, play transparent cards on an invisible table.

Every now and then a child stops to stare but most of the passersby unconsciously give them a wide berth. Even the least magically inclined can sense there's something off about mimes. The Brotherhood just does that to people.

They pause their game and the one on the right stands, a monochrome highlight against a dingy wall. I debate shooting him just because. He mimes something to David, who nods. An invisible item changes hands.

"Put this on," David says.

"Is please an extra word?" I reply. I'm less than thrilled about this.

David just stands there, holding out an empty palm. Sighing, I pretend to take whatever it was. I feel nothing in my hands but apparently the transfer was made because David lowers his arm. I raise my eyebrows.

"It's an amulet," David says.

"Of course it is," I say. Since I've come this far, I might as well go all the way so I pretend to put it around my neck. There's the slightest sensation of weight, but that's it. I look at David, then the mimes, thinking that the mimes might possibly look less retarded. Nope. "All right then," I say, "let's go."

Jerking into motion like a novelty clock, one of the mimes pulls something from the inside pocket of an imaginary jacket. He examines it closely and passes it to the other, who examines it through an imaginary monocle. Don't ask me how I know it's a monocle; the non-existent amulet is probably interpreting for me. Satisfied, they insert whatever-it-is into the wall behind them at waist height, turn it like a key, raise a section of ethereal security chain, and finally open a door. Of course this is just my interpretation. For all I know, they might actually be making a soufflé.

One of the mimes turns to me and bows theatrically. *Aprés vous, monsieur.*

It comes out of my mouth before I realize what I'm saying. "You're *French*?"

David smirks at me, then looks down as I glare at him.

The mime bows again. *But of course, monsieur. What else would we be?*

Then it strikes me that I'm hearing a mime speak. Well, not speak, exactly, but it doesn't feel like telepathy either. It's more like the mime went through the motions and the words appeared in my head like the subtitles to a foreign movie. I don't like it one bit.

"The amulet translates for you," David says helpfully.

"You have one too?"

"While I still need it."

"David, what are you think—"

S'il vous plait, the mime interrupts. *Business awaits*. He bows yet again.

"Now what?" I say to the world in general.

Rather than answer, David steps through the wall.

❀

Apparently there's another world behind this one, a mirror image blocked out in shades of gray. After a moment of disorientation the world turns inside out and colors explode into monochrome. The fake bricks in the wall become solid black, the mortar thin lines of white, and the court streetlights spread billowing clouds of gray. The dispirited crowd is still there, oblivious to the change, but have been transformed into hulking figures shrouded by wispy fumes. Wan globes of light, eerie in the omnipresent gray, spark between the hulks, leaving trails of fading mist. There's also a sense of being watched. Nothing particularly malevolent, just intense scrutiny by things unseen.

I'm about to ask one of the guide mimes a question when he holds a finger to his lips. He walks his right index and middle fingers across his left palm and looks at me. After making sure I'm paying attention, his left palm engulfs his right hand and he pretends to die.

I get the point. Each plane of existence has its predators, and just because humans are the titular top dog on ours doesn't mean it's the same elsewhere. These things might not be hungry now, but there's no reason to attract their attention. I guess even using mimespeak is too dangerous, let alone actual words. Again I wonder what David's dragged me into, but there's no point in backing out now.

As we travel through this shadow Tipton, I'm filled with a sense of dread. The lighting, or whatever it's called, hurts my eyes despite not being very bright and my instincts, recovering from the initial shock, scream that at any moment I'm going to be brought down from behind. The hulking phantoms ignore us and there are no other obvious dangers, but the hairs on the back of my neck try to escape anyway. David's also on edge, which isn't surprising, but the professional caution of the mimes only increases my sense of danger. They stop every few minutes, as if tracking something or checking if *we're* being tracked, and occasionally sign quietly to each other. The invisible amulet doesn't help with that.

Things come to a head near what, in the normal world, would be Alizar Court. Here though, it's a nightmare shadow of harsh white and dripping black, with gray eking out a miserable existence in forgotten nooks and crannies. The phantoms congregate around a central altar which emanates waves of murderous intent. *You're going to die*, it whispers directly into my brain with such certainty that for a moment I feel there's no other alternative, no other way it can possibly be. Despite my mental training, it's all I can do to not scream in defiance and attack. I'm not one to go quietly. David, next to me, is about to break.

Sensing this, one of the mimes takes something from an imaginary pocket and tosses it like a dart. I see a gleam of silver strike one of the misshapen phantoms, which disappears in the gray mist. It bellows in shock and rage, shrill, grating, and inhuman, doubly loud in the dead silence. As if jolted from a trance the other phantoms jerk away inhumanly fast and the black leeches out of the world, leaving behind a stark outline that hurts to see. The black concentrates itself into a malevolent sphere, which engulfs the stricken phantom. A scream, deathly loud in the utter silence, rises in pitch and volume until it becomes too high to hear. The darkness disperses back to its accustomed corners, giving this place a sense of volume once more. There's no trace of the victim.

The certainty of death subsides and I feel a sense of satisfaction, like an ancient predator settling down to a post-kill nap. The remaining phantoms arrange themselves back in front of the altar, acting as if nothing happened.

I look at David. He's shaking a bit but soldiers on like he's seen it before. If *that* hadn't scared him off...

Eventually we reach the analogue of Heironymous switching platform, Tipton's largest commuter interchange. It's always crowded, and the endless phantom people swirl through the gates and concourses like sludge through a chthonic prayer wheel. As they pass through me, a sluggish charge of energy slouches up my spine. The omnipresent advertizing screens, outlined in black and white, break into shimmering concentric circles as we pass. Out of curiosity, I sneak a good look at one of the phantom's faces.

Winding horror envelops me as I see a rotting, alien skull in the process of chewing itself apart. Wriggling bits that look like maggots but are attached to bleached-white bone fight each other, the losers bleeding blackish crud. Their eyes, or the holes where eyes normally are, look intentionally scarred shut but their apathetic gaze holds so much wrongness I have to cast a silent charm to regain my balance. I'm not happy at using magic here, where I don't know if it will attract undue attention, but it's better than the alternative. Even so, I'm left with the desire to blast as many of them apart as possible. It's like looking at them has left a grimy patina on my soul.

I look at David. He's gazing down at the ground, only looking up when necessary. That's probably a good idea but I don't copy him. Ignoring my surroundings, for any reason, will eventually get me killed.

Despite my paranoia, the infinite, hulking crowd of phantoms doesn't spare us even a first glance.

Several times I nearly lose track of our guides—their black and white striped shirts make excellent camouflage in this place—but we make it to a point midway between Astrid and Megabyte platforms. The mimes stop at what's probably a maintenance door in the normal world, but in this place light drips out around the edges and pools on the floor. The one who warned me about speaking pulls out another invisible gadget while the other keeps lookout for who-knows-what. The first mime places his gadget against the wall, the light brightens until the door seems to glow, and then he steps through while the lookout takes up a defensive posture. Taking the hint, David and I follow through.

A series of glowing rings coruscate past us, and then we're there, wherever there is. A sense of relief passes over me. Well, it's not relief, per se, but more like someone removed a smothering blanket from my mind and isn't drooling on it anymore. The new landscape looks like a country field filled with free-standing doors erected at random. Everything's cartoony and still monochrome, but opposed to the shadow Tipton, everything's in sharp, almost painful, relief. The trees are obviously trees, not a jumble of harsh white and black, and are defined in graduated gray. The distance holds a manor unlike anything I've seen before. When the second mime rejoins us, fading into existence like a ghost in reverse, we make our way up a hedge-lined path toward it.

I inspect one of the hedges. The cartoony leaves are razor sharp and I cut my finger. A drop of blood pools, then sprouts wings and flies away. One of the mimes laughs silently. I glance at David, whose eyes are planted firmly on the ground.

The path winds under a series of massive dolmen, stone archways that could have been filched straight from Stonehenge. It's a decent walk, and the manor's front porch seems to materialize from nowhere. We take the front steps and without ceremony enter Olygandr, House of Doors.

Inside, we're led to a comfortable antechamber. Wooden chairs cluster around a coffee table like teenagers around free samples, but the oversized books aren't that bad. I'd have more of an opinion if they were in English, but the stylized patterns of dots and dashes are probably the height of literary fashion in mimeworld. David's still lost in downcast thought and thankfully we're not kept waiting long. Part of me is grateful they're not trying the old "let's keep them waiting to show how important I am" game, but the bigger part of me wonders what game is taking its place, especially when the mime who arrives to usher me in indicates that David will stay in the waiting room.

I'm taken to a genteel, monochrome study. The walls, floor to ceiling, are lined with books, the only exception an unlit fireplace with an ornate mantel. Two easy chairs face each other from the edges of a patterned rug. Seated in one is the most commanding mime I've ever seen. The mime sports a black turtleneck, one designed for fashion rather than warmth, and a black beret. The face paint, while neutral, manages to convey an amused smirk and when the mime rises to greet me there's a feline fluidity of movement which suggests a panther poised to strike. With a nod the mime who ushered me in is dismissed.

Greetings, the other mime says, bowing, and indicates itself. *This is the Unspoken, leader of the Brotherhood. Thank you for coming. Please, have a seat.*

At least we're starting off polite. I sit.

Would you like a drink? Brandy, perhaps? The Unspoken mimics a shape and a bottle appears between gloved hands. Two brandy snifters are created next and each of us is poured a glass. No longer needed, the bottle hangs in the air before fading away. The Unspoken hands me a glass and proposes a toast to the start of an excellent working relationship.

I'm definitely on point. Not only is this place setting me on edge, now this character is offering me something to drink. Travel tip number one when visiting strange and unknown worlds is to never eat or drink anything unless you're ready for a permanent stay. I might be being offensively paranoid but I don't give a damn. David and I are going to have a long talk after we get back.

Don't worry, the Unspoken says. *Speaking for you is perfectly safe here. You haven't taken the vows.* A concerned look crosses painted features as the Unspoken sips what's ostensibly brandy. *Is this the wrong milieu?*

Arms move in an impossibly complicated pattern and the study blurs. I'd say it pixilates, except it doesn't. It's more like everything merges with its own shadow, and then the shadows move. The only thing remaining in sharp focus is the Unspoken's face, brow furrowed in an exaggerated imitation of concentration. I search it for any hints to the mind behind it, and the eyes suddenly open and fix on me. One winks. We're now in a corner office.

Would this be more appropriate? The Unspoken leans back on a swivel chair, exaggeratedly relaxed.

I add another item to the list of things I don't like about this mime. Though the tone's humorous and the face is smiling, there's nothing in those eyes except twinkling, lizard-brained mockery.

"I prefer the study," I say. If the offer's there, I might as well cause a little extra work.

As you wish. Another dramatic flourish, another nauseating scene change, and we're back.

"David says you want to hire me."

The Unspoken cocks his head. *Right to the point. Very well. Would you be amenable to investigating an individual? You are already acquainted.*

"That depends on who it is." But whoever it is, I doubt I'll be interested.

You call him the Goth.

Then again, I might as well hear this out before saying no. "I'm listening."

He is the one importing the weapons you're concerned about.

I nod. I've already figured that out. I'll also have to talk to David about not spreading my business around. It could get us both killed.

It is a prelude to summoning the Archangel of Despair.

Yeah, I think. Pull the other one; it's got bells on. Am I supposed to invest in a bridge somewhere too?

"What do you need me for?"

The Goth already possesses wards against the Brotherhood.

And so they need an outsider to do their dirty work. Great. Next I'll be told a small group can succeed where armies would fail. Please.

Our payment, the Unspoken continues, *will be based on the quality of information you bring back. Verbal information will earn the down payment once over, and physical artifacts will earn double or triple, dependant on their utility.*

"And what, exactly, is the down payment?"

This. The Unspoken reaches theatrically for a rear pocket. Facial features contort as something is searched for and then found, and I'm handed a small, soft bag. I loosen the drawstring and look inside. A night sky full of stars looks back.

"Is this astarum?" I say, a little shocked. My one-time mentor Old Jed mentioned the stuff a few times, that it's used as currency in the more exotic locales. As to its value, a pound of the stuff is more than enough to buy a small island with change left over. There can't have been more than a few ounces in the bag I was holding, but Old Jed's warning rings loud and clear. Long story short, an ounce of that stuff is worth more than my life will ever be.

Yes, the Unspoken says. Am I mistaken or is there actually a slight edge to the tone?

"Quite an expensive fee for information." Not to mention that no one I know can make change, and I don't want to get the attention of anyone who can.

It is up to the client to determine the value of information, is it not?

That clinches it. Something is very wrong. "I appreciate the offer," I say, standing, "but I need to decline."

Your reason?

I hand the bag back. "Personal."

❀

"What were you *thinking*?" I ask David when we're back at my office. He stares at me. "Well?" I say.

There's no response.

"This is the *Brotherhood*," I say. "What can you *possibly* hope to accomplish by sucking up to them? Even *I* don't mess with them. That should tell you something."

David mumbles a few words.

"What?"

"Don't yell at me," he says, louder.

"I'm not—" I take a deep breath. "I'm sorry. Just...why? Everyone's afraid of them. *Everyone.*"

I thought that might have been it, that he's consorting with them to gain respect on his streets, but that faraway look from the greenhouse returns to his eyes and he says, "You wouldn't understand."

I quite literally want to shake some sense into him, but I don't. "Try me," I say.

"They engage themselves protecting those secrets which were never meant to be unearthed. Thus they bind themselves with vows of silence, ensuring life's safety."

That sounds like the old David. I'm not a cult-breaker, but I take it as a positive sign. I think I might get through to him.

"David, everyone says that. The Brotherhood just hasn't found anyone they want to use those secrets on yet. It's better to stay away from people like that." Especially when they're powerful enough that they could wipe you off the face of the earth without even noticing, but I don't say that out loud. David might be rebellious enough to take that as a challenge. All they'll have to do would be abandon him in that in-between world and he'd be a goner. Their power truly shocked me and, if nothing else, I might have just found the topic for Raven's next paper.

"They are both honorable and trustworthy," David replies.

"How do you know?"

He doesn't say anything, but I can see the greenhouse in his eyes. He hasn't been alive long enough to know that beauty doesn't mean a damn thing. Elves are an excellent case in point. They're more than happy to slit your throat while you sleep and they approve of human sacrifice because it means it's not them dying. But people still think they're beautiful.

My phone vibrates. It's a page from the Count's number. Duty calls. I don't have the report done but at least I have enough information that the Count won't see it as a waste of time. I don't know how he'll take the Brotherhood possibly being involved, but I'm about to find out.

"I've got to meet with the Count," I tell David. "Do you want to come? We can get something to eat afterward. I'll buy."

He perks up at the prospect of free food, still a typical teenager in that respect. "Sure."

❀

We take a cab over to Grant Courtyard, where one of the Count's safe houses doubles as thrift store. I ask David to wait outside and the esquire guarding the door—officially, he's providing low-income citizens with a safe place to shop—nods me in. I breeze past the aisles of worn clothing and bins of mismatched shoes and through the Employee Only door at the back. An intimidated assistant manager is doing paperwork in a rough office with an open door. He looks up startled as I blow by, but I ignore him.

After a quick two-story ride, the elevator opens onto a plush hallway. The floor, walls, and ceiling are covered with red shag carpeting. Paintings by Renaissance masters are covered with gauzy red silk. The stained glass door at the far end rests in a gilded frame and sports a diamond doorknob.

Inside, Count Fantabuloso, the Baron Marcus, and the Baron Elmdore are seated at a cherrywood table.

"The Brotherhood is involved," I say before they have a chance to speak. Sometimes, I have to admit, a dramatic entrance feels damn good.

That causes silence. Count Fantabuloso turns a dial set into the table and the R&B music playing in the background fades away. "You have my ear," he says.

I give him an overview of my visit to Olygandr, then relay my suspicions. For whatever reason, the mimes are interested in tanking the elf-dwarf alliance, or maybe they have old business to settle with the Goth. Either way, things could get complicated. The barons exchange a few quiet words with each other.

"What other information have you found?" the Count says.

I start into more detail about the magical research being done at Ablesoft, but before I can get to the adamantium bomb the Baron Marcus wordlessly bolts out of his chair, draw a handgun, and rushes to the exterior door, making sure it's locked. He presses his fingers to his ear to better hear his earpiece. The Baron Elmdore does the same.

"Status?" the Count demands.

"We're under attack," the Baron Marcus replies.

"Who dares the gall?"

"We don't know."

"Summon reinforcements."

"Can't do that, milord," the Baron Elmdore says. "We're being attacked at multiple locations."

"How many forts are besieged?"

The Baron Elmdore goes pale. "...All of them."

The Count swears volubly. Muffled booms can be heard through the walls. Whoever this is, they're playing for keeps.

"May I suggest—" the Baron Marcus begins.

"Yes, yes. Of course. With haste," the Count says.

The Baron Marcus presses the panels in the stained glass

door in a certain sequence and a red, crackling light flows over it, melting it shut. We exit through the other door, pass through a mirrored-ceiling bedroom complete with rotating heart-shaped bed, and into a leopard-print bathroom. The Baron Marcus and I cover the door while Elmdore fiddles with buttons on the platinum-edged hot tub. He mutters an incantation and a sizeable section of the tiled floor fades away, revealing a utilitarian corridor. The metal walls haven't even been painted over. A small, two-door car is waiting.

"Marcus, wait," I say. "There's a kid outside. David."

Marcus shakes his head. "They know the Count's here. None of ours are still alive."

None of theirs. "I'm going to check anyway," I reply.

"Suit yourself." He shrugs and we climb into the car. I'll have to double back anyway and there's no point in walking the length of the escape tunnel. The booms get louder, then fade, as though the assailants know the Count is leaving the building.

Chapter 10

Here we are, back enjoying the Brotherhood's hospitality. I'm not happy about it in the least, but at least we're not in that freaky shadow world. "We" are the remains of Count Fantabuloso's organization, Raven, and me. The mimes picked me up while I was searching the area around the thrift store—by the time I'd gotten back there was no sign of the attackers anyway, just the bodies of a few surprised esquires and a ton of property damage. On the basis of "any port in a storm," the Count's negotiated a deal where his surviving barons and esquires get asylum. When they found out the Goth was behind that steamroller offensive, the Count-Brotherhood relationship soon became a great deal cozier.

Not many of the Count's men survive. Each safe house and weapons cache was hit simultaneously with force. By the time anyone realized what was happening, almost half had been overrun and there was no chance of anyone receiving reinforcements. I had no idea the Goth had grown this strong, and if he was a bastard before, now he owns all the weapons that used to belong to the Count.

When Raven showed up, she brought the information that my apartment had been firebombed and that David had been captured. It figures. The Goth would be the one bastard to ferret out where I live. Swallowing my pride, I tell the Unspoken I'll take their damn case, but not for any payment. Instead, I expect enough support to rescue David. He was in the wrong place at the wrong time because of me and I'm going to get him out. If I can royally piss the Goth off along the way, so much the better. After that, though, I'm out. This is way over my head. Let the Goth, Fantabuloso, and the Brotherhood fight it out while I move to Tahiti.

The days it takes for the Count and the Brotherhood to actually come up with a plan are endlessly frustrating. We're not allowed out of the greenhouse for "safety reasons" and all of my questions are met with infuriating, exaggerated shrugs. Raven tells me to be patient, and tries to distract me with small talk and card games, but I hate sitting around while an enemy figures out how to use me for target practice.

I spend most of my time pacing the greenhouse. At two floors it gives me just enough room to fume properly. Green is everywhere, and I swear the gnarlier vines are looking at me. One particularly ugly fruit, purple and swollen, can't possibly be from this planet. Banks of flowers and herbs curve towards hothouse lamps and there are at least three mimes present at all times, trimming hedges, making cuttings, and for all I know using some of their unspeakable secrets to coerce them into growing faster. Wherever I go I'm surrounded by the smell of heat and earth and green. Out of habit I start tracking the mimes' movements.

Eventually, I notice faint, colored lines painted on the floor. The mimes don't deviate from the paths they mark except to tend to plants. Then four new mimes arrive and do everything in their power to avoid the paths. Days pass, and I get better at telling mimes apart. I realize with a shock that mimes change clothes. I always thought it was part of the shtick, like the makeup, but apparently ancient secret societies also have laundry days.

By the fifth mind-numbingly boring day a sense of meaning starts to nag at me. Watching the mimes move around makes my brain itch, especially when I realize that one in particular, an older woman with a beret and one eyebrow permanently arched, always walks the same path at the same time. I know it's theoretically possible to trace runes in time as well as space, but since no one has been able to create functional 3-D runes the idea of 4-D runes is pretty much ignored except by quacks. Watching the mimes, though, I'm tempted to give the loonies a little more credibility.

What are they doing?

Finally, we're called into the de facto command center. It was once a storage room, and a collapsible table and collapsible chairs have been hastily set up. Hothouse lamps, bags of soil, pots, UV lights, and other equipment still line the walls, and a holographic projector takes up most of the table space, surrounded by paperwork. Right now it's displaying a map of Tipton. Other than the Count, seated at the head of the table, the room is empty.

"What's the news?" I ask him.

"Grim," the Count replies.

"Nice toy," Raven says from behind me.

"Of Brotherhood provenance," the Count says. "The sheer length of their reach may, in quieter times, cause much concern." He absentmindedly adjusts the feather in his hat. "Nevertheless, allies of circumstance are allies still and fate's caprice shan't nullify respect."

"Why are we here?" I ask, not in the mood to sit through more of his affected speech than necessary.

"The Brotherhood found an enemy camp."

"On Lord British's estate," I say. "I could have told you that."

"Dick..." Raven says, trying to slow me down.

"Ah. Ignorance, as always, claims the loudest voice. Lord British remains uninvolved."

"Bullshit. I saw them meeting a few days before—"

Raven cuts me off. "Now is not the time, Dick." She turns to the Count. "I apologize. Please, continue."

He nods. "David is present there as well."

"How long have you known?" I accuse.

"You are anxious to rescue him, I see." Using the holographic map, the Count shows us how to get there, then pompously informs us no assistance can be spared. He does wish us success, and asks that we inform him of our plans when we decide to make the attempt so that we won't be caught in any crossfire.

"Since I'll have to scout the area first, then find some help, there's no telling when," I say. "Plus, there's no way to know if someone's tapping our lines of communication." It sounds a lot like they want to use me as a distraction, and they can go fuck themselves. This is for David, nothing more. I'll go when I feel ready, and if that makes them nervous that's too damn bad. I'm no one's volunteer cannon fodder.

"Communication is essential in this endeavor," the Count says.

"Then start giving me something useful."

He slides a mobile pad across the table. "All the information you need is there."

Raven tries to catch my attention to get me to back off, but I ignore her. "You're still stringing me out to dry," I insist.

"Perhaps..." the Count says slowly, having the gall to act like I'm raking him over the coals, "the Baron Elmatos and two of his esquires can be spared. My arms, such as remain, are yours for the attempt."

"Gee, thanks," I say, a bit less sarcastically than I intend.

❀

"What's gotten into you, Dick?" Raven says, catching up with me.

"Nothing."

"Don't give me that. You just pissed off your best-paying client, and then kept going."

"I said 'nothing.'"

"I realized that." She chuckles. "What do you plan to do now?"

"Well, first I plan to head back to my jail cell and read what they've got. Then I'm going to go to my apartment to see if anything's salvageable. Then I'm going to pick up a few things, rescue David, and move to Tahiti."

"Tahiti, huh? Do I get an invite?"

I glare at her amused smirk. There's a glint in her eyes and, suddenly, I'm aware of how little I know about her. For all I know she could be up to her eyeballs in this, Davenport Irregularity and all, but I force the paranoia down. You can't throw away years of trust just because everything smells rotten. People who do end up living in run-down apartments, eating dog food and constantly sweeping for bugs.

"Sure," I say.

"Good. I'm also coming along when you rescue David. The only reason you survived that last ambush is because I was there."

❀

My apartment is, quite literally, toast. The front door burned to white ash but the surrounding corridor looks completely untouched. When my landlord Frank finds out about this, if he hasn't already, he'll have a coronary. I smile at the thought. It was probably a flashfire spell combined with reflecting wards. Nothing else would have burned hot enough to create this kind of devastation and the wards would have focused the energy and heat back into the apartment, ensuring a more complete destruction. And once my protective spells had burned out, their magic energy would only have fueled the inferno. Raven looks at me questioningly and I nod.

She cups her hands together and a sphere of purple light appears between them. It's a magical pit-bitch, something you send in knowing it'll trigger every booby trap in the area. Clearing the area manually would take too much time and there probably won't be too much that's recoverable anyway.

The sphere saunters through the door and back out a few minutes later. No explosions, no chills crawling up my spine, nothing that indicates a magical discharge of any kind. All that leaves is mundane traps. I probe around the door for trip wires, then carefully tap a ruined part of the door. It dissolves, the ash hanging in the air like powder, but no lasers are visible. After the ash settles, I tap the remains of the door again, harder, to completely dislodge it, and I flatten myself against the wall in case of explosives. Raven does the same.

Nothing.

There seem to be no pressure traps or tripwires, so it's probably safe to go in.

As it turns out, my caution's unwarranted. There's absolutely nothing inside my apartment except for piles of ash and twisted metal and plastic, including some that were probably the remains of my sprinkler system. A thin, burnt tiki-person arm sticks out from one of the piles as if trying to escape. Covering my mouth with my jacket, I head for my bedroom and the safe I keep for emergencies. The hole where my closet used to be is slightly off-putting—there's a tiki person dust shadow on the back wall—but my safe is still present and intact. A surge of hope quickly extinguishes itself when I realize the door is ajar.

Everything inside is gone. My fake passports and credit cards, emergency magical supplies, stacks of cash, concealable weapons...all gone. I know the safe was well hidden; did the bastards burn down my apartment just to get to it? Or is this to add insult to injury?

Standing there with the ruins of, well, not exactly my life because this is just an apartment I'd had no particular attachment to, a feeling of utter pointlessness steals over me. What am I doing?

"I have some money we could use to get supplies," Raven says.

"Why?" I snap.

"David's my friend too," she says. "You're not the only one who gives a damn."

David's not exactly my friend, more like a constant pain in the ass, but I let it slide.

❀

Our first stop is the Hobolympics bazaar. The Hobolympics themselves are almost over, and I haven't been able to catch my favorite events. This is numbly added to my list of reasons to stay pissed off, because I'm definitely not feeling it right now. Most people stay out of my way. They know what trouble looks like and most have enough of it already. We start at Little Benjamin's tent, a mutant mushroom on a steel floor. Little Benjamin is a close-cropped double-amputee. He barely survived losing both his legs and had bought himself the best motorized wheelchair money can buy on the black market. It doubles as a mobile weapons platform.

His tent is huge enough that smiling salespeople could sell appliances underneath, and samples of his wares, carefully watched by armed guards, are set up on collapsible tables. Mostly he sells the smaller weapons, but he also carries smuggled weapons for people he trusts. It might be hypocritical, not letting the Count know about this hole in his network, but I have enough enemies already and recent events have irrefutably shown the flaws in the Count's plan of peace through strictly rationed weaponry. Even so, it's odd that his flashier stuff is on display. It's sandwiched inconspicuously between worthless pieces of crap, but it's still on display.

At the tent's edge and flush with the cavern wall is a building that looks like a group of outhouses have gotten together and decided to try for respectability. Nodding at the guards, I knock on the door while Raven browses the tables.

"Just. A. Min-ute," a synthesized voice says. It's one of Benjamin's wheelchair add-ons. "I'm. On. My. Way." He doesn't actually need it, but uses it whenever he doesn't want people to bother him.

"Cut the crap, Benji. It's me, Dick."

"Couldn't you. Have picked. A. Better. Time."

"I need supplies and am willing to pay for them."

"Hot. Damn. Let me. Put. Away. The lube."

A few moments later Little Benjamin emerges, a stocky man in a gray T-shirt, bright orange hunting vest, and camouflage pants. The edges of the pants are tucked neatly under his stumps and the power supply on the back of his wheelchair constantly makes a noise like a scuba respirator. Indicator lights flash patterns in green and orange and the handguns mounted on each armrest swivel to track me. The chair's bulletproof hood is raised and the nozzle of the acid-sprayer tucked underneath the seat is barely visible.

"Well, I'll be," he says, intentionally blocking my view as he closes the door behind him. "That infamous bastard Dick Richards is actually willing to pay his own way instead of just breaking in and stealing what he needs. I'd be getting a hard-on if they hadn't snipped that too."

"Hal-le-lu-jah," the synthesized voice says.

"What've you got?" I say.

"What you see out there on the tables," he replies. "Is that a problem?"

"Praise. The Lord," the synthesized voice adds.

I scowl. Does he absolutely *have* to do his Southern preacher shtick right now? Even on good days it makes me want to smack him and he knows that.

"Of course," Little Benjamin concludes, "special orders cost extra but I can have it here in maybe two or three days. Is Raven with you?"

I grunt. She's way out of his league. "She's looking through the merchandise."

We both look.

Raven picks up a rocket launcher and fiddles with the crystals set in the launch tube. One of the guards moves to stop her.

"It's all right," Little Benjamin calls out. "She knows what she's doing." He turns back to me. "She knows what she's doing, right?" The background lighting changes from red to purple, and her hair shimmers.

"She's never let *me* down," I say.

Raven finishes inspecting the RPG and sets it down. "You've

got a bigger selection than last time," she says over the tables between us.

Using the joystick, Little Benjamin guides his chair to her. I follow.

"Business has been good," he says.

"Business is always good for you," Raven says flirtatiously. "But rocket-propelled Jamborees? That's impressive."

"You recognized them?" Benjamin says.

"I'm always interested in powerful hardware."

While I realize she's just playing him to get a better deal, this still irks me. It's teeth-grindingly painful to watch, and I'm about to leave when Little Benjamin lets slip something interesting.

"Well..." he starts, in the manner of a man about to impress. "Word under the Under is that Count Fantabuloso bit off a bit more than he could chew."

"Whoever said that's got a big mouth," I say.

Little Benjamin glares at me, obviously wishing I wasn't there anymore. "They're not the only one."

Raven giggles, actually giggles, then raises her eyebrows at me. All right, all right. Time to go and let her do her thing.

"Speaking of the big mouths," I say, "I think I'll check on the results of the 1,000-m pie dash."

"That was a good one, especially the semifinals," Little Benjamin says. "Too bad you missed them. Results are still posted though, so you could catch them if you hurry."

"See you back at the office, Raven."

She nods and goes right back to flirting with Little Benjamin. His body language screams smug superiority, like he thinks he's won something. For a moment I want to tip his chair over and kick him in the head.

❀

Truck Stop Stadium doesn't truly have an exterior. Over the years a small city's grown around it, cannibalizing and rearranging the roads that used to converge. There are building codes, kind of, but those spring from the Great Mantato Tuberfruit's unique genius and overall it looks like a giant earthworm's vomited out a commercial/residential complex. Twisted metal sculptures erupt from unexpected surfaces and enterprising local citizens make it a point to stick tennis balls on the sharper edges. After their makeover, the sculptures look like someone tried to motion-capture a nuclear strike and the dust shadows of the volunteers are still sporting the suits in Hell. Normally I ignore them as familiar background noise but today they annoy the piss out of me.

On the randomly spaced public address screens, lolcats present the Hobolympics results. I have to climb a ladder welded to the side of a building to find the pie dash results. Rampaging Rolf won the gold in the 1,000-m for the fifth time in a row. That man must have a cast-iron stomach. In one interview, he said it was honed from swallowing all the bullshit his government job forced down his throat.

Most pie dashes are simple. You run half the distance, gobble down a small pie as fast as you can, and then run the other half. The 1,000-m, however, has a pie every 250 meters and puking them up is an automatic disqualification. It's a rare man who can eat, sprint, and keep his lunch down. The event is extremely popular; there's nothing the general public loves more than watching out-of-shape humanoids desperately stumbling forward while trying not to vomit. It's a veritable metaphor for modern life.

The traditional close to the Hobolympics, the marathon, is just about to start and I figure I could do worse than kill time watching it. It's held in the official Tuberfruit dungeon, a winding complex a few floors beneath the stadium itself. The multilevel maze of booby traps and dead ends is ceilinged with plexiglass in most places. The good seats are in compartments shaped like glass-bottomed boats but I opt for the public auditoriums instead. Miniature cameras embedded in the walls capture all the action, sometimes in more than one angle.

The auditoriums are set up like movie theaters, and the screen of the one I choose is broken into thirty-two sections, like multiplexed TV. Ushers at the door hand out cheap binoculars while potato-clad peons sell refreshments. I sit near the back.

"Now remember," a mother tells her child, "ten minutes after the last runners go in, they release the attack dogs. Be sure to zoom in on that. The look on their faces is priceless."

I guess it's never too early to start encouraging bloodlust.

The lights dim and the first heat of runners is released. Since the grand prize is lifetime room and board in one of the Great Mantato Tuberfruit's best hotels, everyone—from vagrants looking to settle down to gangsters looking for a base of operations—throws their hat into the ring in the hopes of hitting jackpot.

As the action heats up, the audience starts whooping and cheering. Biting the dust first is a Kenyan runner proudly wearing his country's colors. Fleeing a goblin with sharpened teeth, he turns the corner right into the goblin's mate, who disembowels him with a wicked blow from a shovel.

As the words, red and yellow on a black background, commandeer the screen, a booming voice asks the theater:

"Are you not entertained?!"

The crowd erupts like Mt. St. Helens and food flies everywhere.

The obstacles making life terminally interesting for the competitors include sledgehammers rigged at kneecap height, runaway rotary saws, and a few claymore mines stolen from God-knows-where. Goons in police uniforms patrol the dungeons, brutally savaging anything they come across with their nightsticks. Dispensers at key locations drop every imaginable kind of weapon from toothbrush prison shivs to semi-automatics with no ammo. Medics, easily identified by their white body armor with spray-painted red crosses, cart out the wounded and the dead.

Try as I might, I can't get into the crowd's enjoyment and leave before the roving flamethrower teams are unleashed.

❃

"There you are," Raven says, joining me at my table. I found a sports bar and the privacy's helping me feel better. While the bar is packed, for the forty-five minutes I've been here everyone's been glued to the marathon footage being streamed live.

"How was shopping?" I ask.

Her face lights up. "You wouldn't believe the deals I found. Best of all, I didn't have to give a single blowjob."

I suppose that technically fits the definition of a successful shopping expedition, but other than that I have no idea what to say.

"Oh, don't look at me like that," Raven chides. "Feminine wiles are an internationally recognized currency and exchange rates are always good."

Again, I'm not sure if she's joking. So...moving on. "What did you find?" I say.

The crowd in the bar goes silent.

On the screens, one determined contestant reaches the center of the maze: the Temple of Success. The Chalice of Victory, a spray-painted, nigh-indestructible coffee mug, rests innocently in the Jaws of Defeat, a spring-loaded bear trap.

"I love this part," Raven whispers.

Bleeding from a deep gash down the side of his face and neck that stops just short of his jugular, the lone dwarf inches forward carefully. The feed zooms in on his face; intensity shines in his eyes. Even a grenade exploding in the background doesn't break his concentration.

With a deft, catlike move, he snatches the mug free. The bear trap doesn't budge and he nearly sags with relief.

"ANNOUNCER: [whispering]," closed captioning reads, "What he doesn't know is that the bear trap is never loaded."

"ANNOUNCER 2: The best part is, even if he knew that at

the beginning, by this point adrenaline's burned that knowledge right out of his brain."

Victory almost certain, the dwarf takes the chalice to the Wall of Champions. There are twelve alcoves in the stone and all he has to do is choose the right one. Slowly, deliberately, he reaches out, the Chalice of Victory in a trembling hand. He sets it in an alcove, being careful not to touch the sides. You never know. The view switches to the alcove-cam.

The dwarf's face seems to rise as the alcove floor lowers. His eyes widen, and then the alcove-cam goes blank as the plastic explosives detonate. He's made the wrong choice.

"I'm sorry, what were you saying?" Raven says as the bar watches the instant replays from multiple angles.

"What did you get?"

"Oh, just the usual. Effect crystals, Squeemines, a Field Effect Banishing Rocket."

"You actually bought an RPG?"

"If the Goth really is trying to summon the Archangel of Despair, who knows what else he's yanking out of the ether. Plus, it's dual purpose. Any non-summoned creatures will feel the wrath of a conventional warhead." She says that last part with great relish.

"What about stealth?"

"Women can fit anything they want in their purses. I thought you knew that already."

"I meant cloaks of invisibility, warding charms, black ski masks?"

"You know, Dick, if you'd just cast them on yourself you wouldn't have to beg, borrow, *or* steal."

"You know damn well why I don't." That comes out more forcefully than I'd intended and there's an awkward silence. Raven flags down a waiter and orders a Long Island iced tea.

"Are you sure you're okay?" she asks me after it arrives.

"I'm always okay."

"You haven't stopped tapping your foot since I sat down."

I look down and Raven's right. When did I get this antsy?

"I'll be fine," I say. "How's this? After we rescue David I'll go on a real vacation."

"I don't buy it. If you went to the moon, the moon would blow up just because you were there. You enjoy trouble."

"Not this time."

"That's because this time it's personal and you're losing."

"Just whose side are you on?" I change the subject. "Speaking of trouble, how does Tuesday night sound for crashing the Goth's party?"

"Why not tomorrow?"

"I need to pick up a few things."

Raven laughs disbelievingly and twirls her drink's umbrella. "Who are you going to piss off this time?"

"If all goes well, no one."

❀

I'm actually serious about that. My plan is to break into Ablesoft ninja-style, wake Robert Cunning Anvil up from a dead sleep in the middle of the night, and convince him to loan me some nihilium. They said he destroyed everything, but he's a dwarf. Destroying *all* of it would be like eating his firstborn.

Then, for an encore, I'll storm the Goth's fortress, cut a bloody swath through bleached-out faces, liberate a virgin, and fight my way to safety, fantasy style, though I don't think David would appreciate me getting fresh. And while I'm at it, I'll also rescue a bikini-clad Raven from an evil magician. That last image lingers and I rub my eyes.

I really do need a vacation, or at least a nap.

I plan to spend the rest of the afternoon trawling public databases for any useful blueprints, but on reaching my office there are signs that attackers have tried to break in—scuff marks on the door, rainbow flashes as I step inside—but the wards have successfully repelled them. Raven's fake filing cabinets stand mute under a flickering, yellow light. I kick the pot of one of the plastic plants, tipping it over and spilling marbles on the floor.

My desk/chair is tipped over—had they tried penetrative telekinesis?—and large parts of the drywall are burned away, revealing the protective sigils underneath. They glow dull red, nearly out of juice. I readjust my trophy shelves, just for something to do, then power up my computer and get to work.

I don't find much, but I'm not any worse off than before. Sometimes the best you can do is all you can do. And with my skulking clothes torched, hopefully I'll be in and out in a flash.

The sound of someone outside the office sends me into high alert. I crouch down, draw my handgun, and wait. There's a small click as the outer door opens slowly. I draw down, using an armrest to steady my aim, sighting for where a human's torso would be. That will take care of anything human-size, dwarves and elves will get shot in the head, and trolls will get shot in the crotch. A good bet all the way round.

A dark figure slips inside, easing the door closed behind it.

I pull the trigger once. A glowing blue orb hits the idiot square in the back, and boy does it feel good. He goes down without a sound. I approach cautiously and turn him over with my foot. It's Ezekiel Kanaghy, Amish Special Agent, and that makes me feel even better.

I strip him of his weapons and gear, prop him against a filing cabinet, sit in Raven's chair, and wait. Blues only stun and he'll come to in a few minutes. His limbs will still be paralyzed but he'll be able to talk.

The first thing he sees is me. In the flickering lights I probably look like a serial killer and that's the effect I want: grinning and pointing a gun.

"Well, well, well," I say. "Look at what the cat dragged in."

"You have no idea what you've gotten yourself into," he says.

"Were you planning on telling me?"

He says nothing.

"Then I think I'm perfectly happy with shooting you." I lean closer. "Nice suit, by the way."

"Thanks. Where's Raven?"

"I shot you with blue, Zeke. You know I have red and yellow, too, so why don't *you* answer *my* questions?" Red's mind fog. Yellow is acid.

"I'm serious. Where's Raven?" Kanaghy tries to make his voice menacing but can't muster enough force.

"Tahiti. Why are you here?"

"We thought you might be in danger." I glare at him and a small smirk plays across his face as if to say, *What? You lie, I lie. That's just the way this game is played.*

I stand up, kicking the chair back. "What did Raven do? Pull your fake beard off in public? Tip a prized milk cow?"

"You mean you really don't know?"

I admire his persistence, trying to get me to lose faith in her. But, like I said, you don't throw away years of trust just because of a few really bad days. Raven thinks she has it under control and I have better things to do than pry into her life.

Truth be told, I'm already getting tired of this. I check the slide to ensure a yellow slug is next—knowing is half the battle—and, satisfied, aim for his crotch.

His wristwatch beeps three times, a tiny, digital sound. "I'd wave if I could, Mr. Richards, but our time together seems to be up." A mist condenses around him and billows as if breathing. It's a low-power teleport spell that swaps two objects. If my wards were in better shape it would have no hope of success. As they are now, I settle for flipping him off as he fades away to keep up appearances and I swear to myself that if he's being swapped with explosives I'll hunt all the bastards down.

It's a butter churn instead, with a Bible balanced on the back. King James. With my name inscribed on the front cover in gold leaf. More bureaucrat humor.

❀

Six hours later I'm stuck inside an Ablesoft maintenance crawlspace, waiting for automated security to deactivate. I'd thought it was suspiciously easy. As it turns out, the place is actually loaded with sensors and traps, but those don't arm until an intruder is too far inside to do anything about them. Whoever set these up had a twisted mind. Vents even pump mist in so I'll be sure to notice the laser triggers that pop up ahead of and behind me. They look like standard low-power red lasers so I'm not too afraid of them. It's whatever they're connected to that makes me nervous. With no options, I stay still. Hopefully the whole thing is on a timer and, in an hour so, it'll get bored and shut itself off.

This isn't particularly comfortable. One knee's jammed against my chest and the other leg is stretched out at an angle just short of dislocating my hip. I have to keep my right arm behind my back to keep from breaking a laser. Not to mention the crick in my neck.

Luckily, I know a trick for surviving these kinds of situations. By moving part of your soul outside your body and filling the spaces with a certain kind of energy—it feels the way cotton candy tastes—you can gain all the benefits of rigor mortis without the costs. But to make sure you don't actually die you need a focus to store the displaced bits of soul. Almost automatically my left hand contorts awkwardly, reaching for my inside jacket pocket.

My hopes are confirmed with the smooth crinkle of a candy-containing plastic bag. Pressing my back against the top of the duct to clear some space, I fish it out with my index and middle fingers. Gummi bears. I flick it away from me and amazingly it avoids all the lasers. I'd rather not take that kind of risk but if the focus physically touches you the spell won't work.

I close my eyes and start the chant, heavy syllables from a dead language sounding like the scrape of stone on stone. After the fourth time through it bounces through my brain on its own volition, meaning I'm ready to move on. I visualize the Gummi bears and judge how much of my soul they can hold. Any extra I try to stuff inside will be lost, and I figure there's enough room for maybe 60 minutes of rigor mortis. Good enough.

I pulse the image of the Gummi bears every time the chant's third word pounds its way around my skull. The bag grows larger until it fills my mental vision. The berserker frenzy also grows but it seems a long way off, a side effect of the necromancy. I'm about to seal the spell when a dull clunk penetrates from outside.

I open my eyes. The top half of a dwarf's head stares at me.

"Don't mind me," the eyebrows say. "I want to see what you'll try next."

❃

"What do you think of the system?" Robert Cunning Anvil asks, handing me a mug of spiced cider. He was suspicious initially, but after recognizing me as Charles Darwin he's become a great deal more hospitable. I thought I knew everything I need to know about dwarves, but apparently spying on a potential business partner is an expected part of dwarven culture.

"It certainly caught me by surprise," I admit. We're in his rooms, just a few doors down from his workshop. I'm cramped and cross-legged on the floor, the berserker rhythm still pulsing through my mind, but otherwise glad to be out of the vent.

"It was my idea," he says proudly, clearing some magazines off a table and stuffing them into a drawer. "Why stop them at the walls when we can trap them in cages? I only wish we could have installed cameras without giving it away. You know, to see the looks on people's faces."

I drink some cider and set the mug on the table. "You're a lot calmer than when I met you," I comment.

"Yep." He smiles. "And it's all thanks to these babies." He pulls a silver cigar case from his pants pocket and opens it. It's full of blunts. "You could almost believe the world will turn out all right after a few puffs." He pulls one out, fishes for a lighter in a pile of junk behind him, and tokes up. "We were starting to wonder if you'd follow up."

I look around. Robert is obviously a young bachelor. The signs are obvious in any species: piles of clutter, old clothes, and assorted junk everywhere. The only clear space on the floor, other than where I'm sitting, is a path to the bathroom. I keep expecting to see a fraternity banner somewhere.

"I do have some questions," I say.

"I guess I could answer some before we take you to see Evanek. It'll have to be in chains, though. You understand. Tradition." He offers me a hit and I refuse. Having lived underground for so long, the dwarves started cultivating exotic mushrooms long before humans even dreamed of psilocybin. I'm not sure exactly what's in it, but the musty second-hand smoke is already bringing tears to my eyes.

"You and Julia, was it? Anything going on?" Building rapport first will make the request easier. Otherwise he might get angry and stop talking completely. The prospect of chains also concerns me.

"It's Maria, and gods no. Dwarves aren't slavers, and I refuse to lower myself to her level. They say they're only gnomes, but that's no excuse." He takes a long hit, finally releasing his breath with a combination burp and giggle.

I agree with him. "There are standards of dignity and honor to uphold."

"That's exactly right."

"And it's a shame about what they wanted to do with the adamantium."

"Don't even get me started," he says, then stops to fan his face. "Whoo. I felt *that* in my toes. Everyone thinks that all dwarves are good for is magic weapons and magic armor. Period. Forget about our advances in high-temp superconductors, industrial organization, or baking. Even the...even the...the people who know better hear 'dwarf' and think 'All right! Let's get us a magic bazooka.' Assholes."

"I understand why you got steamed about the nihilium," I say.

"Do we *have* to talk about that? I'm trying to enjoy my evening," Robert says. He sighs and leans back in his chair. I prepare myself for an activist spiel. "It's a dwarven thing, you know. The living bones and soul of the earth. Yes, we mine, and yes, we forge, but we do it with respect. None of this let's blow up a mountain and forage through the remains crap. You humans have many good qualities, but patience isn't one of them."

I get the impression he feels like a born-again Christian surrounded by ravers.

"Take uranium. It's," he takes a hit, "a perfectly fine metal, forged by dying stars. Then you humans find a way to turn it into a bomb. The earth willingly sacrifices her bones so we may build in the image of the gods, not blow craters in her several miles wide."

"I thought dwarves were known for their war machines," I say to keep him talking.

"That's different," he replies in the tone of a religious apologist tired of countering the same argument for the umpteenth time. "War is war, but you destroy your enemies, not the earth itself. Nihilium's mostly compressed magic and a true magic to energy conversion could wipe out the moon. It's like my grandfather said. An unused sword only grows sharper with time." He pauses. "Now you've depressed me."

"I'd be willing to take any samples off your hands," I say. Now's as good a time as any.

Robert looks at me suspiciously and inhales slowly. "Really."

I figure I have nothing to lose by telling the truth. If that doesn't go well, he'll hopefully be too stoned to remember the conversation. Robert listens skeptically, then asks me, "What makes you think I still have some?"

"You're a dwarf."

He grunts. I wait. He closes his eyes.

Finally, he says slowly, "I *suppose* I could let you borrow the grille. All it does is destroy illusions. And even if you're lying, what could you do with such a minute amount?"

"That's greatly appreciated," I say.

Grumbling, Robert stands up and walks into his bedroom. I stay behind to not appear overly intrusive, and dwarven curses ricochet off the walls. When Robert emerges, still cursing, he holds a medium-sized, ornately worked steel chest.

"All this time," he says, "and the *phrexs* knew exactly where it was. *Gav'rikon taxeg!*" Loosely translated, that means "May the demons who cause deep mine explosions use their testicles for fuel."

"How much was there?"

"About ten pounds of unworked nihilium, as well as my research diary for the reactor. Who..."

"Well, I know a good detective who'd be able to find out for you." Trying to salvage things, I take out my own card and am offering it to him when he waves me off.

"No. I know who it was and have a better idea." He walks back into his bedroom and reemerges with a small steel anvil and similarly sized golden hammer. After clearing space on a bench flush with the wall, Robert sets the anvil down and places the hammer carefully on top. He kneels and, folding his hands together, chants.

It's not a dwarven dialect I'm familiar with, so I only catch some of the actual words, but these rituals are all the same underneath. *Oh great and powerful god of craftsmanship, I've been wronged. Nut-punch whoever was responsible until they cough up their own genitals and curse whoever uses what I made. Amen.*

I sigh. There goes that idea. Plus, Robert sounds like he's sobering up as the chant continues and I'm not interested in being presented in chains to anyone, regardless of how culturally insensitive my absence would be.

A glint of plastic near the top of a small pile turns out to be Robert's ID card. I steal it and take my leave while he's still preoccupied, swiping my way out of Ablesoft. Because I'm not a total asshole I leave it at the last security station, telling the guard I was working late and want to turn in a badge I found before going home. Since I'm leaving and not trying to get in, she doesn't question me.

Chapter 11

Raven and I watch the solid double doors, marked "Do Not Enter" in giant red letters, that mark the entrance to the Goth's headquarters. According to the plans she found, this is the only way in or out. The Baron Elmatos and an esquire are hanging further back, covering us.

We're in a condemned district—even the moving walkways have been disconnected—and have already broken through several unmanned security stations. Compared to Tipton's normal bustle, this place is so empty it hums. It's not dirty so much as grudgingly sterile. The video screens are still active, displaying ads, information, and public service announcements to people who haven't been through in years.

There's very little cover, but we had the forethought to acquire some riot shields from the Count's armory. As the Baron Elmatos and the esquire—I think his name is Jacob—take positions behind them, I inspect the door and Raven does whatever it is she's doing with her eyes closed. This was once a popular district, as the ten-lane walkway attests, but we didn't have time to find out much about it.

The Count also lent us all type-II magical body armor. We all wear it. At least, I assume Raven is under her purple jogging suit. Though she cuts such a dashing figure, it's hard to tell.

The spoils of Raven's shopping expedition are much more likely to be useful. In addition to the Banisher RPG—which is slung over the Baron Elmatos' shoulder—and the Squeemines, she found effect crystals, a few multi-purpose sealants, and some hacking runes. Squeemines are one of my personal favorites, and each of us has two for personal use, with the remaining four for emergencies.

"Did you know that nine out of ten women wear the wrong size bra?" the screen closest to me asks. "And did you know that unnecessary chest compression can cause headaches, migraines, cramps, and depression, not to mention an embarrassing fashion faux pas?"

I almost shoot it. All the magic use recently has left me with a persistent, biting headache.

Raven opens her eyes and says, "The door electronics are fused shut. Nothing's wrong with the door itself, but it won't open unless we can bypass the electronic override."

"I must have left that in my other coat," I say. We rejoin the Count's men and tell them the situation.

"You know anything about these, Esquire?" the Baron Elmatos asks.

The Esquire Jacob grins. "'Course I do. We used to slice these all the time. Give me a few minutes and I'll have you breezing." He straps the riot shield to his back and heads to the screen closest to the door. He cracks the frame with the butt of his handgun and fishes around until he finds wires, which he splices to his phone. Its last words are, "Ask your doctor if Philanthropex is right for you."

At the door, he pops open an access panel, then frowns and looks puzzled.

"Is there a problem, Esquire?" the Baron Elmatos says. Everything he says sounds like a veiled threat.

"No wireless here," the Esquire Jacob says. "Normally I'd Google it, but it's no biggie. I can wing it."

While he works, we review the plan. According to the plans Raven's somehow found, this door should open onto the main floor of the Goth's headquarters. It's been remodeled to look like a Victorian manor house. To the left should be an elongated servants' shed that serves as a barracks. Our plan, such as it is, is simple. Blow through the door, blast a way into the shed. Somewhere in the lower floors should be where they keep prisoners. Other than that we're going in blind and hoping for the best. My instincts scream that it's a horrible idea but we've wasted too much time already. This is all the intel we're going to get.

The Esquire Jacob finishes hacking his phone directly into the door's internal computer and we're ready to go.

❀

The doors open slowly, their grinding screech giving anyone inside more than enough warning. When the opening is wide enough for a person, Raven tosses an effect crystal through, a combination flashbang/funhouse mirror. This kind flashes twice to get everyone's attention, then releases a brilliant wave of white light, blinding anyone stupid enough to still be looking directly at it. For forty seconds afterward, it creates multiple images of anything moving through its field of effect.

The Baron Elmatos and the Esquire Jacob rush through, crouched low behind their riot shields, while Raven and I stay flat against the corridor's walls. They immediately take fire. A few seconds later it's our turn. With our magical shields Raven and I should be safe enough in the short term. Again, I don't like relying on magic but again I have no choice.

We burst into a manicured lawn, firing as we go. I use my handgun; Raven uses bolts of black-light flame. Unlike me, she has no problems with magic use. A cobblestone path leads from the doorway up to the mansion, winding between five marble fountains. As expected, the servants' shed is off to the left, but there's a hell of a lot of open ground between here and there.

The baron and esquire are hunkered down about halfway to the first fountain. The ground around them has been swallowed by color, like they're taking fire from a pissed off rainbow. An ethereal hum fills the air, but it's just automated defenses, no actual hostiles. We might actually get away with this. Deciding not to run through the killing field just yet, I edge along the wall, looking for the turret firing on them. We need to take it out before our duplicates disappear. Raven dashes the other way, presumably doing the same.

I pump a few rounds into a dark patch on the roof that shimmers like a mirage. Nothing. I keep circling around and am maybe thirty yards from the shed when I get nailed. Whatever these things are shooting, it knocks me clear onto my ass and I see stars. I roll to my stomach and keep crawling, hoping I have enough time to reach cover. If just one hit did that much, I can only imagine what will happen when twenty of the twenty-four people currently in its sights disappear.

Four black-light bolts hit the mansion. Where they explode, the blinding color filling the air is neutralized and it's possible to almost get a clear view. I look around. Raven is crouched next to, I think it's the Baron Elmatos, slowly canvassing the mansion from relative safety. They've managed to advance to one of the fountains.

I have just enough time to cast a warping field around me before the incoming fire quadruples. A shiver follows the magic as it runs through my body, subtly deflecting the blasts. Like a mental dam had burst, other spells flood out of me automatically. A runic chant to enhance my casting pathways. A healing field to mitigate direct hits. Enhanced senses. Light precognition. Focus and endurance buffs.

Time slows down.

It all comes back like a runner's high, but this is the big leagues and if you're not ready to fight don't throw your hat in the ring. This time, I go with the rage and look forward to destroying as much real estate as possible. A mental alarm sounds, which calms me down slightly. With a song of frenzy and power filling my thoughts I remind myself: all I have to do is get David out. Nothing else.

But first things first. As out of practice as I am, running all of these spells at once will drain me before too long. Where's this fire coming from?

A black-light burst reveals a mechanical shape at the top of the cupola, but that's too easy. Instead, I focus on a seam in the roof where a wing detaches itself from the main body.

Responding to intuition, I roll to my right just before the ground where I used to be exploded, leaving a gash that reveals the metal underneath. *Too slow*, I gloat silently. I have to admit that being back in the throes of magic feels good. My cover, however, is quickly being worn away. I need to do something fast.

Another black bolt hits the roof, and sure enough there's an active turret hidden beneath the overhang. Yelling, I launch a spell and a bolt of lightning, thrown like a grenade, arcs from my hands, through the rainbow maelstrom, and into the turret. The blinding destruction decreases by half.

I grin. Where's the other one? They'll be set up to—a flash of orange light erupts around me, then everything goes black and numb as life energy is diverted from my body into my defenses. This is going to leave one hell of a headache but the healing spell is already working on it. When I regain full consciousness, I'm crouched and running forward, tossing spell after spell at the mansion. I'm not aiming but I don't care. The primal laughter of berserker fury floats through the air and whoever dares attack me will not survive the hour. Siding shatters and windows glow with heat as the mansion's defenses ground the energy. I pass one fountain, then another, until I'm within reach.

There's a slight pressure in the small of my back, and everything goes dark again.

❀

The first thing I notice is rushing in my ears, like the ocean decided to spend the night inside my head. Next there's warmth and dissociation, me floating weightless and comfortable. I open my eyes and am greeted by a soothing field of black.

Hints of dark maroon undulate across the infinity like ley lines.

So this is it, I think disinterestedly. The berserker rage is a long way away. The world will pause, an offer will be made, and I'm going to break the demon in half before accepting the Faustian bargain. I got David into this and I'm getting him out. I don't feel any aversion to the idea, only numbness and disappointment. I hadn't been good enough on my own.

Everyone likes to think they're commanding the forces of the universe, but instead you're surfing the flow, reacting to things you barely understand and hoping you don't drown. Even your instincts are part of the vast heritage of every living thing, and there are beings out there better at channeling those energies than you'll ever be. Maybe Old Jed was right. No one refuses the devil's bargain because they simply can't.

I wait, but nothing happens. It's just me and infinity, staring each other down like bad poker players. Am I not worth it, even to demons? Then vertigo kicks in, stars rush out the top of my head, and suddenly I'm sitting propped against something cold. I blink my eyes a few times to clear the fog out of my vision. It doesn't work.

I hear Raven's voice. "Welcome back."

"What just happened?" Wondering if I'm permanently blind.

"You charged the house looking for the other turret. I had to knock you out to stop you."

"Did I get it?"

"No, but we dragged you to the far side of the servants' shed. It shut down and there's no one else on guard."

"That's not good," I say.

"You think?" the Baron Elmatos says. "What the hell did you spike your breakfast with, anyway?"

"I can't see," I say.

"It should pass by the time Jake finishes setting the mines," Raven says. "We're blasting our way in. Hopefully there'll be no more surprises."

❋

The Esquire Jacob sets the Squeemines at one end of the servant's shed. We're clustered at the other, as far away as possible while still out of the remaining turret's line of sight. Most of the blast is supposed to be directed inward but you never know. The Baron Elmatos plants a riot shield between us and the mines. The other, I'm informed, is now a twisted piece of magically-reinforced plexiglass somewhere on the lawn. It held just long enough to get me to safety. Three direct hits within two seconds had been more than enough to destroy it.

The Banisher RPG's also been abandoned. It looks untouched, but none of us is going to run out there to get it. The Esquire Jacob limps but is otherwise unhurt. I shake my head to clear the rushing noises. That also doesn't work.

When we're set, the esquire pushes a button on his phone. The mines carve into the side of the building with a quiet thoomp. I pick myself off the ground, already starting to ache all over. The spent Squeemines fall to the ground, the baron kicks in a good chunk of the wall and voila. Instant door. On our way in I pick up the copper casings. They might be useful later.

Our entry leads to a small cell, one that might belong to a twisted monk. A sheet metal desk is wedged in the corner, two black light squiggly bulbs dangle from the ceiling, and the remains of a wooden bed frame unlucky enough to be directly opposite the mines lie scattered on the floor. No windows. The door locks from the outside but it's open and we emerge into a hallway tiled with small geometric shapes that don't seem to repeat. The walls have been treated to resemble crumbling stone, complete with moss, and there's no immediately visible access to the lower floors.

The Esquire Jacob brings up some intel on his phone. "There should be a stairwell at the end of the hallway, through the door on the right."

"How come you're never this organized?" Raven whispers to me. I tell her to shut it.

We head down the hall, clearing each room as we reach it. All are unlocked, identical, and empty. The last door, presumably leading to the stairwell, is the only one locked from the inside. A few gunshots later the door is propped against the wall and we head down the stairs.

The lack of resistance puts us all on edge. We'd thought that after blowing our way into the barracks we'd take out anyone resting inside and proceed through the floors. We'd use Squeemines and effect crystals to cause as much damage as possible as widely as possible, hoping that whoever's in charge would focus on where we've been rather than where we're going. With their forces spread out, we could ambush them a few at a time, whittling our way into more favorable odds. With a little luck we'd find David before running into too much resistance. The lack of anyone alive shooting at us, however, quite possibly means they've already set up an ambush and are waiting for us to run into it.

The stairwell only goes down one story and the next floor looks like an industrial sewer system. Unlike the top floor, which is one long hallway, this one branches like veins in a leaf. Every surface is covered with a slick, greenish tinge and trance techno plays in the background, just loud enough to irritate. Circular portholes, sealed with metal doors and bolted from the outside, dot the walls at regular intervals. Damp seaweed hangs from the ceilings. It's unreal.

"I've seen worse in anime—" Jacob starts, but Elmatos cuts him off.

"Focus, Esquire. Where do we need to go next?"

He checks his phone and points to where the tunnel forks. "Left."

We check the first six portholes. All open into nothing more than slimy closets holding upright coffins. All the coffins are open and empty. This must be where long-time cult members are stored, after they've lost enough of their souls to not care about much of anything. After that, we don't waste any more time checking "rooms" and follow Jacob's instructions to the next stairwell. The stairs are just a ladder down to the next level. Elmatos nearly gets his riot shield wedged stuck in the small tunnel, but we free it without too much trouble.

The third level is much the same as the second, and so is the fourth. No activity at all, and the design obviously centers around keeping people in rather than out. I sincerely hope that's the case. Of all the flaws my enemies can have, I like arrogance the most. (To be honest, I appreciate incompetence more, but that's too rare to hope for.) If the Goth really thinks no one would ever break in, and has only put up two turrets as a token defense, this will be easier than I thought. The turrets might even be another measure to keep people from escaping. Then again, an ambush might be around the next corner.

The fifth level drops even the pretense of rooms. There's nothing but coffin after gunmetal coffin standing upright on an expansive concrete floor, most without lids. About half are filled with pale-skinned zombies staring blankly into space. The spiked chokers, fishnet stockings, black leather trench coats, platform shoes and combat boots don't help the scene. Luckily for us, they don't react as we move slowly through the room.

"Cool," the Esquire Jacob says when we're halfway to the next stairwell.

"What is it now?" the Baron Elmatos says.

"I've been using my radar app and the pattern's pretty neat."

Great. Jacob's a nervous talker. My opinion of him drops but I ask to see the pattern anyway. It's the Star of Neferth, a fractal pattern used in summoning powerful demons. I swear. Could the Goth really be...I inspect the nearest empty coffin. A thin layer of cheap velveteen lines the inside, and on the rear there are a few rust-colored stains at about chest height.

I take Jacob's phone. "Does this thing have a black light app?"

"You kidding?" Jacob says. "Let me show you."

"Do you think it's a living rune?" Raven says.

"Maybe."

Jacob finds the app, messes with it for a few seconds, then his phone's screen glows black-light blue.

"Shine it back here," I say. I cast a charm to make fluids more visible.

Sure enough, there's dried blood tracing intricate designs on the rear of the coffin. A double line extends straight down from the runic cluster, forking when it hits the floor. Following the lines, it becomes apparent that all the coffins are connected in an intricate web.

I look at the Baron Elmatos. "We need to get through here as fast as possible. Now."

He nods and the Esquire Jacob looks questioningly first at him, then me. He's probably not used to a baron taking orders from someone other than the Count, but this is the reason the Count pays so well to keep me around. No one in his employ has much experience with the world of raw magic, where angry sons-of-bitches come after each other using nothing but the power of their minds and the elemental forces of the universe. I do and am willing to hire myself out. While most of the time it turns out to be nothing his men couldn't have handled for themselves, the few times reality plunges down the rabbit hole I'm in charge. Period.

Raven usually decides to play along.

The Star of Neferth is one of the nastier sacrificial runes. Unlike others which only take blood, bodily fluids, or years off your life, the Star of Neferth devours pieces of soul. It doesn't care what souls it uses for fuel. Anyone or anything placed on the interlocking points gets consumed, making it great for unwilling sacrifices. Finally, it's fractal. It can be made any size without losing its effectiveness, the only limitation being what will actually fit on the points.

I debate knocking a few of the coffins over, trying to cause a magical short, but given the sheer size of this Star that would be like pissing into a hurricane. Every second we stay down here we risk losing parts of our souls through induction. We don't even have to be on one of the node points.

The manhole to the next level is, of course, located at the very center of the Star. Static fills the air as we head inward, itches crawl through bones. Small auroras flirt with Elmatos' riot shield, and his lips tighten. He's definitely not pleased. Jacob swears as his phone flickers and dies, but by then I've figured out where we are in the layout and know where to go. Raven's grinning, her eyes glowing like a cat's. Purple bleeds from her hair to form a dark aura around her, creating shadows independent of light.

A conversation with Old Jed floats to the top of my mind.

"If'n y'ever be situated whereas power, the power, it lit'rally be making the air hum, make sure y'get some yerself. It's not an opportunity t'be wasted." He'd then walked me through a spell designed to catch and store loose power in an object. "Course, if'n y'have nothing on it, y'can use y'rown body. Just make sure to be storin' elsewhere as soon as able."

We'd been in an abandoned temple dedicated to one of the Old Gods. At least, we'd thought it was abandoned until something, we never quite saw what or who, rang the alarm. The tolling of dead bells filled the squat stone halls and when an impossible wind strong enough to knock a man over picked up, Jed started casting the spell. I followed along, storing power in a canteen on my belt.

"Where does this power come from?" I asked.

He looked at me askance, a hooded expression in his eyes. "Sacrifice souls." He adjusted his backpack. "Let's be leavin' before whatever wakes up wakes up."

Flickering movement in the deeper darkness proved we weren't alone and reality started to bend. The columns tilted inward without moving, the angles between the flagstone tiles changed. A deep vibration, felt through my feet, rose into an audible howl. Time to leave.

Afterward, I learned that when a soul dies, its essence dissolves into pure magic. But the stuff in my canteen was still a soul. Sick to my stomach, I asked him how to return it. Jed exploded.

"What'n you be doin' that for? They done been dead and gone over ten cent'ries. Y'want to call them back, back from the Blessed Lands, if'n you feel shivered and wrong? Let well enough be." That was all he'd say and we continued home in silence. Even after returning to Tipton he wouldn't speak to me for days.

After the storm had blown over, I asked him how people could go to the afterlife if their souls were trapped and devoured.

"Some say souls have souls," he said, cryptically. We were packing for another walk-round, as he called them, and had just finished fireproofing some long johns. He fished out a small, leather-bound book from his backpack, one that I'd never seen before, and leafed through a few pages. For the rest of the day, he only spoke when absolutely necessary.

❀

Below the Star is a temple. The altar's the dead giveaway. A stone circle six feet across and one foot thick, it's supported by four black metal legs spaced near the circumference. A hole in the middle, barely large enough for a person a stand in, lies directly underneath the hole we dropped out of. For some reason, the Goth felt it necessary to stop the ladder between floors at the temple ceiling.

We step off the dais and into the rows of metal folding chairs. White candles rest on long brass candlesticks, forming a backdrop for the altar and hiding in niches around the room. They burn with a cold, unmoving white flame, like starlight. I check. They're not electronic.

"Put that back," the Baron Elmatos barks at the Esquire Jacob.

"This is some freaky shit," he says, leafing through a worn

hymnal. There are at least twenty copies in a cheap bookshelf.

"I said, *put that back*," the baron repeats.

"Oh, we're fine now," Raven says. "The Star won't affect us down here."

"I don't want him taking souvenirs."

"Listen to this," the esquire says. "'The only true peace is sleep, the only true sleep is death, the only true death utter oblivion. Thus we sacrifice ourselves to—"

The Baron Elmatos smacks him on the back of the head and forcibly confiscates the hymnal. "Don't say it! Never say something's name in its own damn temple."

The Esquire Jacob grumbles, fiddles with his phone, then looks up. "What's that?"

The tapestry on the ceiling's been dyed blood red and a rigor mortis face, like a Chinese demon, grins down at us with bug-wide eyes and a beard made from naked human bodies. Jacob snaps a picture of it with his phone.

"It's the welcoming committee," I say. "Let's move on."

I hold the black curtain at the back of the room open. It's coarse and oily, like burlap covered in grease. After everyone's through I wipe my hands on my pants but nothing comes off. Lacking any other options, we press the up button for the elevator at the end of the short hallway.

Inside, there are ten buttons in a pattern that mimics the sephiroth in the Kabbalah tree of life. Our options, marked in crabbed handwriting, are Cupola, Mansion Left, Mansion Right, Kitchens, Arcade, Dining Hall, Men's Wing, Women's Wing, Swimming Pool, and Temple. The Baron Elmatos has to shush the Esquire Jacob several times, but after some deliberation I press the area that Daath, the hidden sephirot, usually occupies. The doors slide shut and we're treated to an easy-listening cover of death metal, arranged for piano and harp.

I press Daath again. Nothing happens.

"Just pick something at random," the Esquire Jacob says.

"Shut up and let the man think," the Baron Elmatos replies. I appreciate the vote of confidence.

Finally, I press the buttons Mansion Left and Mansion Right simultaneously. Daath is sometimes considered a blend of two other sephirot, and sure enough an eleventh circle lights up, right where I knew it had to be. The lights in the elevator dim and turn blue.

I don't make the newbie mistake of assuming the Goth's hideout is laid out according to the elevator buttons and try to feel the changes in movement instead. A misleading layout is a trick used by security-minded architects worldwide and it's amazing how many people fall for it without thinking. Beside me, Raven does the same, her eyes closed. The doors open without incident onto the hidden floor.

All four of us flatten against the walls, weapons drawn, but there's no resistance. Instead, we walk into a science fiction brig. Wide, hexagonal doorways open onto small rooms. Four of the twelve are occupied and we find David in the third. He looks like crap.

"Good to see you," I say.

He looks up weakly. Like the other prisoners, he's chained to a sigil-covered bench. From what I can see, they're meant to drain a person's physical, mental, and spiritual strength. Part of me's impressed he's survived this long. His eyes focus on us for a second, then his head sags. He says something, weakly.

"Don't worry. We'll get you out," I say, but Raven lays a hand on my shoulder.

"He said, 'wards.'"

The doorway looks clear so they have to be magical. Technology isn't advanced enough yet to create force fields. And if it isn't human or dwarven technology, we're screwed. So the wards have to be magical.

"Blast them," I tell the baron. He and the Esquire Jacob aim at the seemingly empty doorway. "Aim for the corners," I snap.

If their shots do make it through, I don't want them hitting David. Jacob corrects his aim and they fire.

A wave of coruscating light annihilates the bullets with soft, popping sounds.

"Again," I say, and the same thing happens. It's obvious they won't be able to overload the wards, but the longer the wards are active the more Raven can learn. I just hope we're not setting off any too-obvious alarms. The lack of resistance coming in, the lack of guards...what's going on? I look at Raven and she shakes her head. She needs more time.

Once more, though, and she's learned all she needs to. She waves us off, chooses an effect crystal, and sets it down just outside the open doorway. Next she calibrates a Squeemine—we have eight left—and walks forward, holding it in front of her. When it reaches the doorway the wards activate. Raven winces, then presses a button on the mine itself before letting go. The ward dims but is still present, shimmering like transparent gauze, and the mine hangs in the air where Raven put it. Seconds later, it detonates, sending all its force into the ward. The barrier of light glows first red and blue, then green, all the way through violet, and finally a painful bluish white. The effect crystal turns solid black and the wards disappear, leaving behind a smell of burning soap.

"We have until the crystal turns clear again," Raven says.

Good enough for me. I'm in there like a flash and shoot the lock off the chains. David sags forward and I catch him, lifting one arm over my shoulder. I get a better look at the sigils etched into the cell bench and I wonder how he managed to stick it out. Most people would be complete zombies after a few hours and he's been here for several days. Was it a trap?

"What about the others?" the esquire asks.

"Leave them," I say, telling myself I'm perfectly justified. They're already way too far gone, we can't carry them all and still protect ourselves, our priorities were getting David and our information out...My intestines still knot up, but we have no choice. "We'll need to go through the main house," I continue, and in response to Raven's questioning look: "He won't survive a trip back through the Star."

Elmatos nods and takes the lead back to the elevator. We select Main Dining Hall. It has the best chance of multiple exits, increasing our chance of escape. I don't want to wander around unfamiliar territory.

The elevator dings and the doors open onto a communal lunch.

❀

There's a moment of silence as confused heads and mascara-framed eyes swivel to look directly at us. Crystal chandeliers hang from the ceiling. A heavy metal soundtrack, volume pumped up to eleven, plays in the background. The reason no one responded to our infiltration was because of shit like this. Forget what I said about incompetence; it makes enemy reactions too hard to anticipate.

Almost in slow motion, the Baron Elmatos drops to one knee in front of us, riot shield ready, and lobs a Squeemine into the room. The Esquire Jacob lobs another and Raven raises her hands, spheres of purple energy engulfing them.

While the teenage idiots clearly weren't expecting this, they recover quickly. A goth near the back of the dining room yells, "Apep prime!"

The Squeemines land in the middle of a long wooden table piled high with fast food served on silver plates. The explosions turn crystal pitchers filled with soda and energy drinks into caffeinated shrapnel, and a kid at the lead table clutches at his neck and drops as a metal spork takes him in the throat. Not a single one could be out of high school, and my intestines ratchet up another notch. Then they return fire with more than lethal force, losing a part of their souls with every spell they cast.

The Baron Elmatos is nearly knocked on his ass by the intensity of the barrage, and his riot shield cracks, but he manages to return fire. I notice four goths sneaking out of the room through the doors in the back but can't do anything about it. The elevator doors close. There are muffled thuds, the doors bulge inward, and then quiet.

I press a floor at random, then pull the emergency stop when we're between floors.

We formulate a plan quickly. They're going to be watching the doors like hawks, but they'll have to guard all of the elevator exits or shut down the power. Either way, they'll need to detach groups to do so, improving our odds. We'll pick a floor at random and Elmatos will take point, hoping the riot shield holds. We'll chunk Squeemines through and while the goths are recovering from the blast, Raven will unload with the sealants. They're supposed to be used for sealing doors shut and other tactical annoyances, but in dire situations they can also be set to explosive expansion. With luck, we'll create soft cover and possibly entomb a few goths. Suffocation is a bad way to go but it's still much better than soul stripping.

I look at David. He's propped up in the corner, as far out of the way as possible.

We're ready to go, but the elevator starts moving on its own, heading back for the dining hall. They must have overridden the controls.

Grimacing, Elmatos takes a position in front, holding the shield up for cover. The esquire and I prime the Squeemines, hoping to take out as many as possible. The doors open and incompetence scores another point. Quite literally all of the goths, including the four that had left, are waiting for us as the elevator doors ding open. If we'd have just picked another floor, we'd be in much better shape. God damn it.

The Squeemines vaporize immediately in the rain of electric blue death heading toward us. Elmatos' riot shield starts to smoke. Where the arcs of energy hit the elevator, they gouge out drops of molten metal, showering us with pain. Raven and I switch gears, casting a defensive shield just inside the elevator doors. I feel the familiar surge of magic yet again, but not battle frenzy. I guess even my medulla oblongata knows charging into that would be suicide.

"Who the hell taught these kids the Devil's Touch?" I yell though there's no need to. Despite the furious special effects display, the Devil's Touch strikes with the absolute silence of the grave.

"Does it matter?" Raven says.

"Close the doors, close the doors!" Jacob yells, frantically pushing the button.

"That's button's useless, dumbass!"

Outside, most of the kids break into smirks. Only about a third of them are actually attacking. The others are waiting and watching behind upturned tables. As the first group starts to run out of juice the next group begins casting. The doors close as the second wave hits and starts to melt away. Then everything stops while the goths conserve their energy.

"Fuck fuck fuck," the Esquire Jacob mutters, mostly to himself. He takes out his phone and starts messing with it.

"What the fuck are you doing?" the Baron Elmatos barks weakly. His riot shield is a brown and flaking crisp and there's a wicked gash along his left side where he took a glancing blow. It looks like thousands of miniature meat hooks gouged an inch deep. The flesh glistens.

"If I'm going to die, I might as well text people goodbye. Fuck! No fucking signal."

The elevator lights and muzak die as the power is cut.

The Baron Elmatos chuckles disbelievingly, the gallows humor of a dead man. Even if we get out, he won't survive the poison. It will feel like garrotes of barbed wire are raking across his bones, then fade to an itch as his nerves die. Seconds after he'll stop breathing and his heart will stop. He knows it, too.

Raven, who's been crouching with her eyes closed, suddenly stands. "I'll take care of this."

"How?" the Esquire Jacob says.

"Get David and Jake out," she continues. "Take the left door out of the dining room, go down the hallway and take the second right. Follow it down past the first branch and through the third door on the right. That hallway leads to the cupola. There's a teleportation ring that leads out."

"How do you know all this?" Jacob demands. "And what about the baron?"

"He'll be with me," she says.

"Fuck that."

The elevator lights come back on—the goths probably realize they need at least some power to open the elevator doors. Their incompetence has finally worked to our advantage. Piano and harp fill the air.

"Jacob," I say. "You can stay here or not stay here, but as soon as those doors open again I'm leaving with David."

"You'll just get yourself killed, listening to this bitch. She's obviously on their side."

That does it. I'm not going to humor this kind of idiocy. I realize Jacob's scared to death and panicking, but now isn't the time for horror movie theatrics.

"Suit yourself," I say, hoisting David across my shoulders. At least the two of us will make it out and I have no worries about Raven.

The elevator dings and the doors are covered in dark, purple light. They open slowly, as if fighting their way through molasses. I look at Raven. Her eyes glow dark blue and her jogging suit inflates like it's holding back a storm. She nods. "Go."

I launch myself for the doors. Jacob can follow if he feels like it. I hit the purple light and swear. It's like jumping into ice cold water and I hope David has enough left in him to survive. He moans and the world slows down even more. The first few words for an endurance chant force their way through my lips before I realize it, and I choke them back as bile rises in my throat. I need to stay in control. Keep moving. Just keep moving.

After what feels like minutes we emerge into the dining hall. Everything moves at a snail's pace. Even the arcing tendrils of the Devil's Touch move slowly enough to avoid and the goths stand as if frozen in purple amber. Raven's really outdone herself this time. The air itself seems liquid but I set that from my mind and head for the correct door. It's slightly ajar and I'm immediately thankful. Even with both my weight and David's slamming into it, it moves like it's stuck in foam, nearly dislocating my leading shoulder. I probably wouldn't have been able to turn the handle.

Outside, my ears pop like I've just dropped several thousand feet in two seconds and my eardrums are *this* close to giving up. Shouting and laughter come from the dining room but they don't seem to have noticed me. I keep moving.

The only other thing I remember about the escape is that the Goth's mansion has some very nice, very red carpet. I also vaguely recall shouting, a numb sensation, and shooting someone in the crotch at point blank range.

Chapter 12

When I wake up I'm too exhausted to be suspicious. My entire body aches and it feels like a sadistic acupuncturist has been using me as a teaching aid. I don't feel like opening my eyes but at least I'm lying down. I run through a mental checklist.

Body parts? I move my arms and legs to make sure they're still attached, and my head hurts too much to be gone. Check.

Clothes? I move my arms and legs again and feel fabric. Check.

Concentration? I try to visualize a hexagram, basic stuff, and it feels like my mind is on fire. In that case...

Weapons? I pat myself down as stealthily as possible. Turns out I'm actually naked, and the fabric is a blanket and itchy bandages. I'm also lying on a mattress, a pretty good indication that I'm with friends. Then again, some people have a sadistic sense of humor.

Dreading what I'll see, I open my eyes and guess what? All I see is pain, beamed directly into my brain from the light overhead. Shading my eyes cuts down on the glare and I see a nightstand with an alarm clock, lamp, and sunglasses. I pick those last up. They're the cheesy, oversized kind favored by music stars on drugs, and are framed with neon yellow plastic to boot.

I grin, then wince from the pain. Raven obviously made it out too, in much better shape than I am if she's leaving me such a thoughtful waking-up present. Now I just need to check on David. I start to swing my legs over the side of the bed, intending to sit up in the same motion, but I only make it halfway before some asshole drops a brick on my temples. I guess I'll be staying in bed for a while.

When the pain fades, I gingerly open my eyes again and take stock of my surroundings. I'm lying on a cheap motel bed covered by a clown-themed bedspread. A pendulum clock in the shape of a black and white cat grins at me as its eyes and curved tail swung from side to side. To my right, away from the door, is a monochrome, pointillist painting of a sailboat in a storm. At least, that's what I think it is. My eyes aren't focusing correctly and for all I know it might be yet another remix of the dogs playing poker.

Several minutes later, out of boredom, I try to get up again. Same result.

Same thing happens a few minutes after that. And after that.

Just before I launch my fifth attempt I notice something hiding behind the nightstand lamp. It's a remote control with only one button. For lack of anything more productive to do, I press it repeatedly.

After I've given it up and called the thing busted, a mime wheels David through the door. He's skinny and emaciated, even smaller than usual without one of his funny hats, but he's alive and there's fire in eyes. A good sign.

"I'm glad you're awake," he says. "We thought you might miss the memorial services."

Normal English. Even better.

"I'm not sure I can make it," I say. I hadn't known the Baron Elmatos or the Esquire Jacob that well, and I don't want to test my strength.

"We have another wheelchair," David says.

"No thanks. I damn near knocked myself out trying to sit up earlier."

"Are you sure?"

"Yes."

David sags, something I wouldn't have thought possible in a wheelchair. "I guess it's your choice, but I was hoping you'd give Raven's eulogy."

❀

No one except the ridiculously rich actually gets buried anymore. Cremation is the way to go. Still, some people prefer a traditional send-off. There might be nothing but ashes to bury, but they can still get a tombstone on a cemetery green.

That's what Raven had chosen, and the fact there's no body doesn't mean a damn thing. Apparently it's been two weeks since they found me in an abandoned corridor, several buildings away from the Goth's HQ, dragging David along behind. After five more days they gave up on everyone else. The Baron Elmatos and the Esquire Jacob I could understand, but Raven? I don't want to believe it, but they show me her will, which was enchanted to only appear after her death. In it are instructions for burial at Pleasant Pines Cemetery.

There are a few hours left before the service. I spend most of those trying to convince myself she's really gone. Even with the will right in front of me I don't quite believe it. She's too smart and too canny to let a bunch of high school kids take her out. Then it dawns on me that I need to figure out what to say.

"She was a competent secretary, excellent researcher, good backup in a fight, and teased me far more than strictly necessary," doesn't seem to cut it, but that's all I really know about her. We were both happy with our boundaries and I refuse to let myself regret not knowing more about her. I could fall back on the standard platitudes—"she was a dear friend and will be missed," "our lives will never be the same," and other bullshit—but people use them because they're easy, not always because they're true.

I honestly wasn't that close to Raven and have no right to give the eulogy, but everyone else disagrees. I try to figure out whose idea it was, but the mimes aren't talking and...well, honestly, it's probably David's.

I can do this, I tell myself, say a few words on her behalf, and it's not like there's anyone else here who knew her better.

❀

Photos of her, the Baron Elmatos, and the Esquire Jacob are propped on a small folding table in the cemetery park, surrounded by floral arrangements. I suppose they're considered tasteful. The Count is here, as are most of the surviving barons and esquires, not to mention a company of indistinguishable mimes. It's a nice spot on a perfectly manicured fake lawn, with ersatz trees providing shade at aesthetic intervals. It feels like the first day of spring but when I look up there's no sign of any sun, and that annoys me. I don't see the sun often, but if Pleasant Pines is going to fake being outside they might as well get it right.

I adjust my ridiculous sunglasses, glare at the mime who's pushing me around, and bring my attention back to the ceremony. It isn't the only one taking place. Other voices can be dimly heard from the other side of the hills but we at least have a semblance of privacy.

The Count gives eulogies for the Baron Elmatos and the Esquire Jacob, sounding like a Shakespearean general. It's all duty and sacrifice, remembrance and honor. Rally the troops for the upcoming battle. With your shield or on it. Brotherhood.

Then it's my turn.

I'm wheeled to the podium. The mime stands a respectable distance away. The memorial table is to my right and I resist the urge to smash it. The mimes have found a hospital gown for me and the last thing I need is to fall out of the wheelchair and flash everyone while throwing a tantrum. I stare at the flowery wreaths for a moment, then out at the audience. They stare back.

"There's not much I can say," I say. "Not much I want to say. In fact, as soon as I get out of this damn thing I plan on kicking that son-of-a-bitch in the nuts and stomping his face in." Some of the Count's men smirk and that pisses me off. "What? You got a problem with that?" I say.

It isn't the Gettysburg Address but nothing else feels appropriate. Raven is—was Raven, and now I'm going to kick the Goth in the nuts and stomp his face in. After I spend the rest of my time silently daring anyone to speak up, I'm wheeled back to my place in the audience. A Catholic priest says "ashes to ashes, dust to dust" in an official way for the Baron Elmatos and a high priestess from some Neopagan religion does something with papier-mâché and amber dust for the Esquire Jacob. An aged priest, dressed in black robes half covered by brown, is there personally at Raven's request. He starts a nonsensical sermon with the gist that, at a human being's innermost core, there's nothing that can really live or die. I don't know why, but that gets my attention.

"If even our bodies are only impressions," he continues in a voice that manages to creak with dignity, "a small voice in a world filled with voices, what then are our memories? What are the fleeting images of joy and love we ascribe to the departed? Do these images reside in bones, in ashes? Will they fade even as grief fades?"

A small murmur passes through the non-mime portions of the mourners. Is this guy telling us our memories are useless? I'm not quite sure, myself.

Oblivious, he continues. "If we cloister them like buried treasures, what use are they, growing moldy in the dark corners of our hearts? Set them free. Set yourselves free."

The murmur grows louder and I decide to like this guy on principle. He's not afraid to piss people off.

"Don't hold yourselves separate. Share these memories, this loss. Lives are fleeting, but life is eternal."

The old priest grips the podium with two bony hands, possibly to steady himself or for emphasis. Either way, his voice doesn't change. "Whatever you treasured in them is also in you. If you miss their smile, smile. If you miss their kindness, be kind. Though we are deceived otherwise, we are, and have always been, complete." He smiles kindly. "The best in them is also the best in you, and there is always so little time."

He leaves the podium with most of the Count's contingent audibly decrying his senility, but a few of the mimes are smiling. Real smiles, not face makeup covering a grim expression. Shuffling away, he pauses a moment, then turns. He moves his brown half-robe out of the way, revealing a glinting ring strapped to his upper left torso, and I swear he winks directly at me.

I watch him until he passes behind a tree, then turn back for the end of the service. I don't know why, but I'd prefer it if the crazy old man wouldn't emerge from the other side, if he'd just disappear into thin air like an angel with Alzheimer's.

❀

Two days later I'm back on my feet. It creeps me out, but the mimes are actually excellent healers. At least I'm not in mime-world. As best as I can tell, I'm in a strange two-star motel that they use as a base of operations.

Even though entry is controlled completely by key-card access, my door still has a chain latch. I spend the first few days alternating between glaring at the feline wall clock and coming up with ways to destroy the Goth. Then, mercifully, I'm able to walk again and am about to walk my ass into some revenge when David, on his own two feet as well, lets me know that the Unspoken wants to see me. Were they just waiting for me to get better?

I reluctantly agree and he leads me down two flights to a dilapidated conference room. Generic landscape paintings hang crookedly on the walls and wide windows at the far side of the room are covered with coarse curtains. The Unspoken and the Count are seated at one side of a long table. I figure there's no reason I can't tell them off on my way out and I look forward to it. This bullshit's cost me far too much already.

There are no chairs on my side of the table, so I take one from where they're stacked along the wall, spin it around, and sit down.

"What do you want?" I say.

"To the point as always," Count Fantabuloso replies, "if rarely sharp."

The Unspoken half-stands and nods. *Your recovery has been swift and much looked forward to.*

"What do you want?" I repeat.

"Silence fits best," the Count says, "for one in my employ."

He looks pretty haggard himself but I don't care. "Didn't you get the memo?" I say. "I quit."

We lock gazes and both slowly start to stand.

The Unspoken makes a sharp gesture with both hands, index and middle fingers outstretched, and I'm glued to my seat. I assume the Count is in the same predicament. *Gentlemen.* He focuses on me. *Please tell us what you saw.*

I do. The air around the Unspoken shimmers and I get the distinct impression the Unspoken isn't happy.

I see. There is another task for you, Mr. Richards.

"Stuff it," I say. "I said no the first time." David, still in the room, gasps. "And not my problem."

"Did I not say knaves will never be knights?" the Count says.

"You can stuff it too."

"Loyalty is woven from such slender threads, does not unravel so much as snap."

"The only reason I'm not snapping you in half right now is because you're not worth it."

SILENCE!

And there is. So complete it feels like ice. The Unspoken's face makeup shimmers as if it's about to crawl away from his face, like his human form is just a suit of clothes that can be taken on or off at will. Each thread in the black turtleneck races to see which can be the first to get away and the beret curls in on itself, dissolving like smoke.

After waiting a few seconds to establish exactly who is in charge, the Unspoken continues.

Trust is an investment, and since it seems to be lacking, here is some capital.

The Unspoken's form settles on human again, the beret reappearing. David whispers, "You shouldn't have done that." I ignore him.

Many have speculated as to the nature and purpose of the Brotherhood of the Unspoken Secrets. The Unspoken mimes a martini out of thin air and I can tell this is going to be a spiel. I watch and listen. I don't have much of a choice.

Ever since humanity learned how to dream, it has dreamt of secrets hidden in the dark. Ancestors with incredible power. Long-lost civilizations. Keys to the meaning and control of life itself.

The Unspoken mimes while speaking. The conference room is replaced by grand vistas and inaccessible locations. So small they can barely be seen, explorers and dreamers from all eras and civilizations test their luck and skill.

And yet, for all the rumors and dreams, ancient knowledge and expeditions, none have succeeded. The best, brightest, most obsessed and quite insane have all failed to find Shangri-La, the Fountain of Youth, or Atlantis.

The Unspoken's gestures widen, becoming incredibly expansive, but still as edged and precise as a blade. A mocking smile hovers under reptilian eyes.

There is knowledge not meant for humanity. The vainglorious were never meant to wield true power, nor the bleeding hearts. Whenever ambition and desperation outstrip humility, the Brotherhood will retain the balance.

The tableaus expand. An arctic-clad explorer, high in the Himalayas, searches for the legendary snow chrysanthemum. Ice blue and delicate as crystal, it's fabled to have the power to resurrect the dead. An avalanche sweeps him off a narrow precipice and he rejoins his wife, albeit not in the way he expected.

Elsewhere a charismatic extreme athlete, out for fame and endorsement contracts, rappels into the crater of the wrong volcano. Unseen hands loosen pitons and his entire team, camera crew included, plunge to their deaths.

In the corner of my eye I see a conquistador being drowned, head held under an ornate fountain of limestone and marble.

By summoning the Archangel of Despair, the Goth seeks to disturb that balance, draining humanity of its hope and fury, leaving them with nothing but numb acceptance. This must not happen.

A brief but powerful image of a gray world, filled with despair, hits me like a punch to the gut, but since this is all magic I don't take it too seriously. Emotions are one of the easier things to manipulate. The grungy conference room fades back into vision.

The Unspoken looks me in the eyes. Finding myself unable to look away, I squint to prevent any psychic connections from fully forming. *We need you to stop the Goth from gathering the last of the components needed to complete the summoning.* The Unspoken waits a moment to let the import of the speech sink in, then nods.

"Basically," I say, able to speak again, "you dropped the ball and now you want me to get it back."

Count Fantabuloso looks like he's about to explode again, but the Unspoken simply says *Yes.* I can deal with that.

"How much are you going to pay me?" I say.

Triple the previous offer.

I was planning to reject him out of hand, but that much money isn't something to be sneezed at, even if it is astarum. I'll be able to buy an island on a plane far removed from this clusterfuck and retire in peace. One last job and then I'll be out. "And an equal amount for everyone I take with me," I say. I also want to see how much the Unspoken is willing to pay.

Do you not feel sufficient to the task? The Unspoken's face is back to a feline grin.

"You don't have the necessary funds?" I fire back.

Very well. Goths are scouring the Jungian Isles for immaculatum.

When you and your associates return, all will be paid.

The Jungian Isles? Sure. Great. Why not?

David follows me out of the conference room.

"Yes?" I say, expecting him to chide me for not being more polite to our rescuers.

Instead, all he says is, "Thanks."

Chapter 13

Beethoven's Fifth, a pub in the Colson district, is a favorite watering hole for postmodern adventurers. It's where I first met Old Jed and where I hope to pick up some backup willing to work without a down payment. That's unlikely, but possible. I step through the heavy wooden double doors set in the aged brick façade, and into a different world.

Neon tubes spread like veins in a place that could have been carved from the grudging hulk of a long-dead machine. Set perfectly flush in the seams, they fill the place with thin light. A breathalyzer, currently reading 0.6, is affixed next to the door at shoulder height, and curtained booths raised a step above the main floor line the walls.

I head for the bar. The bartender, a solid guy I don't recognize despite the scar across his forehead, gives me the standard, noncommittal nod. I tell him I'm looking to hire and he hands me the mic. Behind him, bottles of all shapes and sizes are arranged on shelves transplanted onto a grand organ. Its metal pipes gleam.

I press the button on the mic and a pure tone sounds, getting everyone's attention. Even the waitresses in rough leather skirts and thick blouses, rolling around on inline skates, pause to listen. The pub tables bloom like industrial flowers in a concrete field.

"Excuse me," my voice echoes. "I need people to go with me to the Jungian Isles. The payment is astarum on return."

The heckling starts immediately.

"Astarum? He's not expecting us to return!"

"If you need sherpas, go somewhere else!"

"I don't need a funeral just yet, walker!"

"Walker!"

"Walker!"

The word's picked up by a chant that spreads to the whole room. They even bang their mugs and plates. A light above one of the booths turns blue. They're actually interested.

❀

Like I haven't had enough bad luck already, who's inside but the vagrant superhero Captain Eight and his sidekick/handler, Chernobyl. I'm tempted to turn around as soon as I see them but they *are* competent enough, in their own unique way, and beggars can't be choosers. I need to get this over with.

"Dick!" Captain Eight says. "Long time no see! How've you been?"

The hyper-enthusiastic life of any party, whether the party wants him to be or not, Captain Eight's shoulder length, tightly-wound curls make him immediately recognizable anywhere. The red and black suit, with an 8-ball the size of a grapefruit on the chest, is almost an afterthought.

"Did you hear how we got kicked out of Newark?" Chernobyl says.

He's the shorter of two. At 5'4" to the captain's 6'2" he'd easily be lost in a crowd if not for his trademark suit. It's dark blue, highlighted by blue and green neon flames. He also wears similarly adorned combat boots. Captain Eight says the flames complement the aerodynamic properties of Chernobyl's bald head, helping him run faster.

"Oh my God, it was awesome." When Captain Eight talks, you can almost see the primary colors and speech balloons.

I reluctantly take a seat.

"There we were, chasing my archnemesis, the Ultra-Pirate Lord Captain Uberbeard," Captain Eight continues, almost standing in excitement, "when we realized we were heading into a trap. Being the heroes that we are, we decided to head right for the nerve center."

"By that he means we got blindsided in an abandoned strip mall," Chernobyl translates.

Captain Eight ignores him. "And who turns out to be behind it all but Dr. Rocktopus, the six-armed maestro of mayhem himself, personally overseeing one of the captain's many nefarious enterprises! It was classic. He looked at us. We looked at him. There was so much tension in the air I thought I'd go blind. That happens sometimes and you have to be careful," Captain Eight adds matter-of-factly.

He floats down memory lane, thrilled by his own story, before continuing. "I was about to launch my most super awesome attack when Dr. Rocktopus pulls out not one, not two, but three double-necked guitars. Three! I don't know where he pulled them from and I don't even care! It was just. That. Bad. Ass. Sunglasses appear on his head from nowhere—"

"And remember," Chernobyl adds, encouraging him, "this is in a district with most of the power out."

"—I know. Sunglasses in complete twilight!" Captain Eight gushes, not missing a beat. "He struck a pose and I held my breath. I knew I probably shouldn't let him power up, anime style, but even I wanted to see what happened next."

"We were actually trying to free ourselves from debris a booby trap had dropped on us," Chernobyl asides.

"Whatever. All three of his raised hands dropped at once, and he played the ultimate power chord. And by ultimate I mean *ultimate*. The floor started shaking, pieces flew off the walls, and all of a sudden there was 80s hair everywhere, like someone superglued neon mullets to a horde of cracked-out flying monkeys." Captain Eight stands, eyes closed in the thrall of excitement, and momentarily stops talking.

"I seem to remember you getting hit in the temple with an

energy blast instead," Chernobyl says. Captain Eight holds up a hand.

"Don't ruin the moment." He takes a deep breath. "It turned out the flying 80s hair monkeys were just a diversion from the real threat. Cyborg ninja-monkeys."

Chernobyl laughs. "That's actually pretty close to the truth. They were cybernetically enhanced and wielded some kind of pulse rifles. Dr. Rocktopus had them hardwired into a suitcase-sized supercomputer hidden behind a derelict slushee machine. I figured he was controlling them through the guitars."

A waitress pushes past the booth curtain and sets two plates on the brass table. The table's been welded from sections and resembles a chambered nautilus. Both plates contain a bunned polish sausage resting on a field of sauerkraut.

Chernobyl thanks her, and when she asks if we need anything else Captain Eight says he needs her number or his life will be meaningless. She just laughs and rolls her eyes. She fishes condiment bottles from the wide pocket sewn onto her leather skirt and rolls off.

"Where was I?" Captain Eight says, sitting back down. Sometimes you just have to let him talk, get it out of his system. "Oh yeah. The cyborg ninja-monkeys put up a hell of a fight. I'd dodge left and they'd weave right. I'd attack high and they'd counter low. I couldn't even line them up so they'd take each other out. It's a good thing Chernobyl was there or I might have been toast."

Chernobyl is decorating a polish sausage with intricate patterns of ketchup, mustard, and relish. He's a bit OCD so I don't say anything.

Captain Eight continues. "He did this thing he does, with the glowing hands and the 'foom' and the 'whoosh.'"

"EMP," Chernobyl says.

I nod. An electromagnetic pulse would knock out any unshielded computers.

"They stumbled back, but redoubled their heinous assault. One close blast nearly seared my ass shut. Literally. Not to be dissuaded, Chernobyl redoubles his efforts. Foom. Whoosh!" Captain Eight demonstrates with his hands. "They stagger back, stunned, but seconds later they jerk fully upright, ready to bring the pain. But I was ready for them." He stands up and strikes a pose.

"Captain Eight! Exfoliate!" he shouts. Both Chernobyl and I duck, but the most that happens is that the skin of his polish sausage peels off. His superpower is that he can make any word that ends with *-ate* happen. If that sounds pretty random, it is. Plus, his command of the English language isn't the best. Chernobyl often says that one day Captain Eight will discover a dictionary and that will be the end of us all.

"All of a sudden, pieces started flying off the ninja monkeys. I could see the glow of their guts and Chernobyl hit them again. Foom. Whoosh!" Captain Eight leans in, his voice low for the big finale. "They stopped dead in their tracks, not even falling over. I kicked one in the nuts just to make sure. We won, but Dr. Rocktopus was nowhere to be seen. Then we heard the whine..."

"I disrupted their power cells with that last burst. We had to get out of there before they went critical," Chernobyl says.

"...and, for some reason, Newark authorities don't like surprise fireworks."

"We nearly took out four blocks, Captain."

"Not us. Them. Did our food come yet?"

"It's been sitting in front of you for a while now," I say, irritated.

Captain Eight looks down, astounded, then digs in.

"So, you're interested in going to the Jungian Isles," I say when it becomes obvious neither of them will start the conversation.

"The whosit in the what now?" Captain Eight says.

"The Jungian Isles," Chernobyl repeats. "You remember them. Jungles, frogs, mist."

That surprises me. "You've been there before?"

"I hate that place," Captain Eight says. "Why'd you think we want to go there?"

I want to strangle him. Listening to him is making my headache worse. "When I announced the job, the light outside your booth turned blue."

"It did? We thought you were being social."

"I told you not to wave your arms around, Captain. You accidentally hit the button."

"It's not my fault that's where the button was."

"Look," I say, burying my face in my hands and cutting short their next spat, "if I don't stop the Goth from finding the immaculatum he needs he'll summon the Archangel of Despair and basically take over the world." Hopefully that's simple enough for Captain Eight to understand.

Captain Eight pauses with a half-eaten polish sausage halfway to his mouth. "He'll take over the world?" he repeats, slowly. Chernobyl's already finished his meal and is arranging the leftovers on his plate.

"Or so they tell me," I say. "I'm not sure I believe them, but the pay's good."

"Why didn't you say so?" Captain Eight says, ignoring my reservations. "If the world's at stake, we'd be douches not to help. Count me in."

"And you?" I ask Chernobyl.

"Sure. It sounds interesting."

❀

It's never good policy to leave for the Jungian Isles without updating your last will and testament, or at least setting your affairs in order, so we agree to meet the next evening at about six. I have nothing worth doing myself, besides cancelling all my missing credit cards, but apparently those two have loose ends to tie up. It's probably spending some quality time with their favorite token-operated epilepsy fixes, but who am I to judge?

The last time I spent an extended amount of time with those two I nearly strangled Captain Eight. We all had an interest in breaking into a cult's high-security reading room. I don't know what the dynamic duo had been after, but I was there to find records on a young couple whose families were getting worried about their lack of contact. Since we both needed to get inside, we'd decided to team up.

It was 10 P.M., give or take a few minutes, and the room had shut down. The last of the day guards was about to go home, and we were waiting in a posh café across the court, seated at one of the outlying tables.

"I looked at my deodorant today," Captain Eight had started the conversation. "It said it was 'body responsive.' I'm not sure I want my deodorant thinking of me like that." He was dressed in his version of inconspicuous: his superhero outfit plus a baseball cap and sunglasses. The thing is, it actually worked. Street marketing's gotten so psychotic that stranger things walk by every day.

Rather than take part in another bizarre, pointless conversation, I focused my binoculars on the guards. Five had already left, meaning five more were inside. After three more went home we'd begin.

"You mean you use deodorant?" Chernobyl said, sounding genuinely surprised.

Captain Eight returned the confusion. "You mean you don't?"

"That's not what I meant. I thought you'd..." Chernobyl searched for word, "...invigorate or something."

"I am never hugging you again."

"Unlike your deodorant, I don't think of you in that way."

"Good."

"Good."

"Good."

"Try to look alive, guys," I said. "The last guard just left."

"But I haven't finished my mango smoothie," Captain Eight complained.

"I'm sure you'll think of something."

❀

We caught up to the last guard around the block, out of sight from the reading room. Chernobyl, in street clothes, accosted her with a creepy pickup line. She was short but fiery, and pulled out a can of mace. While she was focused on Chernobyl I knocked her out from behind.

"Captain Eight, imitate." He morphed into a perfect copy of the guard and we stashed her unconscious form out of sight.

Chernobyl and I posed as new converts while Captain Eight escorted us inside. It was highly unusual, but since the woman we'd knocked out was the head of the day shift, the night shift guard nodded us through. Chernobyl fried the guard's systems before he could notify the night shift lead. He was trapped inside the entry booth, unable to even get the doors open. We had about thirty minutes before he'd fail his hourly check in, and then a few more before they'd figure out what happened.

The reading room itself was arranged like a small student library, with bookshelves everywhere. The lights were dim and the informational screens dark.

"They're looking into my soul..." Captain Eight said.

"Who?" I turned, gun drawn, looking for hostiles.

The captain pointed to the pictures of celebrities with glassy-eyed smiles hanging on the walls. God damn it.

"I'm sensing a nuclear power source not too far from here. That's probably where we need to go," Chernobyl said, interrupting before I could take Captain Eight to task for being an idiot. That surprised me. Privately owned nuclear pods are illegal and potentially dangerous, but then again this was a cult. They were probably trying to mutate into aliens from the sixteenth dimension.

We found the secret door and jimmied it open, into the administrative offices beyond. *It figured*, I thought, looking at the cubicle farm. Of course they'd choose the most demeaning office arrangement possible. The superheroes and I parted ways, me to find an HR office and them to do whatever it was they came to do.

Almost immediately I had to duck into a cubicle to avoid a patrolling guard. Other than the usual office necessities, it was bare except for a picture of the cult's founder and a list of the cult's twenty-seven commandments. I ducked under the desk, waiting for the guard to pass, and was about to continue onward when I heard another one coming.

The minutes ticked by without any breaks in the guard pattern that I could exploit. What I really needed was a diversion, and fortunately the superheroes provided one. One of the guards' radios indicated a Code Pink in the reactor room. Bingo. Those two could hold their own and it cleared the space I needed to find the HR manager's office.

I picked the lock without too much trouble and seconds later was in the digitized file system. The passwords Raven had procured were spot-on and I found the location where the couple was staying for "pre-marriage counseling." Time to leave.

I reset the system and was creeping back down the hallway when I heard running footsteps and Chernobyl's voice.

"Run for it!"

They chugged around a corner, headed the same direction I was, and I figured it would be a good idea to keep up. Whatever these two felt the need to run from without making wisecracks about first probably wasn't pretty.

"Did you 'accidently' set the reactor on overload?" I asked, my voice dripping with sarcasm.

"Accidental? There's nothing accidental about it," Captain Eight said. "These guys gooshed an artifact from the Deep Old Ones. We couldn't steal it back so we have to destroy it."

"What about the people all around us?" I nearly yelled, but had the presence of mind to keep my voice down.

"I'll take care of that," Chernobyl said.

We reached the cubicle farm. Twelve guards were waiting for us, weapons drawn.

"We need cover, Captain!"

"Captain Eight, obfuscate!"

There was a pop and a nauseating cloud of yellow smoke started to boil off him. It quickly filled the room, stinging my eyes, nose, and throat. Blind and about to vomit, I barely managed to find my way back to the reading room and out into the court. The superheroes emerged a few seconds later and the compound exploded a few seconds after that.

True to his word, Chernobyl kept the nuclear explosion contained, nearly fainting from the exertion. If I could choose, I'd take him to the Jungian Isles and leave Captain Eight back here, but they're a package deal. Sometimes I think they're lovers; other times I think they're just idiots.

❀

The roof of Donovan Building's been abandoned for years. There's no real reason to be there anymore, other than periodic maintenance, and the roof access shed hums with apathy. The stairwell handrail is starting to rust through and even the graffiti is faded. Sitting on the small landing just in front of the door marked "Maintenance Crews Only. Do Not Open," I wait for the dynamic duo to show up.

Before too long the sounds of nonsensical logic echo upward.

"Regardless of what you claim to know, it will *always* be more cost-effective to cybernetically enhance a ninja than a velociraptor."

"Really? Why's that?"

"The inverse ninja law. Everyone knows velociraptors run in packs, but you'll only ever have to enhance one ninja. Otherwise there'd be no point."

"You know, you might be on to something there."

"Thank you."

"But you're still wrong."

Thankfully their conversation stops before they turn the corner. Captain Eight is as carefree as ever while Chernobyl wears a heavy pack. Everything I've ever heard from Old Jed says that's a bad idea. You don't get hungry or thirsty in the Isles, and you should only bring something along if you don't mind it turning on you.

Captain Eight gives me an exaggerated thumbs-up. His wild, curly hair has been pulled back into a rough ponytail. Both his and Chernobyl's suits are as vivid as ever. It's not natural.

"Let's do this," I say, open the door without waiting for them and emerge skyside. The door's hooked up to a silent alarm, but by the time anyone investigates we'll be long gone. They'll probably chalk it up to ghosts in the machine.

There's some wind, but not much. Donovan's long been surpassed by its neighbors, and walls of glass and steel tower hundreds of feet above us. They look down at us like bored prison guards. Looking up, there's just a hint of dark blue, nearly purple, sky.

Donovan's roof was once a landing pad for suborbital copters, and the encircled yellow H is still visible several yards away. The composite-steel cable the maintenance and flight crews latched themselves to still grids the floor, quietly unraveling and rusting away. There used to be a covered walkway for the safety of the VIPs rich enough to afford private planes, but that's long gone, and so is its footprint on the helipad. At the edges of the roof some safety railing still survives.

"I hate this part," Chernobyl says, panting in the thin air.

Truth be told, I do too. I know the theories: portals to other planes form most easily where reality's thinnest, in the inaccessible holy places of the world. But there's still no reason for one to materialize hundreds of stories off the ground. Until Donovan Building was completed, no one except birds could have possibly gotten to it. Then again, that may be why the Bermuda Triangle eats planes like hors d'oeuvres.

"Can we go yet? I'm getting cold," Captain Eight says.

All magic portals can be opened with a magic chant, after which you have about ten seconds to go through before it closes. Simple enough, except that the Donovan portal isn't actually on the roof. It's ten stories down and several yards out.

"Are you ready?" I say. "Follow me at two second intervals."

"Shit, shit, *shit*! I hate this part," Chernobyl says. As far as I'm concerned, that's a yes. Captain Eight has this wild look in his eyes. "Captain Eight, calibrate," he mutters.

"On three. Two. One. Go!" I start jogging.

Anyone watching would be extremely confused. The way we're spaced, it probably looks like training for the lemming Olympics. There's more time than you'd imagine to reflect on how this is a really bad idea, but giving into the temptation is deadly. I hit the first line in the safety grid and start counting. I'm going a little fast, reaching the second on the count of four, so I slow down. If you can't control your survival instinct you won't survive.

When I hit the fourth line I start the chant. It's nonsense words from a long-forgotten language but it works, so who am I to complain? At least, I hope it's going to work. It's worked before.

The breeze picks up as it always does, sneaking through the surrounding buildings in response to the magic, and threatens to become a wind strong enough to knock us off course. I resist the urge to speed up and get this over with, focusing on the chant instead. It's nice that the proper chanting cadence is also, for most people, the correct jogging rhythm.

Someone long past had removed the safety railing in the section we're heading for, and I could kiss him or her given the chance. I hit the raised lip of the roof, feel the vast emptiness yawn open underneath, and resist the urge to spring off. That would make me overshoot the portal and there's a hell of a long time for reflection on the way to the ground. Instead, I sight on the brass knob at the end of a flagpole as if this is just another run in the park.

Freefalling into open space is surprisingly peaceful, despite Chernobyl swearing in rhythm behind me. Then he too takes the plunge. The surrounding buildings are too far away to touch. There's nothing but sky above and around, and the pompous ring of a restaurant clinging to Donovan Building like the fat rolls of a middle-aged man below. My eyes tear up in the wind and the last thing I see, through the restaurant's clear glass ceiling, is a kid in a booster chair throwing a temper tantrum. That and his mother looking up in sheer horror.

Chapter 14

Travel between planes isn't what most people expect. There aren't any lights or special effects, just a sensation of absolute nothingness. Most of the time people's minds throw up something to protect themselves, usually their favorite neurosis. Dead relatives, visions of the gods, or a chaotic symphony of colors and sounds. It's all the same. I see a big, gray, rippling sheet with a clown face on it, but ultimately your body just jumps from one place to another and only your mind realizes there was something between.

"It looks like we made it in one piece," Chernobyl says, picking himself off the beach and brushing sand off his suit. "It's a good thing neither of us wear capes."

"Speak for yourself," Captain Eight says. "I swear I'm missing a spleen."

"*A* spleen? You've only got one."

"Then that makes it even *more* serious, doesn't it?"

I ignore them.

The beach we've landed on is postcard perfect. There are no waves, and the ocean lies on the beach like blue glass. I can't see any of the other islands in the archipelago, so we're probably on the southern end of Animus, the largest and southernmost of the Jungian Isles. There might be other islands and continents somewhere in the vast, unmoving expanse of ocean, but no one I know is insane enough to go looking.

Further up the beach, a small cairn of stones is filled with water. A line of small ferns grows all the way to the ocean line, but the jungle proper is still a few yards upslope. There's a hint of fog in the air, but the infamous mist of the Jungian Isles doesn't solidify until a few feet from the tree line, where it waits expectantly like a well-trained dog. Hovering above it all like a needle is the silhouette of the Smoker, the impossibly tall volcano of the smallest island, far off in the distance.

"So," Captain Eight says, "where exactly are we going?"

The Goth is after immaculatum, a substance rumored to be the stuff from which minds are made. Old Jed had talked a little about it, and said it could only be found on the Isles. I've always thought it was rumor myself. I guess I was wrong. According to legend, it's only found in a few places and these places change for each person and on each visit.

"There are goths somewhere on this island, and we're going wherever they are," I reply. That's our best bet.

"I see..."

We head up the beach and into the jungle. It feels like there should be life everywhere, bugs, butterflies, brightly colored flowers, small animals darting out of sight, but in our immediate area there's nothing but calm and silence, and a soft sound that can't be waves. And mist. There's mist everywhere. It's probably hallucinogenic, as if a million tree frogs jumped into the air at once and exploded, but no one knows for sure. It won't be too bad at first, but after more than a few days it all adds up and people first turn irritable, then insane. Or so I've heard.

"You got anything?" I ask Chernobyl.

He's fussing with his backpack and pauses. "Nuclear reactions only," he says. "Sorry."

"And you?" I ask Captain Eight, dreading the answer.

He grins and strikes a pose. "Let's find out. Captain Eight, divinate." Nothing happens. He tries a different heroic pose. "Captain Eight, expectorate."

There's a sound like the heavens themselves are coughing up a loogie, then an exaggerated spitting noise. We all dive for cover as a giant ball of mucus, saliva, and phlegm explodes a few yards away, obliterating a cluster of trees. It fizzles angrily.

Captain Eight jumps right back up, undeterred. "Third time's the charm. Get ready."

"Try 'triangulate,'" Chernobyl suggests.

"That's not even a real word," Captain Eight scoffs. "Is it?"

"Just do it," I bark.

He glares at me, but complies. "Captain Eight, triangulate."

His outline buzzes and blurs like he's having an existential seizure. A phantom Captain Eight detaches. He turns translucent, suffused with mist, and the dead leaves under his feet start to crisp.

He regains solidity with a visual snap, drops to his hands and knees, and pukes. Chernobyl helps him back to his feet.

"I didn't even get drunk first," he mutters.

"Do you know where they are?" I ask.

He points.

"How do we get there?"

He ignores me, asking weakly, "What's the word, what's the word, what's the word?"

"Recuperate," Chernobyl says.

"You sure?"

"Yeah."

"Captain Eight, recuperate." A soft, green glow surrounds him and when it fades, he stands fully upright, back to his old self. I ask where we need to go again.

"How should I know?" he tells me. "I'm Captain Eight, not Back Seat Driver Bitch."

"How far away?"

"About twenty miles."

You've got to be kidding me.

❋

On our initial jaunt into the jungle, we pass a carved figure, much like an Easter Island moai. It's covered in moss and vines, with a small shrub growing out of its left ear. It faces the way we came and its eyes are completely shadowed. With its overhanging brow, it looks furious. I run my hands over the gray stone. It's been smoothed but still has a pleasant texture. I rack my brain for any information about these things and a tidbit from Old Jed comes back to me. Check their necks for carvings. Those tell you where you are and where you need to go. But under no circumstances look into their eyes.

I pass along the information and clear away the creepers, thick green vines that have started to grow into the rock. Some of the statue's skin flakes off, revealing a dull, burnt orange underneath. I think I see symbols, a wavy, undecipherable pictograph sentence winding through the exposed rock.

"Come look at this," I say.

Chernobyl does. "I don't see anything."

I look again, but both the symbols and orange rock are gone, leaving behind nothing but mottled gray stone. Great. It's starting already. We continue in the direction championed by Captain Eight, but I can't shake the feeling those symbols had meant "Wrong way, dumbass."

❀

Near the end of the first "night" Captain Eight starts his metal detector shtick. I say "night" because the light here hasn't changed. Oh, there's a sun, which peers like an lecherous old man with cataracts through infrequent holes in the canopy. There's also a moon and, I assume, stars, but it doesn't get any lighter or darker and most of the time you can't see much of anything through the mist anyway.

As for Captain Eight, the shtick begins with "Captain Eight, magnivate," and he spends the next thirty to forty-five minutes picking up various objects and checking to see if they're metal. He does this because he's as mature as an ADD Cookie Monster.

"Is *this* metal?" he says, choosing an object from the ground. He holds it close to his face, stares at it for a few seconds, then pronounces a verdict. So far, he's concluded that a vine, a leaf, and an old turd aren't metal, and that a pebble is close because a pebble is stone and metals come from stone. I have no idea how Chernobyl puts up with this on a daily basis.

"Why yes," Captain Eight says, a bit farther out. "This *is* metal. But what *kind* of metal you ask? Let's find out."

I'm on one side of a fallen tree. Water's collected inside, the perfect breeding ground for mosquitoes or worse. Chernobyl's a little ahead, farther down the impromptu path we've been following. It's little more than a gully paved with mossy stones, and Chernobyl keeps pulling a journal from his backpack, jotting down notes, and putting it back. I hope he isn't trying to create a map. We have no idea where we were to begin with so it would be dubiously useful at best, even if the Isles were known to stay the same between visits. He's already given up on the compass; all the needle does is spin rapidly.

Captain Eight is off to the side, hidden behind a cluster of trees.

"Silver," he says. "This metal is *silver*."

We might as well see what he's found. I call Chernobyl over and we join the captain.

He shows us a silver ankh, saying, "I think they might have camped here."

We do some searching and find more traces. A muddy piece of paper with illegible writing, some markings that could have been runes, and a wet shoelace.

"What do you think?" I ask Chernobyl.

"I thought there'd be more bugs," he says. "There were bugs last time."

Now that he mentions it, it is cathedral-quiet here. Even a background drone is absent, except for the soft, indefinable susurration that seems to define this place. Like most magical worlds, I guess the Jungian Isles can appear different to different people at different times, so I don't dwell on it. But it's still odd.

"Give me a moment," I say. "I'll see if I can't figure out where they went from here. Hand me the ankh."

I'm going to try psychometry.

"Dolor neque sollicitudin elit," I say, and a rush of images flood my mind. I chose the ankh because it's the closest thing to a personal item. People usually forge a close connection to jewelry and the stronger the connection, the easier it is to gain useful information. I see four goths, sense loss and fear, and hear the sound of a river nearby. Shadows dance just outside of vision, but the mist makes it impossible to see where or what they are.

I feel a dull pain in my feet, a reflection of what the ankh's owner felt, then a sharp blossom in the abdomen. Everything goes dark and I'm again surrounded by vine-draped trees in a carpet of green. As the spell fades, it feels like the some of the mist filters into me. Another reason not to use magic if I have a choice.

"Well?" Chernobyl asks.

I tell him.

"Is this what happened then or where they are now?"

"Impossible to tell," I say. Psychometry is far from an exact science.

Captain Eight's voice drifts over to us. He's gotten bored and wandered away. "This isn't metal. It's a *flower*."

I glance up and see a small moai with hooded eyes staring at me from back the way we came. I ignore it.

❀

Several hours in, we reach a river. The underbrush is much denser, almost impenetrable, and it takes us a while to find a clear spot. The river, like the ocean, is motionless, and very wide. It's also tinted green. When we find a broad, flat rock, we stop. Chernobyl sets down his backpack and starts rummaging through it.

"Is anyone hungry?" he says. "I've got protein bars, a few canteens filled with water, a couple sandwiches..."

If I close my eyes I can hear the sound of a rushing river,

smell its watery scent. "No thanks," I say. "I'm not hungry."

"You know," Chernobyl says, "I'm not either, but I'm pretty sure I should be. This place gives me the creeps."

I don't agree with that last part but I say nothing. In fact, this place feels right. A part of me insists that you shouldn't have to eat, shouldn't have to sleep, shouldn't *have* to do anything that takes time away from...I don't know what. Incessant activity feels normal and expected. I think of Raven and David and why I'm doing this in the first place. It's starting to seem far away.

We watch the river in silence. The ever-present mist disperses slightly along the banks, and it's more breathable here. The wet blanket around my mind isn't gone, but it's loose. The river's surface perfectly reflects the overhanging canopy. I think I see a moon and the hint of stars, but my eyes could be playing tricks on me.

"You'd think there'd be more animals," Captain Eight says. "I mean, I'm finding turds all over the place, but no animals. Not even animal noises."

"How do you know they're turds," Chernobyl asks.

"I eat them. Look, if they're turds, they're turds, all right? That's all there is to it. Weren't there animals last time?"

"I thought so, and bugs too, but now I'm not so sure. I guess this bug spray was a waste. Dick?"

I answer without turning my head. "What?" The river's soothing and I'd rather look at it than them. There are no ripples, but the knowledge of where the ripples should be is hypnotic just the same.

"Are there supposed to be animals here?" Chernobyl asks.

"I don't know." Old Jed hadn't told me much about this place. "This mist finds its way into your mind and you can never be sure what you see is real. There might be animals, or there might be only droppings. Who knows. Does it matter?"

"Yes, it does," Captain Eight says. "If anything's going to drop down out of a tree at me, I'd like to know about it."

"Do you think the goths know where they're going?" Chernobyl says after a silence.

"I hope not," Captain Eight says. "Otherwise they'll be laughing their asses off at us while we stumble around blind."

"That wouldn't be a problem if you'd just triangulate again," I say.

"'You can never be sure what you see is real,'" he mimics. "Besides, by the time we get to where they were, they'll be somewhere else." He points to the eight ball on his chest. It's faded from black to a medium gray. "I also need to save power."

❀

"Do you hear that?" Chernobyl says. We're still sitting on the rock, looking at the river. It hasn't been that long.

"What?" I snap. All my instincts are telling me there's a deeper rhythm here, something vitally important, and it's bothering me like a sore muscle. I'd be able to figure it out if people would stop interrupting me.

"That buzzing noise."

"I hear it too," Captain Eight says.

Glaring at them, I realize they're right. It's a slow, building buzz, like distant thunder or a spectacular hard drive failure.

"Let's get moving," I say for no real reason except that the sound puts me on edge.

"Where?" Captain Eight says. "We've got no idea where we're going, no idea where to go, and my ass is starting to chafe."

"Why don't we follow the river?" Chernobyl asks. "We're bound to hit something important."

❀

I wish I knew more about what the Isles are like. I could probably have saved myself the trouble of bringing along company and wandered around by myself just fine. Old Jed said that the Isles have a habit of bringing you where you need to be, but if that's true they're currently being bastards.

The river narrows, then widens into frozen rapids, flecks of water hanging in the air, and finally settles into a wide, glossy sheen like a laminated business card. The mist seems thicker, and there's the hint of a breeze coaxing it into the suggestion of shapes. The river continues to cut deeper into the ground and we're forced away from it by impassable terrain. After cutting through a patch where bright blue flowers sprout from nearly every vine we reach a cliff. Hundreds of feet down lies the ocean. I stare at it for a moment before realizing we've most likely reached the northern end of Animus. The mist is really starting to get to me. The cliffs dimly visible on the other side must be Anima.

"Well, this is new," Captain Eight says. "And brilliant."

"We go left," I say.

❀

Captain Eight is singing "Jungle Boogie" when we find the bridge. It's nothing more than three ropes stretched across the chasm between islands. One to stand on, two for balance.

"Oh *hell* no," Captain Eight says. "I know how this works. As soon as we get to the middle, we'll be ambushed."

"It's not that bad, honestly," I say. "Right, Chernobyl?"

He doesn't respond. We both look at him.

His eyes are blank and he doesn't have his backpack anymore. I don't remember him setting it down.

"Chernobyl?" I say, waving my hand in front of his face.

He blinks back to consciousness. "What?"

"Where's your backpack?"

"It's right here—" He pats his shoulder, then spins around, trying to get a good look at his back. "Where'd it go? I remember buzzing, then laughter, and orange flowers..."

"Do something for him," Captain Eight says, like it's my fault. He sounds worried but is really starting to irritate me.

"I can't. It's the mist."

"Fine. I'll do it. Captain Eight, purificate."

Nothing happens. "Damn it," he says. "I could have sworn it was a real word."

"I'm fine," Chernobyl says. "Just a little groggy. Let's get this done and get out of here."

"There's no way in hell I'm crossing that bridge," Captain Eight reiterates.

"Fine," I say. "Stay here."

I'm about a third of the way across when I hear "Captain Eight, levitate." Seconds later he and Chernobyl float by.

"I thought you had to conserve power," I growl.

The words echo.

Captain Eight flips me off.

There's no ambush.

❀

We stumble across another moai. This one, its eyes also in deep shadow, has a moss toupee and is staring at a tree. Sitting there between two rocks that might have been placed there by intelligent activity, or might have been there since the beginning of time, it looks constipated.

Chernobyl points at the tree. "You think something's up there?"

"I don't know," I say. "Why don't you check?"

"Sheesh. I was just asking."

I focus on the moai, searching for anything that could help us. There's a diamond grid etched on its left temple but nothing else. I rub at the stone skin in case it flakes away. My hands start to tingle, then the feeling passes. I hear a noise like stone grinding against stone.

"You should have checked," the moai says in a deep, gravelly voice.

I jerk upright and realized my eyes are closed. I open them and the moai is gone, seemingly dissolved into the mist. Damn hallucinations.

Chernobyl is up ahead, looking up at Captain Eight. The captain is clinging to a tree trunk, reaching for something tucked in a branch. "I think I found something," he says.

"Good job," Chernobyl says. "What is it?"

"I think it's a bag of Cheetos."

"Don't eat it," I yell. "Don't eat anything you find here." My words are distorted by the mist.

"If you're trying to call dibs," he yells back, "you're too late."

A few seconds later: "Damn it. It's not Cheetos. Just some kind of weird dried vegetable chips."

I sigh. At least we're getting closer.

❀

For some reason Captain Eight is now, for lack of a better word, taunting a moai. They've been hounding us for hours. Every time we round a bend or duck under low hanging branches, there they are, looking supremely uninterested. I just know that apathetic façade is a lie and if we can just get the timing right, we'd catch them staring at us. Part of me knows how crazy that sounds, and that part is what's keeping me from doing anything stupid.

This one is about twice the size of the others. It's wedged into a cluster of tree trunks all sprouting from the same roots like an explosion of bark, and despite its obvious weight it's already been lifted several feet off the ground. It's clearly arrogant, head tilted upward to avoid our smell, and manages to convey in no uncertain terms that the obscuring mist is the only reason it can even tolerate our presence. Bright flowers on long, dropping stalks pay homage from nearby bushes, bushes almost as tall as I am. I want to knock this thing into next week myself, but at least I'm not squaring off with it in a crazy boxing stance.

"Captain Eight, invigorate," he says, puffing himself up and dancing around. The mist swirls closer around him.

"Do you really think you can take it?" Chernobyl says.

"Why not? It's just a big, fat head. Chin like glass."

"That looks more like stone to me."

"Leave it alone," I say. Old Jed hadn't mentioned anything beyond not looking them in the eyes, but I don't want to find out the hard way what they can do.

"One, one-two," Captain Eight says, throwing punches in

the moai's direction. "One-two-eight. Five. Take that!"

Chernobyl looks at me with raised eyebrows and evidently decides this is the best entertainment he's going to see in a while. "Get him, Captain," he says. "Dodge, weave, rope-a-dope!"

Spurred by the encouragement, Captain Eight strikes pose after professional wrestling pose, then lunges forward and wraps one of the surrounding tree trunks in a clinch. "Your henchmen can't save you now, you big fat head."

"Suplex him. Kimura. Make him tap."

Not wanting to participate in the upcoming debacle, I scout the area, looking for clues. We're still after the goths and haven't found much. I don't expect to find much here. The Isles are changeable, and only show you what they want you to see. However, if you please them well they can take you to unimaginable heights of power.

I shake my head. Those aren't my thoughts. They sound like mine but they aren't. It's the mist, rolling into my head and speaking with my voice. I shake my head again. That didn't feel like my thoughts either. I'm a private eye, not some stoned mystic channeling advice from the 45th century.

While I argue with myself, recognition of the silence slams into my brain like a runaway cargo truck filled with ping pong balls. This isn't right. It can't be right. Oh, this place looks like a rainforest, with the dead leaves and the soil and the rocks and the leaves and flowers and grasping trees, but that's just an act and underneath it all, if the damn mist would just clear up, is something vast, impersonal, and very grumpy at being disturbed. I sit down on a non-malevolent rock and look up. Halfway hidden by the mist, the shapeless shadows of the leaves and branches scowl back.

"Why don't you look me in the eye, huh?" I hear the captain say.

"I think he thinks he's too good for you," Chernobyl says.

"Then why don't I just climb up there and *make* him look me in the eye?"

Belatedly realizing what's about to happen, I lurch to my feet and nearly trip over a loose cluster of exposed roots. When I find them again, Captain Eight is clinging to the moai's nose like an orangutan with curly hair.

"Shadows?" he says. "Shadows?! Look at me, you pansy!"

A rumble fills the air.

Chernobyl, at the base of the moai's trees and looking up, hasn't noticed me sprinting toward them. "Uh, Captain?" he says. "Maybe you should stop."

"Stop? I've got him right where I want him."

Captain Eight braces his back against a tree trunk and punches at the moai.

"Still won't look at me, huh?" he says.

I'm several yards away and definitely won't get there before he does something really stupid, so I start casting a spell. It's a simple one, just a focused wave of force. The mist around me cools, like air before a storm.

"Still hiding in shadows?" Captain Eight says. "You bastard."

"I really think you should stop, Captain," Chernobyl says. "The flowers..."

He's right. The drooping flowers on the tree trunks are slowly turning away. Captain Eight, lost in a superhero fantasy, doesn't even look.

"Captain Eight..." he starts.

I launch the spell. The mist fills my mind, tasting like cotton, and turbulent patterns mark the shock wave's passage through the air, gathering momentum like a spectral fist.

"Illuminate!"

The shadows hiding the moai's eyes are stripped away, revealing an angry, bloodshot glow. My spell hits Captain Eight, knocking him out of the trees just before a lance of light sears a white hole through the mist where his head used to be. He stares for a moment, then picks himself off the ground. His hair smokes slightly.

"I thought I told you leave them alone," I say.

"I didn't think it would do *that*," he protests.

Chernobyl steps between us. "Well now we know. No harm, no foul, right?"

"Fine," I say, but inside I'm gloating. Not just because I saved the captain's life and we all know it, but because I've finally gotten the chance to knock his retarded ass flat out on the ground.

❀

For lack of any better option, we head in the same general direction as the beam of light which nearly decapitated Captain Eight. When we find another river, it's a godsend. Not only that, but we find more traces of goth activity, so we have to be on the right track. While the walking is much tougher, with vegetation crowding the shoreline like hobos at a food kitchen on Thanksgiving, the mist is much thinner. Captain Eight solves the plant problem with "Captain Eight, dehydrate," and a huge swatch of jungle simply dies.

He stumbles a few minutes later, and Chernobyl lunges forward to keep him from falling into the river. With Chernobyl steadying him Captain Eight sits down slowly, making an attempt to clear the withered husks of dead plants out from under himself.

"You're almost out," Chernobyl says.

"Then juice me." His voice lacks its usual frat-boy joie de vivre.

"You might want to stand back," Chernobyl tells me.

"Why?" I say.

"Let him stand where he wants to stand," Captain Eight says. "If it fries him, too bad."

I reluctantly back off and peer over the banks. I think I saw fish down there, spurts of color flirting with the mud and flitting around exposed stones. I'm tempted to reach in and grab one, maybe demand some answers, but something tells me that's a really bad idea. The tang of lightning in the air catches my attention and I look back.

Chernobyl is glowing light blue, and holds a gray metal disk in both hands at arm's length between him and Captain Eight. It's about the size of his palm. Abstract shapes in the mist spiral around him. "Ready?" he says.

Captain Eight brushes his hair out of his face and nods.

"Good. On three. One, two—"

"Captain Eight, integrate!"

Chernobyl bows his head in concentration. The glow shoots into the metal disk, making it fluoresce orange. The harsh light doesn't change the surrounding illumination. Instead, it funnels toward Captain Eight, enveloping him in a pulsating cocoon. It builds to blinding intensity, then, as quickly as if someone flushed an astral toilet, it swirls into the captain. Chernobyl drops to a knee. The ground between them is covered in soot and the mist, which retreated from the display like it had been burned, jealously closes in.

"That took a lot out of me," Chernobyl says to no one in particular. "I must be more tired than I thought."

Chapter 15

The goths we're watching have been pinned down by the river, fighting off unseen assailants. At least, that's what we think they're doing. There's no reason for all the shouting and flailing otherwise. We peer over a small embankment at the group of six misunderstood teenage rebels who are industriously trying to set the rainforest on fire. But each time their spells set the trees ablaze, the mist condenses and chokes out the flames. I almost feel bad for them, but watching them run around like headless chickens is pretty funny.

If I squint a certain way, it does look like there are menacing figures in the mist, darting between trees and using vines and moss for cover and camouflage. I can even almost hear the zwipping of blowdarts. But the group ahead might also simply be having a falling out with their imaginary friends from the realm of shadows.

"Should we help them?" Chernobyl says.

I don't know why I'm surprised at the question, but I am. "The state they're in, they'd shoot us as soon as look at us," I reply.

Captain Eight belly-crawls forward.

"What are you doing?" I say.

"There was something rotten under my leaves. It tried to crawl into my hair."

"As long as you're not trying to eat it," I say.

"Are you sure we shouldn't try to help them?" Chernobyl repeats.

I look again. The pierced faces are panicked and extremely pale even though their makeup has long since worn off. They frantically cast spells in every direction while one, an overweight girl with a pink Mohawk, tries to maintain a semblance of order. The others aren't in any mood to pay attention. When people are frightened for their lives, rational thought goes out the window.

"Do you think they can see us?" Captain Eight says.

"Nah," I say.

We have an excellent hiding spot. A blue-ish yellow group of vines has not only wound their way around all the nearby trees, but they've branched around each other as well. Smaller, puke green vines wrap around them like wrestlers going for a submission, and the resulting net is extremely efficient at catching leaves and other detritus. The end result is more a mattress of rotting things, but regardless of what you call it, it's good cover.

The bottom of the mattress extends a few feet over our heads. The damp, earthy smell is quite pleasant and despite the heat and humidity a sense of camaraderie billows up from the ground. It's probably the mushrooms.

Blue-white nets hang from grey disks fringed with orange and perched on slender stalks. Their spores would probably be illegal in most countries, but what can you do? The feeling's a welcome change.

"Want to get closer?" Chernobyl says.

"Nah."

"Why not? They're not fighting anything real."

"What if they are?" I say. "Do you really want to draw whatever it is's attention?"

"They could tell us something useful," Chernobyl insists, "like where the rest of them are. What do you think, Captain?"

"I thought this place didn't have bugs," he says.

"What does that have to do with anything?" I say.

"One's staring at me. It's small and white and has fifteen million eyes."

"Just ignore it."

"I think it's plotting my demise."

"Then squish it."

Farther up the river, the goths' situation gets even more desperate. Their defensive circle is extremely tight, a few are even back to back, and they're about to be forced into the river.

One unlucky soul, a kid in a black trench coat, takes the first step. His combat boots hit the water. I don't hear a splash, but there's a look of absolute horror on the guy's face and he spins around wildly before exploding into dissipating mist. We look at each other and add "stepping into the river" to our collective list of things not to do.

It doesn't take too much longer for the other goths to suffer the same fate. After waiting a few minutes to see if anything else happens, we inspect the battle site and, finding nothing useful, continue on.

❀

We keep following the glassy river for lack of anything better to do except trust the Isles. The lack of a firm direction irks me but I don't see a better alternative. Captain Eight still refuses to triangulate again. The bonhomie has faded and we're paranoid about not touching the water. The mist grows choking and thick. I could swear I see figures dancing around us, taunting and teasing and just out of sight. If bugs were missing before they're certainly here now, making up for lost time with vengeance. The droning, buzzing, biting pests come from everywhere at once and Chernobyl's grinning like he's been personally vindicated.

"See? I told you there were bugs." He pulls his bug spray out of his pack and sprays it on triumphantly. "Good thing I brought enough for everyone, huh?" He pulls out two more cans and tosses us each one.

"I thought you lost your backpack," I say, "back at the bridge."

"It's obviously right there," says Captain Eight.

"Now that you mention it, I vaguely remember that. I

thought I was dreaming...” Chernobyl looks at his backpack speculatively.

“If you lost it then, why is it here now?” I glance around suspiciously. The figures in the mist are no closer than they have been.

“Isn’t it good enough that it’s here?” Captain Eight says.

After some discussion, we conclude that none of us are thinking clearly and that it would be a good idea to tie ourselves together. Who knows what might happen if one of us wanders off. Chernobyl pulls some rope out of his pack for that purpose.

While I vaguely realize this is a sign of something wrong, I’m not really worried.

“Amazin’, ain’t it?” Old Jed says, “trampin’ around out nowhere with nothing on’t but two sideshows. Are y’at least makin’ pay?”

I stop immediately and look around. Captain Eight, who’s tied to me, gets jerked backward and swears. I look around, the mist obscuring everything more than a few feet away. A tug on the rope gets me moving again.

“Oh, y’ain’t see me. The mist’ll drive ye mad. If’n ye must, I’m behind ye.”

I look. There’s nothing. “What do you want?” I say.

“I want you to shut up,” Captain Eight replies.

“Na’ much. Just to know if’n my protégé, Dick Richards, is doin’ swingin’ his nuts out here in forsaken land.”

“Go away.”

“I’m trying.”

“Sorry. So...how much pay *do* ye be makin’? If’n I could cut me in.”

“Go away. I’m hunting goths.” And apparently hallucinating.

❀

The rock formation spanning this particular river looks unstable as hell, but we make it across without problems. On the other side, Jed starts laying into me again.

"I don't want to hear it," I say. "I'm doing this for a reason."

"Oh, beggin' pardon. If'n that be?"

"Saving the world."

"Ye daft fool! What in do y'expect t'accomplish? Assholes to buttplug, shit piles up, and there ain't nothing to do fer it."

"I know, I know. You always drummed that into my head."

"Ain't nobody and no one worth struggle."

"Yeah. You always took the easy way out."

"Easy? Easy?! Ye think crossin' the river of souls be easy? After all I've learned ye this be thanks? Ungrateful whelp..."

One some level I know I'm arguing with myself, but that doesn't make the hallucination any less real.

"Thankful for what? I couldn't go back home after what you dragged me through."

"If'n I recollect, ye were running away initial-like."

"If I'd have known..." I say, not willing to concede the point.

"Bullshit," Jed says. "Ye wanted out. I just painted the door."

"Then why? Why show me? You don't stick your neck out for anyone, remember?"

He chuckles. "If'n I was goin' soft. If'n I didn't think ye'd survive. If'n y'and I seemed kin."

"We're nothing alike," I say, and try to ignore him, focusing instead on an upcoming break in the trail. If the island doesn't drive me crazy, Jed will.

"That be obvious," he says. "I wouldn't waste myself running' around butt-fuck jungle."

❀

Captain Eight's lost in his own personal ode to joy, singing at the top of his lungs. I'd catch up and punch him in the head but at least it's drowning out Jed.

All around is jungle, jungle, jungle, and more mist. We've run out of bug spray, no longer have any idea where we're going, if we'd had any in the first place, and Chernobyl's stopped talking completely. All he'll do to communicate is gesture and make faces. I want to smack him too. We might have been here for minutes, days, months or even years. With the light never changing and the mist everywhere, it's impossible to tell. I hope we'll still be in time to stop the Goth, but the larger part of me no longer cares.

Along with insects and Old Jed, I've started to hear animals off in the distance. Birds, mainly, going quiet when we get close. I'm also arguing with myself, trying to convince myself that no, losing myself here wouldn't be a good thing. I hadn't expected to be out here this long and it's grinding on me.

Captain Eight sings the chorus to his made-up song for the millionth time and that is it! I'm going to murder him. I surge forward, fist cocked and arm drawn back. The rope jerks me back—I guess Chernobyl doesn't realize he's supposed to run too, the idiot—and I fall backwards. I grab the rope in front of me and yank. If I'm going down, so will he.

We roll down a hill—add that to the list of important details I failed to notice—in a big ball of swearing and ineffective hand-to-hand combat. Twigs, leaves, mold, moss...it all flies by in a misty blur and occasionally rocks stab up from the ground. I hope Captain Eight cracks his head open. That will save me the effort of ripping his throat out with my teeth.

We land on sleeping bags. I only notice when I launch myself at the captain and, instead of flying forward in a haze of fury, I fall down again as the ground slips out from under me. The impact does knock some sense into me. Just enough to help, but not enough to really matter. I look around and voila. Sleeping bags, some canteens, and even a tent. The mist is much less thick now; I can almost see like normal. After the anger drains I feel pumped up, superhuman. The buzzing outside matches the buzzing in my head, and it feels right. Comfortable. I remember Captain Eight is an ally. Temporarily.

"What the hell was that for?" Captain Eight says.

"This is a camp," I say, changing the subject. "Still set up.

That means we're close."

❀

The ground, which starts out sloping gently, steadily grows steeper until we climb more than we walk. I start to cast a spell which would let me climb like a gecko, but the mist congeals around me and the clammy feeling puts me on edge, shakes some sanity back into me. Captain Eight has the same problem when he tries his powers and we climb as best as we can. It's arduous and dizzying, which for some reason pisses me off more. Before this trip, I'd thought there was a limit to how angry I could get.

"Why ye be out here again?" Old Jed says. I can see him now, and he's floating next to me, wearing his travelling clothes. He looks, like he always did, like an escapee from a low-budget sci-fi Western.

I pull myself onto a thick branch and search for my next handhold. There's nothing but moss and vines which don't look like they'll hold my weight.

"I fucking told you. Saving the world." I'm not sure if I sound sarcastic and I don't know if I mean it to be.

Captain Eight mumbles something back at me but he's drowned out by Jed.

"Why? What good could possibly come of?"

I see a crack in the rock which might be a good finger hold. "I'm getting paid, aren't I?"

"Ye're on yer last legs. Literally. There—"

"I know, I know. There are millions of wonders in the universe, none of which bring a man back to life."

I swing myself up and scramble onto a path. Here's some walking. The path ends after a few steps. Damn it.

"Cut yer losses. Survive. Start anew. All do't. That's all ye can hope fer."

I turn to punch him but he's no longer there. I nearly overbalance off the ledge.

"Watch it, asshat," Captain Eight calls down.

I don't think I've done too badly for myself and when this is over I'll ride off into the sunset. Tahiti still sounds good. I'll even take David with me.

There's a kid still naïve enough to think the world could be a better place. It never will be, but if he's going to be disillusioned he might as well be surrounded by women in bikinis when it happens. The kid deserves at least that.

❋

We finally climb high enough to be out of the mist. Thankfully, Jed's nowhere to be seen or heard. The three of us pause on a wide ledge to catch our breath and our bearings. I don't know how long we've been climbing, but we still haven't cleared the tops of the trees looming over the forest like hippies on stilts. But we're finally clear of the mist.

Around us, life refuses to give up, every crevice with even the smallest hint of soil hosting a shrub or flower. The places that can't, give it their best shot with lichens and moss.

Able to think more clearly, I feel the sense of urgency return. We need to stop the Goth from fucking up the world for everyone else.

Chernobyl points at something and I look. I don't believe it at first, but there's definitely smoke coming out of the mountain we're climbing.

"A volcano," I say. "Wonderful. Marvelous. Let's all go jump in."

Chernobyl shakes his head and points again. Several hundred feet above us there's a trail winding its way up this side of the mountain, and making their way up it is a group of worn, bedraggled goths. Most are shouldering bulky, tan packs, and they aren't moving too fast, but something about them indicates purpose. If they've found what they're looking for, we've found them.

"Excellent," I say. "Let's take them out."

"Wait," says Captain Eight.

I'm so far beyond exasperated I'm ready to toss him down the mountain. "What? What can you possibly say that will keep me from annihilating them?"

"Since we don't know whether they've found the immaculatum, why not follow them to make sure? Then we can take them out."

I grudgingly concede the point. "Fine," I say. "But no funny business. If you manage to blow me off the side of this mountain I *will* come after you."

Captain Eight gathers Chernobyl and shepherds him along. At the far edge of our ledge there's the beginning of a trail. Hopefully it's the same one the goths are on. I don't think they've noticed us so we have the element of surprise.

But not for long. Between Captain Eight's flamboyant personality and Chernobyl's voodoo zombie shuffle-run, we're about as stealthy as an elephant with Tourette's. I'm not doing so well either. Despite "clandestine" being part of my job description, everything that could possibly make noise when stepped on finds a way to end up under my feet. When we catch sight of the goths several minutes later they're only a hundred and fifty feet away. They've just crossed a rope bridge across a deep cleft, and are about to disappear again around a corner shrouded with bushes.

The angle is awkward, but I'm certain I can get at least one of the bastards. With a burping splort, a bolt of gray vomits itself from my hand and tumbles slowly toward them. I can't help but stare. Whatever I was trying to do, it definitely wasn't that. It hovers in the air like a hungover UFO, wobbling slowly toward its targets. All the goths are out of sight before it hits the rock face, which explodes in a shower of pebbles and moss.

"What the hell did you just do?" Captain Eight demands.

Rather than answer, I release myself from the rope binding us together and hurtle after the goths. The buzzing becomes a throb, then a boil, but I'm too busy buffing myself with spells to care. The berserker rage builds like a flashfire, becoming sheer, unadulterated joy. Suddenly I know that I've lived my whole life for this: hunting down assholes with no need to play by the rules. The siren song of power and rage flows through me, becomes me. I can feel my body burning. The bridge, filled with half-rotten planks, feels like concrete beneath my feet and the air turns cool and fresh. A small mental alarm says this is the mist but that feels right too.

The goths are nowhere to be seen so I hurtle on, ready to unleash everything I have. There's a well-defined path and I follow it through twists and turns. Small purple flowers hug the ground like commandos. The path finally straightens and I sprint the last few yards up the slope and over the lip of the volcano. Far below, molten lava burbles in its cradle. Green rock veins the entire place. Immaculatum, I presume. The closer it is to the lava, the more it glows.

The only way down is to climb from ledge to ledge. Everything else is crumbled away. Simple rope bridges with wooden planks enable easy crossing, and goths are everywhere. I don't see the group I'm chasing but the focus of activity is a camp halfway to the lava's molten surface where they're quarrying the immaculatum. I take it all in at a glance, then grin in anticipation of the upcoming mayhem. It's showtime.

There's a shout as I'm noticed and the bridges fall away, their support lines cut. The odds are fifty to one against me with no cover, which is exciting. Bringing my wards to full strength, I cast Joachim's Cudgel.

A solidified disk of air hurls toward them at thirty miles an hour. It catches two goths by surprise, turning them into pierced, fleshy pancakes. Next!

A group of three goths, casting a joint spell, aren't paying attention to me. Perfect. I hurl another cudgel their way. A dim warning sounds in the back of my mind but that only infuriates me more. These buggers are going to die.

Predictably, the electric blue fingers of the Devil's Touch arc toward me. Is this the only spell they know? I wouldn't put it past the Goth. I almost wish I could set them straight, but as long as they're shooting at me they're going to die.

I launch myself outward, at an angle toward the next ledge, just as the rock behind me melts. Acrid smoke follows me down as I cast yet another cudgel, this time using the air around my feet. In the spur of the moment I aim for a third ledge, where a goth exiting a Porta-Potty is trying to hastily erect magical defense. I rush toward him like a surfer of doom. All his effort really does is slow me down enough to get a look at the light fading from his brown eyes as his chest is crushed to splinters. An ankh amulet dangles from his neck. Eternal life indeed.

A barely-felt impact knocks some sense back into me. What am I, a one trick pony? I know thousands of spells, all ready and primed. I do the three shimmying half-steps of the Prism Dance and suddenly there are seven of me, one for each color of the rainbow. The split of fourteen eyes all seeing superimposed at once overwhelms me at first but this is vindication. Fuck you, Jed. You thought I'd never master the spell.

(I'm briefly aware that all of this power, it's not mine. It's the Isles and the mist conspiring to push me so far past my limits they'll claim me forever, but I don't care.)

Thinking that only one of the Dicks is real, the goths try to concentrate fire. Too bad they're all real. Like thoughts underwater we attack, each spell a supernova in a surreal nursery of stars. Ice shards, rock plumes, sonic phantoms—every nightmare imaginable and more. I am Death, destroyer of worlds, and I do not suffer fools to live.

Their counterattack begins in earnest. I laugh, enjoying the metallic thrill of near misses and the effervescent hiss of my shields deflecting yet another attack. This is *life!* Slinging everything you have at something which gives as good as it gets. Die, motherfuckers!

I run, I float, I fly, and there's nothing and no one my equal.

Then the pit drops out of my stomach and I'm treble-visioned, then double, and finally myself. It's impossible but...I'm losing. The inside of the volcano looks like it's lost a bout with explosive acne and there are human dust shadows on the caldera walls, but I'm still losing. I'm more curious than alarmed at the idea and I pause a moment to see what the ants opposing me are up to. Those left are all on the ledge with the main camp, huddled behind canvas tarps. Two are trying to capture my attention by launching spells, but they're far too tired for the Devil's Touch and their other spells are easily defl—one hits me in the gut like a lead bowling ball.

I drop, realize belatedly I was still floating in mid-air, and the fury returns in full force. I mindlessly unleash wave after wave of energy, but the canvas dissipates it all with the telltale purple glow of adamantium. The air gels. They're casting a portal out of here.

I. Will. Not. Fail!

With a well-aimed mental boomerang I knock out the two giving cover fire. They plunge into the lava like crash test dummies but I still can't get past the adamantium.

"Cowards!" I scream.

One of the goths, from under the protective cover of the canvas, flips me off.

Captain Eight and Chernobyl finally appear over the lip of the volcano, dull swatches of color against a light blue sky. Excellent. Destiny *will* prevail. After all, we're saving the world.

"They're cowering behind adamantium," I yell.

"Great," Captain Eight yells back. "Now we're all fucked."

"Chernobyl, adamantium is radioactive!"

He doesn't move.

"They're getting away. DO SOMETHING!"

Getting the picture, Chernobyl raises his head and arms. A slight pressure wave, and the canvas begins to glow. First a dull purple, then a piercing violet, and finally a painful black-light white just visible enough to grate chunks off your brain. I unload everything I have left. Captain Eight finally gets something right and unloads too.

Striking the obligatory pose, he yells, "Captain Eight! Obliterate!"

❃

The entire crater becomes a shimmering void of angry red and bubbling white. Everything quite literally ceases to exist, recreated moment to moment by sheer force of will. A hurricane of impermanence whittles fake memories out of thick air, exhilaration merges with oblivion, and in the distance I see Captain Eight dragging an unconscious Chernobyl, one arm around his neck, through mud. I turn the other way. The world swivels like a hyperbolic snowglobe and I see the portal the goths created.

"Come on!" I yell, hoping my words reach him. "We don't have much time!"

Willing the portal to stay open, I lunge for it. As I get closer I slow, getting mired in the sparkling fog, weighed down by a greedy universe.

With a snap, the universe decides I'm not worth it and I fly forward into the featureless gray between planes.

Something isn't right. I get an image of a door slamming shut and my mind threatens to fly apart. Oh shit. The portal's been closed on the other side.

One last piece of Jed's wisdom fights its way to consciousness. It's impossible to stay stuck between worlds and people almost always end up where they're going, but only after making absolutely sure that the first exit is truly and irrevocably closed.

There's only one thing to do in a situation like this:

Curl up tight and hope you bounce.

Chapter 16

The next few hours, days, weeks? are filled with neon dreams. Dwarf slave labor toils away in forbidden, eldritch mines under the harsh whips of network weathermen. A seventy-foot-tall gnome forged from used magazines, ancient DVDs, and duct tape chases bedraggled elven refugees across a river into a forest of glass and steel. Death, astride a pale horse, canters up to souls built into a wailing wall of flesh and asks them if they have the time to take a marketing survey. "On a scale of one to ten," he says, "with one being one and ten being ten, how would you rate your current situation?" A familiar laugh comes from everywhere at once.

Above it all, a monochrome cat with a glassy-eyed smile grins benevolently down. It wears a clown nose. It waves its hands in a complicated fashion and a world appears. The cat winks, then devours the world whole and explodes into red confetti, leaving behind a scent of lavender. Like a phoenix out of her own ashes Raven, with angel wings, rockets for the edges of the universe without so much as a look behind.

"Is he awake or does the knave feign sleep?" someone says with a voice like barbed wire.

Hard to tell. Most likely, not all of him made it back. This second voice is the pillow used to muffle dying screams.

"Very well. Inform me when his sojourn behind the veil is lifted and complete. Fate's raiment will never compass patience."

Feathers explode and I'm running through an endless stream, splashing across water like a treadmill. Old Jed, wearing a leather trench coat and brandishing a golden ankh, turns into my father and speaks in stereo:

"What does pride matter anyway?"

A dark figure beheads him and salutes. No blood.

"Is he dead?"

That's the wrong question to ask.

Chapter 17

I wake up in a foul but hollow mood. It's a lot like waking up in a bathtub full of ice and a ten-inch long surgical scar, but the organ that's been removed is the one which lets you be pissed off. Judging from the creepy birthday wallpaper and the unmistakable motel smell I've been "rescued" again by the mimes. Fabulous. I swear, but my heart isn't really in it.

I don't feel that weak so I prop myself up on an elbow. The bedspread shows Wynken, Blynken and Nod attacking a space station with their up-armored flying shoe. Magic burns through my blood like acid and the only thing that stops me from setting the bed on fire is a sudden and overwhelming surge of apathy. The mimes would just buy another one. Or more likely, the Unspoken would theatrically flourish and every apartment from here to Antarctica would find itself bedecked with spooky furniture. There's no point in pointless action.

I blink and find myself staring at the ceiling. I'm now too weak to lift my head and my pillow smells like sour sweat. My arms, despite being silently cursed to within an inch of their lives, refuse to move. The past few weeks flash through my head, but instead of the fury I expect there's only the dull tones of sadness and apathy.

I know it as suddenly as if a switch was flipped. Now is the time to leave this clusterfuck behind. No finishing up business, no getting more money so I can set myself up even better elsewhere. Just go. All the unanswered questions—the extent of Ablesoft's involvement, how the Goth managed to smuggle in so much firepower, getting the chance to punch Lord British in the face—nag at me but, but try as I might, I can't make them seem important anymore. This has cost way too much and regardless of anything I do the goths and the mimes will be at each other's throats for a long time to come and I don't want any part of it. I went to the Isles, did their dirty work, and now I'm going to take David and if anyone even thinks about starting any problems, I'll personally hold their head underwater until they drown.

❀

I wake up again. A female mime with close-cropped hair, a black waistcoat, and top hat stares at me from the foot of the bed. She sits with folded legs by an IV stand, perched in the air like a phantom.

"What do you want?" I say.

She stands quickly, and in the same fluid movement removes her hat and bows. She straightens and the hat remains where it is, upside-down in front of her, and she taps it like a magician. After waving an invisible wand, she pulls out a small, dark blue bag and flips her hat back onto her head.

The Unspoken would like to convey that, despite your failure, you are not personally blamed.

That's real nice of him. I take the bag.

Given the circumstances, your effort was nothing short of monumental and you prevented our foe from acquiring all the immaculatum he desired. Your assistance with the upcoming campaign is also requested.

I glare at her.

You will have compensation, of course, and also be given time to recover.

With all the sarcasm I can muster I say, "Tell the Unspoken that while I appreciate his generous offer, I'd rather break into Hell than help him clean up his own mistakes."

She bows again. *Of course.* But I can see the accusation in her eyes. *They're your mistakes too*, it seems to say.

After she leaves I lever myself out of bed and limp toward the bathroom. My right hip feels slightly dislocated. I open the bag. As expected, a considerable amount of astarum lies inside. More than enough to retire on. My reflection is drawn, haggard, with highlighted raccoon eyes and stubble.

True to form, the Brotherhood's supplied me with a razor and shaving cream. There's also ample amounts of face paint and an industrial-sized bottle of mouthwash by the sink. Figuring I might as well take the hint, I swish and gargle for a full minute. Either it's not actually mouthwash or the inside of my mouth is also numb.

I'm wearing a striped shirt but, thankfully, no suspenders. I guess my clothes didn't make it through. Good riddance. I don't need any reminders.

I set the bag of astarum next to the mouthwash and stare at it for a long time. I'm very tempted to pour the glittering dust down the drain as a final fuck you, just so they won't think to look me up years down the road and ask for one more favor.

But I do have David to consider. Money talks and the kid deserves a nice life after all he's been through. I weigh the bag in my palm. For how light it is, I wouldn't be surprised if it floats away.

❋

The mime motel is a hive of activity. Mimes everywhere prepare for war. A grim faced, monochrome defender of reality juggles invisible balls as if his life depends on it. On the balcony below, two test each other's invisible walls. Interspersed like beetles, the Count's remaining men stride purposefully with blank faces. From the looks of things, the centuries-old agreements keeping most of humanity blissfully ignorant of the magic around them are about to be brutally torn apart.

Once again I'm glad to be leaving it all behind.

I don't see David, but with his curiosity he's probably in

thick of things, making a nuisance of himself. I amble through the motel, humming to myself. Peeking into the conference rooms, I see the Count Fantabuloso place a large metal case on a table. The clasps click open.

"Unbeknownst to those of Gothic manner, I have acquired a fine selection of AlterReal weaponry. This case, and those akin, were missed during the raids."

The mimes nod appreciatively as the Count reveals an empty case, filled with foam and the outlined shapes of weapons.

I move on before I'm noticed.

At the front desk/command center, two polite but firm mimes let me know in no uncertain terms that if I'm not part of the solution, we will have problems. Figuring I might as well go with it, I park myself on a bench outside, watching the ebb and flow of bodies.

When my patience wears thin, I flag down an esquire.

"Do you know where David is?" I ask.

The esquire looks at me blankly.

"You know...scrawny kid, reedy voice..."

"Oh, I thought you knew. The ceremony's about to start and a mime was supposed to escort you there."

Ceremony? What in the world has David gotten himself into this time?

"What mime?" I say.

"He was supposed to be outside your room."

I thank the esquire and, sure enough, when I head back upstairs to my room there's a mime waiting outside my door. I clear my throat and he exaggeratedly jumps to attention, contriving to appear like he's been there the entire time.

"A ceremony?" I say, suspiciously.

This way, please. He tosses off a goofy salute and pivots sharply on the balls of his feet.

On our way to the shadow world gateway, the hordes of Tipton commute past us as though nothing's happened. Disdain rises in my throat like bile and I'm glad when we step through the door between.

Once again, Tipton is rendered in harsh shadow and unreal light, all color and life unwillingly compressed into monochrome. My guide silently, and unnecessarily, warns me not to speak. I'm saving everything to bitch at David if need be. The inhabitants of this Tipton—grotesque, roiling phantoms held together only by malice—seem fitting. More accurate. More real than the polite charades of everyday life. I'm too tired to be truly on edge. Just put some sense into David, I remind myself, and then we can both be out of here.

After passing through a novelty neighborhood twisted into a schizophrenic north pole, we pull up at a row of three doors.

Knowing what's about to happen, I watch my guide closely. He knocks silently and a glow ripples out from his knuckles, like he's tapped the surface of a fluorescing pool. Theatrically, he reverses his hand and rests his palm flat against the surface. The ripple reflects inward from the door's edges, coagulating around the outline of his hand. From there the glow spreads to the entire door, then spills out onto the floor.

Satisfied, he opens the door, then salutes me again and waves me through.

❀

Once the coruscating rings disappear mimeworld fades into place. The surreal cartoony black-and-white accuracy surrounds me and I'm not at all surprised to realize that, despite coming via a different route, we arrived at exactly the same place. It's probably a security measure. The countryside full of doors stands proud, tall, bucolic and mute. Olygandr, at the end of the hedged path, is barely visible in the distance but my guide heads the other way.

He's relaxed, is even smiling, as if this is his natural environment. I wonder what could twist a human being that much. At the second hill he veers left off the path, and, predictably, we end up in front of one of the omnipresent doors. It appears to be wooden, with four inlaid panels arranged two long over two short, and the doorknob's on the left side. The doorframe is missing, but a small fifth panel, a rounded rectangle at the door's apex, is carved with a picture of a blade of grass in bas-relief.

The mime plucks a blade of grass from the ground and holds it up to its carved counterpart. The panel flashes green, a startling and intense splash of color against the monochrome world, and I feel rather than hear a click. Nodding, the mime opens the door, revealing a shimmering portal of light. He steps through. Not quite sure what to expect, and not quite sure I care at this point, I follow him.

The trip is instantaneous and uneventful, and I emerge in balcony seating, which curves in a semi-circle and hangs in a gray void. The nothingness beyond is so vast and mind-numbingly blank it has texture, tantalizing hints of existence and reality. Despite my best intentions I'm awed. The emptiness tries to devour my mind like a black hole and I quickly cast a charm to protect myself against it. My brain rebels against the strain and before I'm sealed safely away I sense a ravenous hunger which sets me on edge.

There's color here, but not much. Just a hint of muted brown.

The balconies could hold over two-hundred people but, except for one figure standing front and center, are completely empty. My guide excuses himself and for lack of anything better to do I head to the front.

As I get close enough, my hackles rise. The figure, though its back is turned, radiates smugness.

"If you've done anything to David," I begin.

The Unspoken turns to face me, head swiveling like a marionette. *Talking is permitted here, if frowned upon.*

"Where's David?"

The ceremony has already begun. He would have been glad to know you came.

Now I do get angry, and it feels like the emotion bleeds out into the void. "What are you talking about?"

The Unspoken gestures out into the void. Below us is a small cobblestone path, perfectly straight and straight-edged, leading to a circular platform. That's where David stands, back turned, head bowed. Surrounding him at some distance away from the platform, eight identical mimes float in a pattern that tugs at my mind, but I'm still too tired to focus correctly. I start to yell, to demand what the hell he thinks he's doing, but my voice is frozen.

I apologize, Mr. Richards, but this rite is sacred. The Unspoken bows and turns back to the scene below.

A silent gong reverberates and David's head rises. His back is still turned and I can't see his eyes. In a clear, but still reedy voice, he proclaims, "My name is David Anthony Clark and I accept the Rite of Initiation."

Belatedly realizing just what he's about to do, I try to vault the railing and knock some sense into his thick skull, but my body won't move. The Unspoken studiously doesn't react, but I can feel the radiating smugness. Bastard.

Six of the mimes begin to move. The ones directly above and below David remain motionless.

In the maddening silence, David speaks again.

"Henceforth, I sacrifice the word 'I.'"

The three mimes that form a triangle above David rotate clockwise. The three below, also forming a triangle, rotate counterclockwise. The two stationary mimes begin to spin in place. My gut sinks and bile rises in my throat as I recognize the pattern. They form a double tetrahedron, the Merkaba, with David at the center.

"This one willingly sacrifices voice."

David touches his throat. All eight mimes do likewise without interrupting their movement. David tilts his head and continues in mimespeak.

This one willingly sacrifices memory.

He touches his head and is again mimicked perfectly by the floating mimes. With unmoving expressions painted on their faces, they pick up speed. I struggle against the control the Unspoken imposes, but am too weak to break free.

This one willingly sacrifices all.

David throws up both arms and the mimes increase speed until he's lost in a gray blur nearly indistinguishable from the void. The Merkaba is a multi-pointed crystal, a pinched compass needle pointing directly to damnation. What the hell is David thinking? Doesn't he know this is the same as suicide? You *never* throw your hat in with something that might not let you go.

Without appearing to slow, the rotation stops and the Merkaba disappears. Nine mimes, identical in motion and dress, file back along the floating, cobblestone path. Shock follows disbelief is followed by a cold, crystalline rage. The Unspoken, satisfied at gaining another puppet, turns to me.

Pity is irrelevant when one moves past the merely human, but this may be of comfort.

The Unspoken looks out at the void and almost seems to be struggling for words. I say nothing.

Most of those who join the Brotherhood do so to run away from empty, wandering lives. All those lost and lonely who believe in annihilation.

"And you dangle some kind of community in front of them and wait for them to bite?" I say. Apparently the ban on speaking has been lifted.

I give them options. It is, as always, their choice.

"You're no better than the Goth." I want to do something, I honestly do. Throw a punch, threaten his life, blast him, but it all seems so utterly pointless. It's not fear and it's not apathy, more an overpowering sense that there is absolutely nothing I can do. I hate the feeling, but I hate myself more.

The Unspoken continues. *The one you called David was instead headed toward something. In the end, that may be his salvation.*

"Really?" I ask sardonically.

He wanted to be like you.

That lands like a punch to the gut. I take the bag of astarum out of my pocket and stare at it. Numbly, I loosen the drawstring. Even in this washed out, subdued world, the dust inside still glitters like a vibrant night sky. Not knowing exactly why, I decide it's never been worth it.

With a nod to the Unspoken, I launch the bag over the railing. The glittering dust spills out into the void, tracing a thin line of night into an infinite tinged-with-brown gray, and fades into a cloud of dying stars.

I don't know what I expect, but the Unspoken's head tilts back in silent laughter. A mocking, reptilian, and above all *knowing* smirk flits across a monochrome face.

❀

Back in my room, I try to convince myself it's no big deal. It's not like I'm David's father. Then, because I knew he was drifting in this direction, I wonder how he could have possibly thought I'd approve, why he'd thought this was anything close what I'd do. But I know.

After the Hobolympics, when he did show up to pester me, David kept asking about my motivations. At that point I couldn't back down and it was obvious that "Put all assholes in the same room so they kill each other and nobody else" somehow became, in his mind, "Sometimes protecting people means playing bastards against each other." That apparently morphed into "Protecting others requires sacrifice." I figured he'd grow out of it but then he got captured by the Goth.

I want to blame it on the Brotherhood, on the Goth warping his mind, on Raven for not saying the right thing when he needed to hear it. The thought of Raven thumps like lead on my skull. She dies saving his life and he repays her by throwing it away? Now he won't have a chance to grow out of it.

And the way the Unspoken casually tossed those words out.

The more I think about it, the angrier I get.

The rage feels good, and for once it's not magical fury. Jed was right. Once you start on the Path there's no turning back. Regardless of what you think you want, you'll eventually leave your world behind.

I lean on the nightstand. The clock on the wall, a grinning, black and white cat, leers at me so I blast it despite my headache. It falls to the ground in pieces.

There's a knock on the door. I don't answer.

Whoever it is knocks again, sparking a flare of irritation. I didn't answer the first time. Don't they have enough sense to leave me alone?

On the third knock I think about smashing the door in their face, but it opens inward so I settle for shouting, "What!"

"I'm sorry. I didn't know if you were in here." It's Chernobyl.

"What do you want," I say.

"Can I come in?"

"Is Captain Eight with you?"

"No. Can I come in?"

"Fine. Sure. Why not?"

I keep the chain latch secured and open the door, making sure he's telling the truth. I'm in no mood to deal with the captain's antics. After confirming his absence, I let Chernobyl inside.

"What do you want?" I repeat.

Chernobyl looks at the wreckage of the wall clock but says nothing. "I just wanted to say, well, thanks."

"Thanks?" I say, incredulous.

"Yeah. Thanks. For saving Captain Eight's life."

"I didn't do it because I wanted to." That's the unvarnished truth.

He stares at me like he's trying to read my face. Taking another deep breath, he continues. "I also wanted to say thanks for putting up with him."

I nod curtly and wait for Chernobyl to leave.

"He hasn't been the same since he got his powers and not

many people..." Chernobyl trails off and scratches the back of his neck. "He's not the most stable person anymore."

"Was there anything else?" I say, looking meaningfully toward the door.

"Yeah, actually. The captain and I are siding with the Brotherhood. The Goth needs to be stopped and we'd appreciate your help." Chernobyl raises his arms, palm out, before I can respond. "Whoah. Your eyes flashed blue and gold there for a second. You're not going to nuke me, are you? I'll fight back."

"I'm through with this bullshit," I say. "Now are you going to leave or do I have to throw you out?"

"I understand," Chernobyl says after a pause. When he reaches the door he says, "Good luck," and closes it quietly behind him.

I narrowly restrain myself from bursting through the door and throttling him.

Chapter 18

The next few days are surprisingly peaceful. I don't have any money, but it's easy enough to cloud people's minds and make them believe I do. I'm using more magic than I have in the past few years, but the song of power's died down to manageable levels. Maybe some part of me broke and it all leaked out. I don't trust it, but I don't question it too much either. Signs of the upcoming disaster are everywhere. Pawn shops associated with the esoteric have closed their doors. Boutiques and salons with elven connections are suddenly sold out of all but human-made products. The dwarf-run garbage routes run late. But none of it is my business and that feels damn good.

I wonder if the residents of Tipton have any idea their world is about to break apart. Something I once heard from dwarves suddenly rings very, very true. Human beings, believing themselves masters of technology, have become extremely arrogant. With nothing and no one to oppose them, most instinctively believe themselves lords of the universe. I look forward to the shock when their world completely and utterly falls apart, when humanity isn't the only one with guns to wield and an axe to grind.

The TVs in the bar I'm in are playing one of the innumerable daytime talk shows. The hostess, little more than a photogenic smile hovering above a well-tailored business suit, is interviewing a self-help guru clad in flowing clothes. Halfway through his spiel regarding the power of positive thinking, the station cuts abruptly to Tipton News 7.

It must be important; this guy is obviously at the top of the news anchor food chain. His toupee alone could make or break an intern's career.

Closed captioned words scroll across the bottom of the screen. "This just in...Authorities are attempting to contain a gang altercation in shiveson district. Two as yet unknown groups are fighting in and between the abandoned warehouses. For more informartion, we take you live to Mackenna Jules, the News 7 reporter on the scene. Mackenna?"

An attractive female reporter, wearing a functional but sporty coat, embodies excited concern. Behind her, police pods block off the multi-lane walkway entrance to a court. She opens her mouth and the words appear a split second later.

"Thanks, John. Behind me is Dialed Court, where authorities are attempting to subdue to rival street gangs. There's not much information yet, but police chief Nathaniel Hawking says the situation is contained and arrests will be happening shortly. Just behind me the police cordon—"

"Holy shit what's THAT!"

Mackenna glares at the camera, furious at the interruption, but the cameraman zooms past her to where a cloud of dust is settling.

A misshapen human form, dressed in the height of Gothic fashion, picks itself up, roars and charges on all fours toward the camera. It easily vaults the police barricade and runs through the police pods parked in front. The flashing lights, however, remain superimposed on the scene, revealing them to be digital effects the studio is adding for dramatic effect.

"I don't believe this—"

"Don't talk, you stupid bitch, run—"

The view jerks as the cameraman abandons his equipment. Two pairs of feet can be seen sprinting for safety. The flashing lights, now completely disembodied, hover like UFOs.

Luckily for them the transformed goth has just enough humanity left to understand cameras. It gently lifts the camera, still on live feed. Despite the unibrow; sharp, sloped forehead; and drooling, demonic grin, the face is recognizably female. Red streaks show where piercings had burst through flesh.

I wonder if, back when this goth started learning the "dark arts," she realized this is where it was all heading. Eh. If she'd been suicidal enough she probably wouldn't have cared.

The automated closed captioning makes a valiant attempt, but all it can come up with is "Gbrkthpprakcis," which I guess is the abomination equivalent of "Hi, mom!" The view blurs and the camera is once again on the ground.

Seconds later, gloved hands drift into frame, pick up the camera, and center it on a black-and-white face. A mime, disheveled and bleeding, slowly and hypnotically wags its finger.

"Times are changing. Don't be fools," the caption reads.

When the station cuts back to the top-dog anchor man, he leans over and throws up behind his desk. His toupee falls off. They cut to commercial.

Some wag says, a little too loudly in the deathly quiet, that this is just a ratings hoax. Finishing my margarita, I quietly see myself out. No one notices.

❀

I could leave, but I figure a few days spent seeing how things play out can't hurt anything. I might come back eventually and having a heads-up could be useful. As I thought, the war simmers quietly for almost a week, then explodes. There are too many people with too many grudges for someone *not* to take advantage of the opportunity. I even see the Mantato Tuberfruit's potato-clad "associates" wandering the walkways and courts. True to form, they wear front-and-back LED-board signs proclaiming that the end is near. The panicked masses ignore them to the point where they have to defend themselves from getting trampled, but the expressions on their faces make it clear that they consider clotheslining panicked bystanders to be one of their job's definitive perks.

Tipton's mayor declares a state of emergency and, after a personal visit in an armored car that's nearly taken out by a pixie rocket launcher, the governor does so as well. I guess seeing an angry pixie come screaming at supersonic speeds toward his bullet-proof windows in a whirlwind of sparkles and wings overcomes his disbelief. And a close encounter with a small dwarven war machine, with its glowing eyes and eerily realistic teeth, is enough to make the staunchest secular humanist reach for lithium.

I'm struck again by how this is no longer my problem. It still feels damn good.

❃

After stealing Gummi bears from an automated kiosk, I consider going back to my office to tie up loose ends but there's really no reason. For all I know, one of the magically-enhanced aluminum foil hats from my trophy shelf will save someone's life. Even the butter churn might be useful. The panic's largely faded. I'm in one of Tipton's upper floors and, while the walkways are filled with less than the normal shoulder-to-shoulder press common to civilized areas, most people go about their business with the expectation that someone else will get things under control.

I do have to hand it to Tipton News 7. They've already found a way to turn the magical war into a gimmick. The chaos and violence are bubbling from the Under up—the only exception being Ablesoft's headquarters, which last I heard is under heavy siege—and some enterprising graphic designer has created the Apocalypse Thermometer. A stylized outline of a skyscraper, its lower regions are filled with frothy red for the floors considered part of the warzone, a cool sea green for those that aren't, and a yellow glow at the disputed boundary. When the red boils all the way to the top all hell will, quite literally, have broken loose. It's visible on every available screen, interspersed by cutting-edge, live-action breaking-news reports, and there's even an interactive version on the website.

The closest interplanar portal is several floors down, at solidly yellow depths, but like the idiots around me I'm not too worried. Unlike them, I have good reasons not to be.

I stash the Gummi bears in my coat's inside pocket. At first, the centuries of buried hatred and resentment exploded upward, consuming nearly eighty floors on average, but after that any further extension of the warzone required planned maliciousness rather than unfocused rage. Centuries of wariness about pushing humans too far are hard to overcome. In some places, the police and National Guard cordons are even holding their own.

It doesn't matter who wins or loses; Tipton will never be the same.

I wrap my travelling cloak around me and make sure my travelling pack is strapped tightly to my back. I'd found both in the wreckage of a retro-neo-hippie store. I have enough dried food for a few weeks and four water canteens to boot. A knife hangs at my belt, but as for everything else I'm travelling light. Various tools and crystals are tucked away and my hat, its wide brim interwoven with mithril thread in protective designs, probably makes me look like some kind of space hobo, but soon enough I'll be away from people who'd care.

Moving into partially abandoned levels, I head down a stalled escalator and into a semi-functional food court. Everything that isn't broken or smashed still has power and the fast food signs beam down on the broken glass and upturned furniture like bemused but still benevolent gods. A few teens, thrill seekers by the looks of them, play death metal heroes in the wreckage, boasting as to who has the least fear. Like being fearless will do any good if goblins get a hold of them.

Past that court and down a wide hallway whose walkways run in gasps and spurts, I come across a shopping center turned strategic choke point. A makeshift armed compound's been built in the center of the four-story court. Surrounded by glittering window displays, it lurks like a constipated mushroom, all rough angles and angry black scars. I can't tell which direction it faces, but someone with a wry sense of humor has glued colored underwear to the largest flat surface, creating a penis with wings. Sigils and runes dot the remainder and I sense enough wards and traps around the court that I know there's no easy way through. Unfortunately, where I need to go is on the other side.

I could backtrack and find another way around, but I'm in no particular hurry. Plus, the men standing guard outside are the Count's. Even discounting the official uniform it's hard to hide that distinctive, angry slouch. I pause just before the closest ward and watch. Sooner or later someone is going to walk a patrol.

When they do, it's a pair, one in the black jeans, combat boots, and sport-mesh shirt of the official uniform and the other in street clothes. I guess the Count's held a recruiting drive. I can't see the pin on the uniformed one's ski mask, but knowing the organization I assume he's an esquire while the other is a lower rank, possibly a private. They both wield submachine guns, which hang from shoulder straps in an overly casual way. Hip holsters hold sidearms. They aren't particularly stealthy, but that probably isn't the point. The stealthy bastards are out wreaking havoc on goths, commando-style, and these two's job is to ensure the safety of the compound by becoming targets if necessary.

The patrol spirals around the encampment, first clearing the ground floor then disappearing at intervals as they make a circuit of the second, third, and fourth floors. They cautiously pick their way through the junked-up hallways and balconies. When they come close enough that they can't reasonably mistake me for a goth and start shooting, I step fully around the corner and raise my hands above my head.

"What the hell are you supposed to be?" the private asks a moment after they both train the barrels of their submachine guns on me.

"I'd like to pass through," I say.

They shoot glances at each other. "And what makes you think you have a snowball's chance in hell of doing that?" the private says.

With my hands still over my head—I'm playing nice—I reply, "Because I know the Count."

"You and every two-bit wannabe. You don't look like a goth or some kind of goblin freak and that's the reason we haven't shot you yet. Why don't you turn around before that changes, punk?"

I look at the other one, who's obviously enjoying the confrontation. "I thought *you* were in charge, Esquire."

He raises his chin, appears to consider me. The private keeps talking.

"Yeah, and he told me to shoot your dumb ass if you so much as blinked funny, and that was back on the ground—"

"Take off your hat," the esquire interrupts.

"My hat?" I say.

"That's what I said, ain't it?" he replies.

Slowly, and with raised eyebrows, I comply.

"Man, put them eyebrows down before I shoot them off your fat head," the private says.

"Shut up," the esquire snaps. "Look at his face."

"I am. That's where I plan on shooting."

"No, dumbass, *look* at his face. It's the Priestess."

"Oh yeah. There *is* a resemblance."

They lower their barrels slightly. No longer directly threatening, but still ready.

"Come with us, the esquire says. "And by the way," he points to his insignia, a silver plus sign with solid circles in the upper corners, "it's Knight."

❀

While waiting for the Count to see me, I learn two things from listening to people talk as they walk by. First, the Count's been cut off for a few days but is about to make a push to rejoin the main Brotherhood forces. Second, the loudmouthed private who, incidentally, is also the one guarding me, really thinks he's that funny. All attempts by his parents to smack it out of him via the back of his head have apparently failed.

I ignore him as much as possible. From the inside, the makeshift fort is even more constipated than it looks from the outside. The corridors, the rooms, even the lighting, everything is angular and cramped. The room they're holding me in is devoid of anything but a makeshift bench welded to the far wall and a squiggly bulb dangling from the ceiling. The bench can't be more than six inches wide so I opt to stand. The private, now that it seems I'm no threat, is leaning against the doorway, smoking a cigarette and annoying the shit out of everyone who passes by. They're all buzzed about finally getting some combat action, but at least half of that has to be the chance to listen to something besides the private.

"You're lucky," he tells me. "Another second of your lip and I'd have blown your head clean off. Then again, they'd probably make me clean up the mess so you might have been safe anyway. Hard to tell."

I remind myself he's irrelevant. A few hours, maybe a day or so tops, and I'll be out of here. Instead of responding, I mentally plan my itinerary. Most of it's hearsay, and most of it's from Old Jed, but I might as well. My first stop will be the bustling marketplaces of Damask, nestled low in the husk of an old forest. The oldest, towering trees, hundreds of feet high, are treated every six months with an alchemical compound that hardens the bark and gives them a deep red sheen. It also prevents them from growing new limbs from the stumps of the old ones that have been pruned away, but as it doesn't otherwise harm the trees, even the elves tolerate it. High above those bronzed stumps a tapestry of leaves and vines filters and cools the harsh sunlight. They say there are families who spend their entire lives in the clouds, cultivating the multicolored plants and weaving them into tableaus of gods and goddesses visible from the ground below.

The markets themselves are built from treated wood and lay open to infrequent breezes. Even constructs that only appear in a mad wizard's wildest dreams can be bought here, but most important are the quartz singing bowls lovingly crafted by the hidden artisans of Dei Sera. Less than an eighth of an inch thick, when played correctly they put even choirs of angels to shame.

(Make sure you get the double-bulged model that sings at D-flat below middle-C and F-sharp above, Old Jed had said.)

The Damask markets abut a harbor of clear green where giant cargo ships fitted with astral sails lie moored to wide docks. Ill-tempered captains argue about cargo manifests and the sails are mostly for show, technology having advanced quite a bit over millennia, but when the sun sets, the canvases, interwoven with gold and mithril thread, erupt into blossoms of fire. They're always happy to take on another deckhand, moving port to port like a hitchhiker across space and time, and even if they won't appreciate it when you jump ship, there's nothing they can do about it.

After buying protective clothing at the orbital city of Trichar'nak, find a way down to the surface of the frozen methane plant it orbits. It used to be a gas giant, but millions of years ago a rogue star flung it out into an impossibly wide orbit. The gas that wasn't stripped away condensed and froze. When it was colonized by the long-dead Illi, they named it Zili'ach'thra, "a cripple's hope," and strip-mined the dense and precious gases to build their city and fuel their empire.

No one has any reason to go to the surface anymore, but there's always at least one daredevil looking to build a reputation and willing to pilot a solar glider down. Touch down as close as possible to 77º 13' 5" N and 35º 26' 12" W. There, where the distant sun always shines at diminished noon, you'll find the frozen falls. Auroras dance feverishly here like whirling dervishes entranced by ancient visions, and caress any travelers with wisps of light.

(Jed said once it was more like molestation. Even with protective clothing, the charge in the air would make you taste metal and set your pubic hair on edge.)

Take the singing bowl from Damask and bury it to its mouth in methane slush. It may take a few tries to find the right spot but when you do, you'll know. If the bowl is well made, and not one of the cheap knock-offs hawked by unscrupulous merchants to the unwary, it won't crack. Instead, it will sing loud and pure, a tidal wave of sound enough to bring you to your knees and sear itself forever into memory. Wait for the purple aurora lightning to strike, then for the song to fade away. If done well, the quartz will be shocked golden and turn harder than adamantium. The bowl will never sing again but if you look inside while in a dark room, you can see an echo of the aurora resonating inside.

It won't last forever though, so as soon as possible launch the glider on a magnetic thermal, return to Trichar'nak, and by hook or by crook find your way to Mktn, a planet so ancient its very name is guesswork and superstition. Its inhabitants spent millennia transforming its surface into one gigantic, interconnected earthwork. Massive labyrinths become sculpted deserts whose size and artistry put even the most accomplished Zen rock gardens to shame. Elaborate structures of colored glass, always transforming in intricate patterns, are powered by machinery still in perfect working order and continually trace symbols of power in four dimensions.

No one knows what happened to the builders. When their sun began its slow, bloated slide into oblivion they simply vanished, leaving the work of a planet's lifetime behind. The sun grows larger every year and soon, as stars reckon time, it will engulf the planet and explode, but for now that distant destruction may as well be an angry hiss across eons, entropy's evil eye hungrily stalking a world it's poised to devour.

Most days it hangs low in the horizon, but on midsummer's eve it rises as far as it will ever go and forms a perfect line with the world's two diminutive, desiccated moons. On that day, find the Labyrinth of Souls. This name is just the latest of a long line of names, but the labyrinth still retains its original power. Follow it and inside you'll see many alcoves in the walls where statues used to be, before the time of fragments and shards. Ignore them until you find the one, close to the center, where "R.C." has been carved in crude, jagged letters underneath. Place the golden quartz bowl here, at the crux point, and the sacred geometry will turn the entire planet into a resonant chamber. There is only one other such spot, several miles away, and it is here you must reach by sundown. Then, when the solar wind is strongest and the whole planet is literally thrumming with power, stand on the cracked altar of dust and pray. As soon as the swollen sun disappears below the horizon, a planet's worth of hope and dreams, all the power of a vanished race, for one excruciating moment, will be channeled into you.

Most die. Many more go mad. But in that one instant when your soul is rattled loose from its mortal cage you will see what most choose to call God. If you survive the return trip, the howling dogs of time will no longer be able to track your scent. You will not age, you will not get sick, and you will not die. You are now immortal, or close enough that it makes no difference.

Don't go looking for the golden quartz bowl. It won't be there, having been consumed by the power. Instead, as you stumble off the dais, there will be a small shrine to the left where planeswalkers through eternity have left offerings of thanks if it struck their fancy. The shrine is ancient, but palpably new compared to the planet itself. More riches than some will see in a lifetime are gathered there, but take nothing. These gifts are only left by survivors, and immortals have long memories, becoming quite attached to the way things are supposed to be.

I stop at the end of the oral history. From there, there are a million different places to go. The marshes to the east of Ghost Elven lands, or so I've heard, contain a flower. Its extract, when properly prepared, vastly increases strength and metabolism, but at the cost of a shortened life span. Then again, if you're never going to die of natural causes, that won't matter.

Other points of interest include the relativistic particle refineries of Jinari-ni-Sokar, orbiting a black hole; the master-weavers of Ug; the sea-coral of Anatheymia; and the mirrors of the Hite Plains. I could go on, but as I do my upcoming journey sounds less like an escape and more like a grocery list. I can even imagine the infomercials.

"Get your vintage Issakar chronoscope now! Able to sense magical disturbances at sub-Planck lengths, no discerning planeswalker should be without one. Imagine the frustration of your enemies when they realize you can not only find, but shift to planes with nanosecond coterminancies! Best of all, we've rummaged the ruined cities for you, so instead of running for your life, you can explore the imaginable!" Was everything already tainted by greedy and grasping familiarity?

When Count Fantabuloso is ready to see me I'm more than ready to talk. The private guarding me is also my escort and he insists on using his nonexistent social skills. He actually dares me to try something and then calls me a punk when I ignore him. How insecure can you get? After passing through an angular corridor I'm led to a squat room where the Count is seated at a metal table, flanked by two esquires standing guard with submachine guns. Other than a few grease pencil marks on the walls and exposed light bulbs overhead, the room is completely bare. Count Fantabuloso looks unhappy in the bleak light, but is nonetheless in his element. He's also wearing the street uniform of his men; there's no room for frippery here. However, as if protesting the lack of his usual sartorial stylings, two long black feathers are pinned by the shafts to his rolled-up ski mask, and nine silver circles in an offset grid mark his rank. The Differance Stick lies across his lap.

He looks more comfortable than I've ever seen him, a warlord to the bone. A warlord who's futilely tried to train people to peace, but a warlord just the same, and never more comfortable than in a war.

"Milord!" the private barks as we enter. He stands to attention. Kind of.

The Count dismisses him with a wave and focuses on me.

"Perhaps returning prodigality has been severely overrated," he says. "Regardless, welcome to the Flying Fuck."

That would explain the underwear dick with wings. A part of me is impressed he managed to say it with a straight face.

"Nice to see you too," I say. The two esquires standing guard stiffen at my tone.

"Perhaps you were ill or under-informed," Count Fantabuloso continues, "as to the terms of our agreement."

"It was at will. Terminable by either party at any time."

"I am not speaking of contractual provisions, but rather of creation. A Count's prerogative may elevate, recognize those who tread uncommon ground. When last we met, brought low by loss, I'm sure offense was mutual. Nevertheless, the stands of honesty command their due."

Really. I always figured we were business partners at best, and now he claims he was thinking about giving me a title in his organization. More likely, he wants my help and is trying to bribe me for it. Too bad I have absolutely no interest in that whatsoever.

"However," the Count continues, "dress as yours intends elsewise."

There's no need to confirm the obvious, so I say nothing. I'm leaving, so why should I care?

The Count shuffles some papers in front of him and waits. When I continue to say nothing, he stands slowly and leans forward, filled with quiet intensity.

"Does this menagerie of fools mean naught?" he growls. "This endless mazing maze of ill intent, confounding all dreams to perish abed? A restless rage only sleeps for so long."

Even now, he still believes. "Do you really think you can force everyone to stop fighting?" I say, incredulous.

"Forever never lasts, but long enough."

"Look at you," I say, tired of the bullshit. "Just look at you. Your organization is fried, you had to ally with the Brotherhood to keep yourself alive, and now you're so low on manpower that you're letting anybody in." I can tell that stings his pride.

"The future," the Count says slowly, "is worth any prize."

That does it. After all that's happened I'm not going to be lectured. Besides, I doubt he believes this schlock himself. It's probably just a show for his men, something that sounds good which lets him sleep at night. He's tried, it's obvious he's failed, and now it's time to move on.

"Just because people believe in fantasies," I snap, "doesn't mean they need to die for them."

After a long moment, with his men just waiting for the order to cut me down, Count Fantabuloso sits back down and makes a decision. "If you wish to pass, like night water go. May you stand fairer in Fate's sight than mine, but before you scrub yourself from this world you should know what stains follow you behind."

He holds out his hand; a guard deposits something in it. He slides it across the table to me. It looks like an oversized pack of cards. What am I supposed to do with that? Play spades by myself when I get bored?

"Proceed," the Count says. "It's yours."

"No thanks."

"Repetition is not a wise man's folly."

Rather than piss him off more, I take the package and stow it in my inside coat pocket. I got what I wanted; damn the rest.

❋

An hour past the Flying Fuck and a few blocks from the portal's location, reluctant curiosity gets the better of me. I open the package and am mildly disappointed when it's just a thin pack of Tarot cards. Just the major arcana, the trump cards, in fact. A macabre, death-centered design adorns the backs, and when I turn the first card over, as expected there's the Fool, about to walk off a cliff, with a little dog barking either encouragement or warning. However, instead of the Fool's normal oblivious, dreamy look, there's a knowing, sarcastic grin. This Fool also sports a black turtleneck and is clearly the Unspoken.

It's a trick used by armies the world over. Soldiers get bored and play cards. Put important information on those cards and the soldiers will absorb it by osmosis. The Goth being a pretentious asshole, he's used Tarot cards and put me on the list. I shuffle through the cards and sure enough there I am, right at number II, the High Priestess, dressed in drag and gazing out at readers with a retarded look on my face. I thumb through the remainder.

Count Fantabuloso is in there too, as are a few of his barons and some mimes nearly indistinguishable from each other. When I get to number XVII, the Star, I stop to stare. It's clearly Raven, with her preferred purple hair, face painted on the naked woman with one foot in the water. She's smiling, of course, and looks like she's just about to burst into laughter.

My first thought is "Raven doesn't have a figure like that," followed immediately by "How would I know?" I feel a surge of elation at the possibility that she isn't dead, but then reality crashes in. Knowing the Goth's style, this is more likely an ornate taunt. Or, for all I know, the Goth isn't entirely sure what happened to her either and wants to cover all his bases.

I'm angry, shocked, confused, and, truth be told, hopeful, then immediately furious at the thought. The world isn't like that, with happy endings handed out like welfare. The emotions flash through me and leave a dull, thumping rage behind. This isn't over. This will never be over. It's time to let the Goth know that I'm not going to roll over, not for anyone or anything.

Chapter 19

It's surprisingly easy to sneak back to the Goth's headquarters. With all the scattered fighting throughout Tipton it's impossible for any faction to fully occupy any territory for long, and the deeper I get into goth territory the more infrequently I encounter their patrols. As for the last leg of the trip, they probably think the headquarters is as secure as it needs to be and doesn't require extra guards. The house itself certainly kicked our asses last time.

There are, however, signs of a skirmish in the long hallway just outside. Several of the screens lining the walls are cracked and in some places the walkways themselves have detached. Electrostatic links, ripped from the walkway surfaces, lie scattered like shrapnel. The double doors marking the entrance to the headquarters itself show dents but are otherwise unperturbed. Whoever tried to crash the gates failed.

The overhead lights flicker and an unseen electrical short silences the remaining advertising. The ventilation system shuts down, and the absence of its barely audible susurration reminds me just how alone I am. The place smells crispy, like bacon or burnt flesh. I cast every enhancement spell I know, preparing to wreak havoc. My heartbeat pounds in the back of my head and I welcome the extra strength the now-muted berserker rage gives me. I'll need all of it as long as I can keep my wits. Not that I have much of a plan.

I cast Joachim's Cudgel and send the plug of solid air slamming toward the doors. The doors creak and bend a little on impact.

Another try cracks them open, and a third knocks them far enough ajar for me to walk through. I step forward and see...

...an army. Spectral forms fill the courtyard beyond. They're everywhere. On the path, next to the fountains, even on the roof of the Victorian mansion. No wonder this place doesn't have human guards. Translucent and standing at attention, they manage to convey every kind of melodrama imaginable. Then they see me.

Rippling like drops of water, they charge.

I back into the hallway and prepare for the worst. I'd planned on ending it. Maybe I should have specified that *I'm* supposed to win.

The first spectral apparition emerges through the doors and I blast it with what some joker long ago dubbed Astral Caulk. It seals ghosts and spirits firmly into the beyond and has given aspiring badasses millions of opportunities to make retarded one-liners, usually before they screw up the spell and die screaming. Silvery bubbles encase the phantasm, harden into a waxy coating, and fade.

It's still there.

I back up slowly as more filter through the doors, advancing with bored expressions on their faces. They flood the corridor like zombies and those on the leading edge raise their heads to look at me. At eye contact, a shiver runs down my spine and I know exactly what they are.

They're not undead, because souls don't exactly die. Instead, they're a pale, twisted reflection of what souls actually are, the residue left behind when everything worthwhile has been drained away. These hollow specters advance like an intelligent swarm, fighting with their sheer presence, emanating the bitter despair of dreams that refuse to die before dragging someone else along with them.

I retreat before the press and am preparing to book it when I notice they're still entering one at a time through the gap in the doors. If they're physical enough that they can't float through the walls, they're solid enough to be hurt by fists and magic. And, I grin, physical enough to be hit by the magical turrets on the other side. Reinforcing my magical shields, I charge.

More accurately, I jump and cast Joachim's Cudgel, using the air around my feet, which rockets me toward the doors like an extreme athlete surfing across an angry Styx. When my invisible board slams into the spectral soldiers they stagger back as if hit by a strong wind. Good enough for me.

Dispelled a split second too late, the cudgel doesn't quite fit through the opening between the doors. I jerk forward like a crash test dummy, then go flying as the spell dissolves. I clip my right arm on the way through and land in the middle of the phantasms apathetically waiting their turn to step outside. There's no moment of surprise. They close on me immediately. The turrets open fire.

I roll to my feet, cradling my arm, and the room dissolves into a cacophony of light and emotion. When I'm unable to avoid their attacks, the touches of the spectral soldiers burn like ice and I feel my memories being devoured. Take as much as you want, I say, I have more than enough and business to take care of. The phantasms themselves diffract the turret blasts like prisms, giving me enough time to keep moving, stay on my feet, and avoid direct hits. The blasts don't dissipate, however, and continue to ricochet from specter to specter, multiplying and attenuating into ever finer threads of color, with me at the ever moving nexus.

It's scintillating, blinding, and I can't feel the ground through my feet. For all I know I could be floating. Superimposed on the soldiers' disaffected expressions are contortions of anger, sorrow, and pain, screaming and struggling impotently like insects bound and liquefied alive by a spider too vast to comprehend. Their movements seem to slow, but become more purposeful, almost desperate.

Now they attack with a searing need. At each unavoidable touch, foreign memories leave burning trails as they riot through me and dissolve. This, I sense, they feel is their chance, their one chance to change their destiny and live again. Instead of just devouring me, they also want to force their memories, their former personalities, into a living body that still has a past and a future.

For a brief moment I wonder why. Why would anyone, given the chance to send a message back from ultimate oblivion, choose to bequeath their suffering, their frustration, their fear? With each touch the memories of pain and despair build up, slowly draining my will to fight. Is this really all they have, all they are?

A feeling of ultimate heartbreak blindsides me and I almost lose myself in the festering, emotional miasma before I right myself, angrier than before. It's a nice trick but this is *not* how I'm going to die, turned into an emo puppet for a worthless master. I chase the foreign emotions away.

Spell after spell cascades from my fingertips as I fight the specters closest to me. Some, unable to bear the tension of remembrance, disintegrate under my assault, but there are always more eager to take their place, materializing from the whirling, psychedelic background. I hear laughter, and realize it's me.

After an eternity fending off these pale mimicries of souls, I notice they're only coming from one direction. Something solid is at my back. Reaching out cautiously with one hand, I find a door handle. At least, I think it's a door handle. My mind is going numb with effort and it feels like there are thick, woolen mittens on my hands. I try to open the door but it doesn't budge, and my lapse in concentration almost gets me killed.

Looking into the contorted faces of the spectral soldiers closing in, I give it everything I have, launching explosive flares into their ranks. The phantasms drop back half a step, enough for me to try the door again.

"Push, not pull," a familiar voice says, laughing at my idiocy. As I stumble inside and frantically kick the door shut behind me, one last touch steals the memory of where the voice came from.

❀

I expect a grand Victorian foyer, complete with winding staircases and delicately ornate chandeliers, but when sight returns I'm inside the servants' shed. The tiled pattern on the floor still does its best to crawl out of sight and I can hear howling like a muted hurricane through the closed door. I check the lock for a way to jam the door, but find nothing. Hopefully doorknobs are outside the spectral soldiers' realm of competence. A scratching skitter in the back of my mind could be an invading presence or simply nerves. I don't remember which end of the hallway holds the stairwell down, but I decide against opening random doors. The fist-sized dents bulging outward on all the ones I can see suggest they've been locked for a reason.

Reaching one end of the hallway, I look over the doors on both sides. The one to the left slowly swings open. I freeze, spells ready, but inside there's only a sheet metal desk, wooden bed frame, and a death metal poster hung crookedly on walls treated to resemble crumbling stone.

Feeling like I've just dodged a bullet, I turn to the door on the right. It's the only one with hinges on the inside, so it has to be the stairwell. I kick the door down. After a few good jolts, it clatters open and I descend into the industrial sewer system.

Despite his obvious insanity, I like the Great Mantato Tuberfruit's vision of the underworld much better than this one. Every surface here is still covered with that sickly green sheen, as if the metal itself is rotting, and while I believe there was music last time the current deathly silence is just as effective. Rivulets of slimy water ooze down the branching tunnels and circular portholes line the walls as far as I can see. All of them are open.

Ducking under a strand of seaweed hanging from the ceiling, I look into one. The coffin in this cell is tilted, leaning against the walls with its lid askew. Checking a few more reveals similar signs of struggle. My teeth grind together.

It takes longer than I'd like to find the ladders down through the next levels. Almost lost in the maze of slimy green, I wish the layout wasn't as good at thwarting invaders as escapees. I don't know how much time I have and I want to make all of it count. Constantly looking over my shoulder in case the spectral soldiers catch up to me, I have no idea how many times I cover the same ground twice. Everything looks identical and my head's still ringing.

Then I hear noises from up ahead. I hustle as close as I dare, then flatten myself against the wall. It feels as grimy as it looks and I peer around the corner. Nothing. I stand up, then whirl around, spells ready, as a light touch grabs my shoulder, but again there's nothing. I glance around hurriedly, in case specters start pouring out of the walls, then scan the floor and ceiling.

I swear to myself, then remove the overly friendly piece of seaweed from my hair. My heart's beating so fast I get lightheaded. A few deep breaths reel it in as calm as it's going to get.

The noise repeats itself, louder and with less echo. At least I'm closer. It's still too distorted for me to get a good bearing. Almost certain that I'm walking into a trap, I follow it.

I round a corner just in time to see a pale figure disappear into the floor. Eyeing the floor in what anyone else would call a paranoid fashion I advance, then breath a short sigh of relief. It's the ladder to the next level. I catch a glimpse of a head just before it moves away from the opening and it's definitely flesh and blood. Ghosts and zombies aren't in the habit of sporting Mohawks. I give the goth about half a minute, then head down myself. A feral grin spreads across my face. They won't know what hit them.

❀

Making sure my defenses are on full to protect against the Star of Neferth, I move from coffin to coffin, hiding myself from those ahead. Two-hundred-odd goths are focused on a line of screaming kids held bodily by their stone-faced compatriots. They struggle like they finally see the oncoming train at the end of the tunnel but it's too late.

Their inarticulate yelling and pleading is interspersed with shocked silence. I have a hard time advancing without getting seen by the onlooking goths and when I finally get a good vantage point there's only one victim left. She can't be more than fifteen, and wears a flowing white blouse above a knee-length, shiny black leather skirt. But while she thrashes as wildly as she can, she's held off the ground by each arm and leg, one impassive goth to a limb. Though she tries she can't even bite them.

The procession of goths takes her to one of the gunmetal coffins and orients her upright. She stops fighting and starts crying.

"Jake?" she pleads. "You know it's me, right?"

No response.

"Please...don't do this," she says. "Jake?"

When she's oriented perfectly to fit the coffin, the goths holding her pause. She goes out of her mind.

"Is this because I wouldn't give you that blowjob? I'm sorry—" she starts, but before she can finish the sentence the four goths toss her inside.

She hits the back of the coffin flat. Sheer, desperate horror flashes across her face as she vaporizes into gray mist. After a few seconds, the mist brightens to pure white and forms itself into another spectral soldier which shoots straight up, darting through the ceiling to join the army above.

As if with one mind, the remaining goths spread out until each stands in front of a coffin. At some unheard signal, they take one step backwards and soundlessly die.

Though I hate to admit it, I'm actually a bit frightened of dropping down to the altar level. I have no idea what I might find and jumping to another plane sounds extremely appealing right about now. There's absolutely nothing between me and the exit and no shame in admitting defeat.

My feet have almost decided to run for me when I realize those aren't my thoughts, aren't my feelings. I've seen worse, kicked worse in the balls. The need to piss my pants diminishes slightly and I feel pressure in my mind, tangible now only because it's eased up. There's an intelligence behind it, one calculating enough to realize that its first tactic didn't work and consider other options.

I creep cautiously toward the center of the Star and the ladder to the temple below. It's time to finish this.

"I wouldn't recommend that," the thing in my mind says telepathically. It's silky, conversational, and filled with self-satisfaction.

"The Archangel of Despair?" I say out loud. If I speak instead of think there's less chance I'll mistake its suggestions for my own thoughts. Given my state right now, the last thing I need is to give it more of an advantage. The throbbing pain in my right arm and ringing headache help me stay focused. A little.

"In the flesh," it replies, "as the case may be."

"And why wouldn't I?" I say, reaching the ladder.

I receive an image of the temple room, distorted as if seeing it through a fish-eye lens. Even though I know they curve, the edges of the circular stone altar seem straight. Thick, black smoke lounges in the center, expanding and contracting like it's breathing. Whoever they've imprisoned in the center is about to become host to a demon, and, well, there's no hope for the poor bastard. The summoning is too far along. And jumping down there will only make me a host to the demon as well.

"Of course, if you'd like to join me, I'd love the company," it continues. It doesn't mention the elevator, even to taunt me. It doesn't have to. If I'd gone through the main mansion and taken it I'd be able to access the temple level and have more options. Now though, I need to stall while I think of something. If it wants to talk, let it talk. Monologuing is occasionally useful.

"Oh? We'd be BFFs?" I say. Still staring down the ladder, as if it would make a damn bit of difference, I smell myrrh and burning fat. Smoke starts to climb.

The vision of the temple disappears. "It's been so long," it says, "and slang has never been my strong suit."

"Best friends forever," I say.

"I like that." It laughs like an uncoiling snake. "Forever... such a delicious idea."

"What would we do?"

"You're trying to probe my motivations? Let's just say it's the lack thereof."

Great. This is one of the *smart* demons. Think, Dick, think.

"I am the Archangel of Despair, after all," it continues.

"You want the entire world to write bad poetry?"

"That will be an added bonus, but no."

I look at the empty coffins surrounding me. Nothing but gunmetal and cheap lining, connected by invisible lines drawn in blood, they nevertheless might have something that could help. The demon interrupts my thoughts.

"By the way, your attempt to stall for time is commendable, but I enjoy nothing more than extinguishing hope. The coffins are fused to the floor and the lining is simply pretty."

"Pretty?"

"Just the right consistency to smother dreams."

The smell of burning fat grows stronger, is now mixed with sulfur. I push it from my mind. This self-styled archangel is trying to confuse me and I need my senses as clear as possible. My injured arm hurts as much as it helps. The nearest coffin is actually stuck to the floor and the lining, when I try to remove it, tears into useless shreds.

"There's no shame in failure," the demon says, consoling and saccharine.

"Oh?" The next coffin is the same as the first.

"And what would success do?"

Here it comes, I think, rolling my eyes.

"You've seen these people you're trying to save," it gloats. "They're shallow, petty, and foolish." I feel it rummaging through my mind and can't stop it. "Children rebel against the injustices of the world, but once that injustice tilts in their favor they defend it like maniacs. It eases the knowledge they're nothing but feral imps, slaves to greed, anger, and self-indulgence. As long as it happens to someone else, they're fine. It takes courage to be evil when you know the world is watching and most people don't have even that."

He is, quite literally, reading my mind but I'm not going to let him win. "And you're going to put us all out of our misery? You certainly know how to sweet talk a girl."

The smell of burning is getting stronger and I can feel I don't have much time until it gains so much control of my mind that I won't be able to stop it even if I figure out how. I glare at the room, willing something to appear.

"Of course not," it says happily. "I'm just going to take away your illusions, the excuses that let people kill themselves one day at a time."

"Some people might thank you," I say. What else is there? I pat myself down, but my pack was lost in the fight with the spectral soldiers and the few crystals I have on me aren't powerful enough to do anything besides tickle this thing. Oh, there's a package of Gummi bears in my inside pocket. I'm saved.

"After all the work I'll be putting into it, I certainly hope so. Or maybe I'll keep those spiritual band-aids. Despair has quite the bouquet when filtered through self-deception and willful ignorance. What do you think?"

Wait...there were shelves with hymnals in the temple, but not in the vision this thing showed me. It was lying and—now what? I still can't go down there, for exactly the same reasons as before. And now the summoning cloud is starting to billow into *this* floor.

"Very good. Very good," the demon says. "The truth will set you free."

"Get out of my head," I snarl.

"Why fight the inevitable?" it says, but surprisingly it backs off. The fear it's projecting becomes more manageable.

Suspicious, I quickly check the inside of my mind. Nothing but headache. Why would it back off? Especially when it should be increasing the pressure?

More out of the refusal to give in than anything, I head back to the ladder. Thick, black smoke spews out of the shaft, already extending several feet out. The coffins nearest the ladder are barely visible.

Then it clicks. I don't know how, but it does. The demon wasn't playing along while I tried to stall it. It was stalling me.

There's no one in the middle of the stone altar, just empty space. I know I have it; I just need to think it through. I lean against a coffin to steady myself.

Normally, the lack of a material focus, either a victim or a magic circle, will cause a summoning spell to fail. However, a strong enough concentration of energy can cause a small tear in reality. That's how portals to other planes form. Put the two together and...it's brilliant, actually.

A Star of Neferth this size, powered by the lives of thousands, could easily punch a hole into the beyond. And if that astral rip is created in just the right place, exactly when the summoning ritual requires a focus, the demon conjured would...bounce, for lack of a better word, off the rip. The smoke, smelling sweet and burnt, *is* the demon. And since there's no material focus to contain it, the summoning will never stop. It, quite literally, will fill the entire world and be able to do everything it boasted about. All the spectral soldiers will need to do is immobilize people long enough for the smoke to engulf them.

But that means there's also one way to stop it. I grin. Summoning spells *always* look for a focus. It's how they're designed. If I can give it one, the demon will be sucked into that and, since it would then have a physical body, it could theoretically be killed.

Even if I'm wrong, there are no other options left.

A coffin would do the trick, but I can't pull those out of their mountings. The scraps of cloth from the linings aren't solid enough. Of the few crystals I have on me, the quartz is my best bet. I damn sure won't make myself the focus. I want to kill the bastard, not become it.

I boost my flagging shields as much as I can, hold the quartz tight in my left fist, and charge. The burning smell almost overpowers me as I plunge into the cloud. I expect to be burnt by millions of floating cinders, but it feels liquid, almost peaceful. I have a moment's doubt that this is the right course of action—maybe this is something it had planted in my mind and wants me to do—but it's too late to back out. I start to choke, but who cares?

"Why?" the cloud whispers. "It's not like anything can make the world a better place."

I stumble to the ladder shaft leading to the altar room, almost falling in. As I double over, retching, it has just enough control over me to make me hesitate, and I'm bombarded with images. An abused wife defending her husband from the police. A soldier pretending bloodlust is patriotism. Drug addicts feigning redemption. Serial killers. Politicians. Day time talk shows. It's a mosaic of self-deluding animals reveling in their idiocy.

It's probably meant to be overwhelming and soul-crushing, but something inside me smiles. The demon's absolutely right. People aren't angels and most wouldn't even notice if it took over.

But unfortunately for this so-called archangel, I've had enough of being pushed around. I don't give a damn about the world but I'm standing right here, right now, with the power to stop it in my hands, and as it turns out I *am* the bigger bastard.

I look at the quartz crystal, its outline barely visible in the congealing smoke, then toss it aside. Instead, I pull out the package of Gummi bears. I hold it over the ladder shaft, grin, and then it's Bombs Away, Sucks to Be You.

There's a high-pitched scream of rage as the demon realizes

it hasn't stopped me. A tidal wave of force hammers against my mind and I collapse, puking my guts out. The nauseating cloud pulses violently, then is sucked back down the shaft.

It doesn't stop there, though. As I stagger to my knees, the room collapses around me. Wanting, needing more power to escape, the demon claws at the Star of Neferth itself, trying to consume it for sustenance. But since the coffins, as it so smugly pointed out, are welded to the floor, the only way it can do that is to tear the building apart.

I'm impressed that the Gummi bears can handle so much magical energy. Then again, they're indigestible in the best of circumstances and these are probably stale.

The chaos around me is small stuff compared to the chaos at the Jungian Isles and I figure I'll just shield myself and find a quiet corner to hide in until it blows over. I cast another protection spell and...nothing. My mind is out of ammunition. Click. Click. Click. Nothing in the chamber. I can still snap the fingers on my left hand—not that it helps even though I do find it a bit funny—and then exhaustion hits like a steamroller and I figure I might as well sit down and watch. It's not like I'm going anywhere.

The walls and ceiling crack open. Steel beams moan. Water from the pseudo-sewers above pours down, electrical wires split and spark, and the floor continues to buckle. Above it all, a piercing demonic screech screams defiance. Coffins tear themselves free with anguished groans and fly through the air like military poltergeists as the Goth's HQ collapses around me. There's no way out now and even if there is I can't get to it anyway. My legs don't want to move. They don't hurt, but they won't move. Eh. I didn't need them anyway.

I do, however, note how well the torn, velveteen lining matches the reddish tint of the coffin slamming into me.

❀

I'm not sure what I expect. My life flashing before my eyes.

A sudden sense of peace and oneness with the universe. My dead relatives lining up to tell me I'm still an idiot. But there's nothing, just a field of fading black. I guess I wasn't even worth the Bargain.

I do, however, suddenly understand something Old Jed often said.

"If'n there be no Heav'n fer folk like us, God willin' there'll be beer."

Fuck you, Jed.

Fuck you, and fuck us all.

Epilogue

Two figures dressed in Spandex dig through the rubble of collapsed floors.

The first, clad in red and black under a mop of unruly curls, turns to the second and says, "Why are we—Captain Eight, excavate!—doing this again?" Several pieces of twisted metal, far too heavy for normal human beings to move, fly onto a growing pile. "Nothing could have survived that and he'd have been squished flat."

The other, skirting around an exposed bundle of wires, replies, "He did kinda just save the world, you know."

"I bet he didn't do it on purpose. Besides, he's an asshole."

Throwing his hands up in exasperation, the second says, "He saved your life."

"Without my permission."

They dig in silence until the second decides to speak. He sighs, and the neon blue and green highlights in his suit, patterned after flames, catch the movement and shine dimly in the flickering light.

"We're heroes, Captain. This is just what we do."

About the Author

Not yet award-winning author Chris Wong Sick Hong is the proud owner of two cats, one dog and half an MFA in creative writing (but it's the good half). In other about-the-authors, he's been plugging the publication of *Dick Richards, Private Eye*, but since this is *Dick Richards, Private Eye*, that would just be weird.

http://www.chriswsh.com
http://www.thedickrichards.com

www.ingramcontent.com/pod-product-compliance
Lightning Source LLC
Chambersburg PA
CBHW022002010726
47494CB00003B/858
9781897492444